The Celine Bower Story
Chronicle Two

The Celine Bower Story
Chronicle Two

By

Carly Brown

mosaicPRESS

Library and Archives Canada Cataloguing in Publication

Title: The Celine Bower story : chronicle two / by Carly Brown.

Names: Brown, Carly, 1977- author.

Identifiers: Canadiana (print) 20220280835 |
Canadiana (ebook) 2022028086X |

ISBN 9781771616485 (softcover) | ISBN 9781771616492 (PDF) |
ISBN 9781771616508 (EPUB) | ISBN 9781771616515 (Kindle)

Subjects: LCGFT: Novels.

Classification: LCC PS8603.R6775 C452 2022 | DDC C813/.6—dc23

Published by Mosaic Press, Oakville, Ontario, Canada, 2022.

MOSAIC PRESS, Publishers
www.Mosaic-Press.com

Printed and bound in Canada.

ONTARIO ARTS COUNCIL
CONSEIL DES ARTS DE L'ONTARIO
an Ontario government agency
un organisme du gouvernement de l'Ontario

Funded by the Government of Canada
Financé par le gouvernement du Canada

Canada

ONTARIO CREATES

MOSAIC PRESS
1252 Speers Road, Units 1 & 2, Oakville, Ontario, L6L 5N9
(905) 825-2130 • info@mosaic-press.com • www.mosaic-press.com

OTHER BOOKS BY CARLY BROWN

The Celine Bower Story: Chronicle One

To Chris,

Acknowledgements

Thank you to Jessica Cavezza, my editor extraordinaire. Thank you to Chrissy Dunker for showing me things I would not have otherwise known. A special thank you to Superintendent Cliff Sexton (Retired), Niagara Regional Police, for patiently answering all of my questions.

To my publisher, Mr. Howard Aster—Howard Aster found my book in a pile of slush and decided to take a chance on me. Thank you, Howard, and God bless.

To the Port Perry 'Timmies Crew', ladies, I cannot thank you enough for your love and support. To my grandparents, Clifford and Evelyn Trapp (R.I.P.), thank you for giving me a soft place to land, I will never forget it.

I meet many different kinds of people on my travels, it is often the kindness of strangers that gets me to where I need to go, thank you.

To my husband, Chris and my mother, Dianne-- I cannot thank either of you enough.

Chapter One

The wake was shorter than he anticipated, and darker. There were even fewer people there than he thought as he walked in the assigned room. He raised an eyebrow as he looked at all the empty seating and wasn't overly saddened by the grim reality that they weren't going to allow that many people to be there. In fact, Troy Alexander knew exactly how his father and her immediate family would have handled the news of his mother's death. Truthfully, the suicide was not unexpected as anyone outside of his closest family members would be allowed to believe. His father and her caretakers had been dealing with his mother's illness for as long as he could remember. In all the years, he surmised as he stood there, it was all he could ever really remember anyway. Even if someone in their household had ever claimed that she was getting better or making progress, Troy knew deep down by the way she looked at him when he caught her staring, that empty and chilling look in her eyes, that nothing had changed. As he stood there looking at her shiny, black coffin, he was surprised that she had even made it to her last birthday.

Sometimes his mother would come back from those overpriced, private clinics and look a little more vibrant, somehow brighter, the color a little more noticeable on her usual pale and sunken cheeks; people would have recognised that she was a real looker back in her day. But he knew all he had to do was be around his mother for any length of time and her true state of mind would escape out into the open. Then she would be whisked away to her own bedroom, till the new concoction of 'miracle' drugs had time to be in her system and take effect. Troy was so used to that broken-record of a story that he didn't even need to hear the words of how his mother's stay at whatever new clinic was and the promises her doctors made to keep.

After he got the phone call about his mother's death, and the details about the service he was to attend the following night, Troy hung up his phone and retreated to his oversized bathroom where he spent no less than two hours meticulously grooming his entire appearance. Every stray hair was clipped or cut or combed into place. He selected the appropriate salon- quality products from their shelves and counter space and exfoliated, buffed, and toned. He slowly shaved the five o'clock shadow that had appeared on his cheeks and chin and then stepped into his massive glass-enclosed, imported marble shower for an hour of scrubbing and soaping and luxuriating under the massaging streams of warm water. He used a loofa that he had purchased from a luxury goods website and imported from Australia. The soap had been tissue-wrapped and directly imported from France and apparently, because of the soap, he knew he shared the same taste as more than one internationally known movie star and rapper. He washed and conditioned his hair with the products his stylist had chosen for his hair type and when he finally shut the water off, he toweled dry with his favorite Egyptian cotton towels. Troy stepped onto the bathmat and studied his appearance in the bathroom mirror. As soon as he saw his reflection he knew he had a right to be satisfied; Troy had also spent the afternoon at the gym, doing the series of workouts prescribed for him by his personal trainer, it had been a leg day. But-- he was careful not to stare for too long, he didn't want his skin to dry too quickly before an application of his favorite serum and lotion cold help capture his own natural oils to save his skin from premature aging. He was gentle as he patted the skin around his eyes, and he made sure he massaged his elbows and knees quite thoroughly. He was lucky he did not ever have to work because of the amount of time it took him to be ready to leave his home. And finally, a light misting of his favorite cologne was sprayed while a selection of his favorite tunes played in the background. He put on his favorite Armani suit and walked out the door.

Chapter Two

"You're drunk." his father said as he sidled up next to his son in the dark room.

"Not exactly." Troy said, without looking, moving slightly away.

"Well, you stink like booze." His father said as he leaned in close, his nose scrunched.

"What do you care?" Troy said venomously.

"I care because your entire family is here," Troy's father said as he leaned in close and hissed in his son's ear. "And your mother's only child shows up an hour late and reeking of alcohol."

"I'm surprised *you* showed up at all." Troy said angrily as he turned to his father. "But I guess you really need to impress my relatives with your stupid suit, and your fake tears, and your stupid, blinding love. Making sure you tell them your side of the story. Why don't you just leave me the fuck alone, *man*… so I can grieve my mother in peace?"

"Hey, you watch your mouth, pal. I loved your mother and *I am still your father*." Troy's father said angrily as he turned to look at his son. It was all he could do not to slap his son's face, but he didn't; they were at a funeral for his wife and he would not conduct himself like that in front of her family, or anyone.

"Yeah, that's great, *Dad*." Troy said mockingly. When was the last time we even spoke before you called me yesterday?" Troy said and quickly wiped a tear from the corner of his eye.

"What's that go to do with anything? This is neither the time nor the place to have this conversation." Troy's dad said then took a deep breath. He leaned in close to his son and whispered in his ear. "If I remember correctly, you were invited to my birthday dinner three weeks ago and you never responded to our message. So, don't go pointing your finger at me." He hissed in his son's ear, a bright red color rising from his neck up to his cheeks. They looked identical in their expensive suits and clean hair.

"Yeah, that was a nice text from… what's her name, Coco? Kiki? What number is she now… the one who sent me the message? What was her name again? I really just cannot seem to keep them all straight in my mind. It actually took me a few days to figure out who it was that *even* sent the message." Troy said and laughed bitterly.

"You sound ridiculous. Maybe you should go home and sober up." His father said as he grabbed his son's arm and whispered fiercely in his ear. "And don't even think about coming to the funeral drunk… I will escort you out myself." His father said through gritted teeth. Then watched as his adult son pulled his arm away like a five-year-old child.

"Don't tell me what to do." Troy said as he turned to his father. "And don't ever touch me again. *I don't need you for anything*, asshole." Troy said as he straightened up in his jacket. His father casually following suit, suddenly becoming aware of the turn in their conversation. It never took much, but both men were raised properly, and knew there was a time and a place for every conversation, and not all were to be had in public, especially at his beloved wife's funeral.

"Rich talk from a guy that's never worked a day in his life. Go home and sleep it off. Be here tomorrow at two. Try to look like you care that your mother is dead." Troy's father said quickly as another mourner appeared, an older woman, to greet him and give her condolences.

"Fuck you." Troy said under his breath as he turned and walked away.

Chapter Three

Troy Alexander walked out of his mother's wake feeling a lot smaller than he felt when he walked in. He did not want to fight with his father but the last few years, the feelings of abandonment that surfaced after his father moved out did nothing for his feelings for the man, and it did not encourage happy tidings when the two were in the same room together. Troy decided that he hated his father on sight after walking into the wake and seeing his dad speaking so candidly, so warmly to his mother's close friends and some of their old staff that it made him sick with contempt for the man. He couldn't deny that his father loved his mother very much, and if he was a bit older and a lot less bitter, it would have been easier for him to understand that his father did all he could in the many years his parents were married. He would have accepted that his father struggled with his own demons when faced with his mother's mental illness. Her problems tested his father's strength over the years, and eventually he left the marriage and their family home a broken man set on finding an easy relationship as payment for all the years he spent trying to fix a woman with a psyche that would always be broken. It tore their small family apart and Troy Alexander had been alone in the world ever since.

The weather station had been reporting a storm heading in their direction for the night and the rain was steadily becoming heavier as the wake dragged on inside the funeral chapel. He quickly found his car where he left it in the parking lot, got in and sat down. He pulled a small silver flask out of his jacket, unscrewed the cap and tilted his head back for a deep swallow. Troy put the cap back on and traced the inscription on the front of the antique canister. He couldn't find any symbolism in the meaning; he had come across the antique flask when he was going through his grandfather's desk and belongings and decided to make it his own. Troy figured as he sat there tracing the silver pattern that his grandfather probably wouldn't be needing it anymore anyway, considering he was long dead and buried, so Troy cleaned it up and saved it for special occasions. He had been sipping out of it before he got to the wake and once during the time he was inside. Maybe his father was right, he thought. Maybe he should just go home and sober up in preparation for the funeral the next day. It occurred to him as he was walking out of his mother's wake, that he would spend the night at his grandfather's place. Even though it was out of the way, he thought he would get comfort from the idea of just being closer to and surrounded by the things that reminded him of happier days. Troy still couldn't get used to calling the mansion his, it just didn't feel right. The mansion was too big and felt too empty. Troy never brought any of his girlfriend's there either, knowing from a few unpleasant and uncomfortable experiences just how women reacted to a man's wealth, and he couldn't be bothered sifting through all the users and the takers. The apartment he had in the city was closer to his school and a lot more convenient. But, for the sake of the night being what it was, Troy would go where some point of his life he had been a part of a family. It wasn't a perfect family by any means, but it seemed to him, even at young age, that everyone tried. There were those times of course, that left him scared and confused, but he still held onto the memories that he could consider normal. He was so young to ever understand properly what was different about him and the way the other kids he knew grew up. And by the time he was thirteen, he did grasp a different understanding of what his wealthy grandfather had tried to do.

His mother was beautiful, and considering all the money her father had, she was considered quite a catch. The problem was her mind; she should probably have been institutionalised from a young age, but her father could never bite back the shame and acknowledge that *his* only child was somehow damaged, flawed. Selfishly and perhaps just a sign of the times he was in, Troy's grandfather did not want people to know his beautiful daughter was mentally ill and completely incapable of looking after herself or of being left to her own devices. The grandfather could always, well almost always, maintain control of his daughter's wild, unpredictable, and sometimes dangerous behavior while she was under his roof. They had 'minders' of course, staff that could be blended into the surroundings at a moment's notice, and always introduced as 'family friends', that was how they could function daily, but he needed to set the stage for his dream of a perfect life's legacy. A determined man, he set himself on a mission to find his daughter an acceptable suitor, so that she could live a 'normal' life, and he could have somewhere safe to leave her; it wasn't going to get any easier and he knew it. He was worried; he wanted his daughter to produce an heir to his fortune and he knew he would have go to great lengths to make that happen. Troy's father was the best candidate, the old man could tell. After they were introduced through family connections (it was on a 'good day'; his daughter looked most beautiful then with the sunlight in her long, blonde hair, her behaviour calm and jovial, as she had taken all her medication that morning.), they would spend their summer afternoons on the large stone patio, laughing, eating, and dancing into the night until the couple were to be married. The couple had their only child, a son, the following year.

Troy put the flask back in his suit pocket and started his car. He maneuvered out of the parking lot and drove cautiously in the direction of his grandfather's home. The night was dark and quiet, and his mood was a mixture of calm and anger. His interaction with his father and the anticipation of facing all of the people who knew his mother at the wake had drained all the energy and emotion from him. He just wanted to shower, eat and watch television for a few hours. Troy drove along and looking out the window he noticed the storm pick up outside. He had no fear though, his expensive tires gripped the slick black roads. Although Troy did suddenly become very acutely aware that if he were to be stopped by the police and given a breathalyser that he would probably be pulled over right there on the side of the road. That would cause an avalanche of bullshit that he did not need in his life the night before his mother's funeral in a single phone call. He did not want his father to be right about anything. Troy took his foot off the accelerator just as he was driving around a wide bend dotted with yellow signs. He turned quickly when he thought he saw a girl walking dangerously close to the curb carrying a large cotton bag over her shoulder. The girl turned as his headlights shone in her direction. She smiled brightly as she stuck out her thumb and stepped closer to the road. Troy didn't think about it for a second; he slowed as put on his turn signal and pulled over to the curb.

Chapter Four

Troy Alexander drove a beautiful car and the hitchhiker knew chances were good that it was definitely warmer in the car than outside in the freezing rain on her current path. When he rolled down the window, all she saw was a very nice-looking guy in a suit with a shy smile on his face. The girl shimmied over to the car window a bit more and felt a faint gust of warm air mixed with expensive cologne come from the opening. The girl was young, sopping wet, and when she leaned in toward the open window, he smiled at her and she smiled back. She was momentarily taken aback by his appearance; raindrops were dripping off her hair and running down her nose, but she stopped because she thought that he had the most beautiful eyes she had ever seen. She couldn't believe her luck. She was shivering, wearing only a hooded sweatshirt, jeans and boots. She had her bag over her shoulder and was holding it back with her arm. She leaned in closer and smiled like she knew him before saying hi.

"It's pretty wet out there." Troy said, looking out at her smiling, then reaching over to turn down the radio.

"It sure is." She said with a laugh and tucked her long, wet hair behind her ear. She was holding her bag behind her, but it was heavy and wet and kept slipping forward.

"Do you need a ride somewhere?" He asked nicely, looking forward to the direction she had been heading in and seeing nothing but roads and some scattered houses with large yards in the front.

"Well, yeah and no." She said, wiping her face with her hand while turning forward but leaning her body slightly on his car.

"It really looks like you need a ride somewhere." He said with a burst of humorless laughter as he looked around the area behind her then back to her face. "Where *are* you going, by the way?"

"Well, I guess I'm going to the bus terminal." She said and sighed loudly, then let out a soft moan as she shifted her feet.

"Downtown? You're going to walk all the way there in this weather? It's three miles from here." He said then leaned further over the passenger seat to hear her over the sound of the pelting rain and traffic, and his idling engine.

"I know... it wasn't raining before I left." She said and smiled a perfectly white smile. Even though it was clear from how wet she was that she had been out in the rain for some time; her long, blonde hair was completely slicked down on her face, nothing could hide how beautiful she was.

"Look," he said as he smiled. "Why don't you just let me give you a ride? It's pouring rain out there and I'm going in that direction anyway."

"You don't mind? Really?" She said eagerly, not needing to be asked twice. "That would be great. I tried to get a cab, but none would stop. And my phone is dead." She said as she shoved her bag back over her shoulder again.

"No problem. Get in, you're completely soaked." He said and leaned over and opened the door for her.

Chapter Five

"Wow, thank you so much for stopping." She said as she stepped over the curb and sat down in his car. The girl squeezed her heavy bag down at her feet and was using the sleeve of her sweatshirt to dry her face.

"I think there's some napkins in the glove box, if you want to use them." Troy said and turned on the interior light so she could see what he was talking about. She immediately reached forward, opened it, grabbed a handful of tissues and began patting her face dry. He smiled, switched off the light, and looked in his mirror before pulling away from the curb into the flow of traffic.

"So, what's your name?" Troy Alexander said to the girl as he looked out to the road.

"This is a really nice car." She said at the same time as him, then giggled nervously as she looked around the darkened interior of his car.

"You go first." She said smiling and turned to get a good look at him while he was concentrating on the road. His focus was on driving and although he could feel her looking at him, his eyes remained on the road in front of him. The windshield wipers were at a low setting and the radio hummed quietly in the background.

"I just want to know your name." He said keeping his hands on the wheel but looking momentarily at her face. "Mine's Troy."

"Oh, I'm sorry. I'm Morgan. Morgan Dallas. It's nice to meet you, Troy." She said and took a breath, smiling inside because the girl could not believe her luck; she runs away and the very first person that stops for her is a young, hot guy driving a really nice car. Not some old pervert in a dirty van, like her parent's had warned her about.

"It's nice to meet you too, Morgan. But tell me, what is a pretty girl like you doing out there in the rain, anyway?" He said as he followed along with traffic.

"I told you, I'm going to the bus terminal." She said defiantly, then shook as a shiver coursed through her body. He smiled, then reached over and adjusted the heat on the dial.

"Okay, that's cool. So where are you planning on going when you get to the bus terminal?" He said casually, he was watching the traffic but he wanted to get a red light so he could get a good look at her face. He could smell her wet clothing and a faint hint of strawberries emanating somewhere from her person.

"I know you're going to laugh," She said as she looked out the window. "Well, maybe not," She said then turned back to him. "But everyone says I'm really pretty, so I'm going to California to be a movie star." She said smiling proudly and moving a stray hair off her face.

"Wow, really? And you're leaving tonight?" He said and cracked an easy smile.

"Yup, pretty cool, right?" She said as smiled and fixed more of her hair.

"Yeah, it is really cool but, is that all you're taking with you?" He said and nodded in the direction of her bag shoved in at her feet.

"Yeah, I'm gonna travel light and once I get there… I can get a job and buy whatever I need." She said breathlessly. "Plus, it's really warm in California, don't you know?" Morgan said with the authority of one who may have learned all she knew about the place where she was going from TV and movies.

"Yeah, I've been to Cali, actually. It's cool. I'm just wondering how old you are, if you don't mind me asking." Troy said, as he was driving and trying to get a look at her face. He figured the strawberry smell must be coming from her long hair.

"How old do I look?" Morgan said flirtatiously leaning her back toward the door and facing him smiling. She was tilting her head and had a beautiful smile and a small brown mole on her right cheek that emphasized the milky paleness of her iridescent skin.

"I don't know," Troy said slowly, looking all over her face. "Maybe 19 or 20?"

"What? For real? Wow... thanks." Morgan said turning abruptly then pulling down the sun visor to reveal the hidden mirror. She looked at her reflection momentarily before fixing another stray hair then slammed the visor shut.

"Why? How old are you, really?" Troy said as he turned to face her. They were stopped at a red light for the first time since she got in his car and he took the opportunity to get a good look at his attractive passenger. With the extra seconds he got to look at her a shiver momentarily coursed through him because he noticed quite unexpectedly how much Morgan Dallas looked like someone that could be a younger, healthier version of his late mother.

"I'm sixteen." Morgan Dallas said proudly and smiled, as if fooling a complete stranger was an accomplishment in and of itself.

"Really?" He said in a low voice, raising his eyebrows and tilting his head, clearly not believing her for a second.

"Okay, I lied." Morgan said with a charming half-smile.

"I'm fifteen...but I'll be sixteen next month." She said as the light turned green and he began to accelerate with the flow of traffic.

"I'm not sure exactly but, I'm thinking that they may not let you go to California by yourself if you're only fifteen. I'm just saying that you might want to check it out before you buy your ticket." Troy said solemnly.

"Really? Shit. My friend was right. Darn it…now what am I going to do?" Morgan Dallas said, sounding immensely disappointed with her current predicament because things were just getting shittier by the second. She was looking from Troy to the window to her belongings at her feet. Morgan turned toward the passenger window again to discreetly wipe a tear from her eye.

"But… your friends are right. You are really beautiful…you could be a model, or something." He said quickly, trying to ease her obvious disappointment and becoming increasingly more interested in her story and what could have brought her, soaking wet and crying into the front seat of his car.

"Thanks," she said, with a hint of a smile, then looked around at the interior of his car. "This is a really nice car, by the way." She said as if noticing for the first time the sleek, black leather interior and the huge screen on the console. "Is it yours?" Morgan said perhaps a little too seductively. It was like a switch had turned on and she realised as she looked at him again that maybe her luck *had* turned. (He was older, he looked great and he had his own car. Something she didn't see too much of at her own high school, or the mall.)

"Yeah, it's mine. I got it last year when I traded in my old one." Troy said blandly, his leg twitched on the gas pedal as he continued down the dark road.

"Wow, must be nice to have a car like this. You don't look old… what kind of job do you do?" She said, stuffing the wet tissues in her pockets and readjusting the bag at her feet.

"I didn't buy this car. My parents gave it to me. I don't work, I'm in school." Troy said as he navigated the city streets with the flow of traffic. He realised quite suddenly as he took a deep breath that he wasn't drunk anymore like he was at his mother's wake. In fact, he thought as he stopped at a red, that he was tired after all, and he just wanted to go home.

"Wow, nice parents! You're lucky. My parents would never buy me a car. Two feet and a heartbeat for this girl. My dad says my bus pass is the only car I'll need until I get a job and buy one myself." Morgan said then laughed bitterly. She looked out the window at the raindrops on the glass then turned to Troy and said, "Do you go to school around here?"

"Yeah, I go to the university in town. Listen, I don't live too far from here and if you are not in a hurry to catch the bus, do you want to go to my place and hang out for a bit? I live just around the corner... I can take you to the bus terminal later or call you a cab to take you anywhere you want to go." He said suddenly, changing his mind about having company. It was completely out of his character to do something so impulsive, like picking up a hitchhiker but things seemed to be going well so Troy figured with the time he had just had that he would go with it. "There are lots of extra rooms and you can have something to eat if you want."

"Okay..." Morgan said slowly, evaluating her options, which were none. She didn't have a bus ticket, and the idea of sleeping in a bed all to herself sounded amazing considering she had spent the last few nights crashed out on the floor of her best friend's bedroom. And Morgan wouldn't dream of spending the night all alone on a cold plastic chair in the bus terminal with all the weirdos creeping about, waiting for a bus that she didn't even know if she could get on. Morgan Dallas certainly didn't want to admit any of this to the handsome, young stranger that sat beside her that was beginning to look more and more like her own personal knight in shining armor.

"That sounds pretty great actually." she said and smiled, also thinking that a few hours in a nice, warm house would give most of her clothes a chance to dry. And Morgan Dallas might finally be able to do something with her hair while she figured out her next move...which she concluded quite quickly did not involve going home to her damn parents.

"Good, it's settled. We're almost at my place. Just a few more minutes." Troy said and smiled, then pushed down on the accelerator.

"Do you have room-mates, or anything? Is anyone gonna care if I'm over there with you?" Morgan said apprehensively, sounding exactly like her fifteen years.

"I live alone, so don't worry about it." He said, charmed at her sincerity.

"You look really good." She said plainly, as if noticing his attire for the first time. "Where were you tonight, some wicked cocktail party?" She said with a laugh and reached over and touched his suit on his shoulder.

"Not exactly." He said as he jumped at her touch then made a sharp right turn. Morgan reached for her door handle to steady herself then looked out her window at the houses that they drove by. She hadn't been paying any attention to the drive over and they were no longer on the main road where she had initially hitched her ride. They were driving down some residential streets that she didn't recognize at all and she was taking it all in because they were all so beautiful. Morgan noticed the sizes of the houses on the street and the types of cars in the driveways and figured this was a 'ritzy' part of town. She loved the manicured lawns showcased, even in a dark storm, by the massive spotlights beaming from the homes or the decorative lamps that lit up the pathways that led to garages and front doors and back yards and figured this was exactly what Hollywood must be like. Just then the car she was in started to slow down and Morgan watched as Troy pulled into a large driveway of interlocking brick that could easily hold twelve cars.

"Whoa, this is your place?" She said impressed, unable to mask her surprise.

"Yeah." He said quietly as he steered the car into the driveway in front of one of the four doors of the large four-car garage. Troy hit a button and the door slowly began to open.

"Holy shit, nice house." Morgan said, then covered her mouth and giggled.

"Thanks." Troy said blandly as he parked his car in the empty, spotless garage.

"This is *your* house?" She said incredulously, taking a much better look at him, her eyes wide with disbelief.

"Yes. It's *my* house." Troy said to her with a straight face; his mouth was as dry as cotton and all he could think of was going inside to get a cold drink.

"No, like 'your house' and you live here with your parents, right? What are they out of town for the night, so it's 'yours' until they get back, or something?" She said quickly, her head tilted to the side, trying to put all the pieces of the puzzle together in her head: the car, the house, his nice suit. She was hoping he wasn't making fun of her intelligence and lack of sophistication; Morgan knew from experience that some guys automatically assumed that attractive girls were stupid and easily dicked around, sometimes just for fun.

"No." Troy said as he switched off the engine, undid his seatbelt then reached for his door. He smiled at her as if encouraging her to do the same. He opened the door, stepped out, and with one foot on the garage floor, he continued. "What I mean is: this is my house. My parents don't live here."

"Oh, come on." She said as she grabbed her bag and heaved it over her shoulder as she stepped out of the car. "How can a guy like you, a *student*, have the money for a place like this?"

"I inherited it." Troy said as he walked around the car and headed in the direction of the door that led to the interior of the house. Morgan shut the car door and watched him for a moment before following closely behind him. She could smell his cologne from where she walked and noticed how tall he was and how muscular his shoulders looked from the back.

"From who?" She said as she stopped a few feet behind him and looked around the garage as he opened the door and walked through. Automatic lights turned on from somewhere over his head in the cavernous room and she noticed he was standing in what could only be called a gourmet kitchen filled with shiny stainless-steel appliances.

"From my grandfather. Do you always ask so many questions?" He said as he stepped in further then held the door open for her to walk through as he untied his shoes and slipped them off.

"Yeah, sorry. I'm like, the nosiest person ever, I can't help myself. My mother always tells me it's going to get me in trouble one day. So, anyway… like, it must be nice to have such a rich grandfather." Morgan said as she smiled and placed her bag down on the floor then bent over to take off her boots. "Where do your parents live?" She asked as she stood up and looked around the kitchen, then smiled at him. He was standing near the kitchen island watching her.

"My mother is dead." He said uncomfortably and realized that up until that moment he had not once said those words aloud to anyone.

"Oh my gosh, I'm so sorry". Morgan said quickly in a pained voice as she placed her hand on her chest, tears forming in the corners of her eyes.

"It's okay… actually, to answer your question from earlier, the reason why I'm so dressed up is because I was just at my mother's wake." Troy said as he looked her in the eye then turned and walked in the direction of a doorway on the opposite side of the kitchen. He turned quickly when he realized she wasn't behind him and beckoned Morgan with his hand to follow him into the house.

"Oh my gosh, I am so sorry. I didn't mean to be so nosy. Are you sure it's okay for me to be here? I mean, I don't want to impose, or anything. Should I just go? Actually, if you want, I can just call a cab and get outta here. You know, leave you in peace. You must have had the worst day ever and I'm here bugging you." Morgan said breathlessly as she hurried across the kitchen to keep up with Troy.

"No, you don't have to go." Troy said as he stopped and turned abruptly to face Morgan. "I would rather have company tonight, if you don't mind staying. I can call you a cab whenever you're ready to go. I don't know if the bus terminal is open, I guess it would be, so you just have to let me know when you want to leave. Hey, I don't know about you but, I could use a drink. Do you want to have one with me?" He said as he looked her in the eye and turned to lead her into a room toward the front of the house.

"Sure," Morgan said quietly as she followed behind him. She figured he was probably really upset so therefore wanted some company. And, well, she figured slowly that the worst thing that could possibly happen to her was she didn't leave for California until the next morning. He turned and looked at her for a response and Morgan spoke. "To both, I guess. I don't mind staying for a bit if you want company and I will definitely have a drink. Whaddya got? Any wine coolers?" Morgan said as she followed Troy through his beautiful home. Not many of the lights were on making it difficult to see in fine detail but Morgan could tell by the plush carpet under her feet and the grand look of the touches in the home that it was immaculate. She thought if she ended up sleeping over that she would get up early and explore the place from top to bottom.

Troy had led her into a room that she thought would be called either the library or the den. Morgan had never been in a home so elegant before; no one she knew lived in this exclusive neighborhood and most of her references about homes like the one she was in came from reality TV shows and movies. There was a book-lined wall and leather furniture on one side of the room and a huge wooden desk and a stone fireplace on the other. And if she remembered correctly, and had to guess, she would be willing to bet the carpet in the center of the room was the one people called a Persian Rug. When she walked into the enormous room, she saw Troy standing at the desk with a large, heavy crystal decanter in his hands. He smiled when he saw her and placed two crystal glasses in front of the decanter.

"I don't have any wine coolers, so I hope whiskey is okay. There's some cola in the kitchen fridge if you want to mix it." He said and took the top off the decanter and poured the brown liquid into both glasses. He handed one to Morgan as she walked toward him and put it in her hand. She smiled and sniffed at the glass.

"Oh my gosh. What is this? It's so strong, like an old man's drink." She said and laughed, then plugged her nose with one hand and attempted to take a sip. With no shame to be seen for miles at her lack of experience with the finer things in life, Morgan coughed wildly as the aged whiskey burned all the way down her throat.

"Its whiskey, it's some of the best there is. I can get you a cola, there's some in the fridge. Give me your glass, I'll fill it with some ice. I could use some ice, too." Troy said and walked back out of the room in the direction of the kitchen. Morgan could hear him at the ice dispenser at the refrigerator, so she took the moment to look around the room. There was a long thin table behind the desk that had a beautiful assortment of framed photos on it. She looked and saw the only person she could recognize in a handful of the prints. She heard the ice cubes in the glasses before she saw Troy walk into the room. She turned and smiled at him as he walked in, remembering as soon as she saw him that his mother had died only days earlier. Her smile was warm and gracious and when Troy walked in and saw her standing behind the desk with her eyes focused on him, he almost dropped the drinks he was carrying on the very expensive rug. Troy could not believe how much Morgan resembled his mother. He couldn't believe he missed how closely he was standing to a person he was going to bury the next day.

"Oh my gosh, Troy. Are you okay?" She said as she watched the color drain from his cheeks while he nearly spilled their drinks as he walked. She reached over for the one he offered her and took a sip.

"That's better. Thanks. Hey, are you okay? You almost spilled the drinks everywhere. That would have sucked. Who cleans this place, anyway? Not you, right?" She said and laughed as she took another sip of her whiskey and cola and smiled.

"Nope, cleaners and a maid come in all the time and make sure everything is in order. There's all kinds of staff for this place because of the size and the fact that I don't stay here all the time."

"Wow, that is amazing. I wish I had people to clean at my house. I guess *I'm* considered the staff there." She said with a bitter laugh and smiled at Troy who was watching her closely.

"What about your dad? Where does he live?" Morgan asked shyly, feeling somewhat guilty for prying into his life when he was probably at his lowest moment on earth.

"My father has a place about forty-five minutes from here that he shares with multiple girlfriends… and I think he has a dog. I've never been to his new place and he never wants to come here." He said coldly.

"So, like, you never see him?" Morgan said quickly.

"No, not really. The last time I saw him before today was about three months ago." Troy said as he looked over his glass at her face, noticing for the first time, the tiny smattering of freckles that dusted her cheeks perfectly. He knew right then that if she did ever make it to California, that she would indeed be crowned a 'Beauty Queen'.

"Wow, must be nice."

"What?" Troy said and finished his drink in three large gulps. The ice clinked against the glass and he walked over to the desk to pour more whiskey.

"Wow, thirsty much? I could never drink that fast. I'm not really much of a drinker, actually. My friends steal shit from their parent's all the time, but I just have one wine cooler in a night and that's enough for me. Whiskey is strong, right? I can already feel it in my legs. Do my cheeks look really red? They feel hot. Do they feel hot to you?" Morgan said to Troy who was leaning on the desk watching her as she looked from him to the books on the shelves.

"Your cheeks don't look bad… don't worry, you're still really pretty." Troy Alexander said then threw his head back and drank his glass of whisky in one swig. When he righted himself, he was looking Morgan straight in the face. Stomach acid had crept up his throat and he had to turn away from her to keep it and the whisky down.

"Why don't you live with your dad? You can't be that old that you don't want to see your own father." Morgan said sincerely, letting out a long, sad sigh.

"My dad and I have a hard time getting along. You must know what that's like, right?" Troy said then sniffed the air in annoyance.

"How do you know?" Morgan said sipping her drink and looking at him over the rim of the glass. Tilting her shoulders, she was posing with the most innocent-looking face she could muster. She had been practicing her poses in her bathroom mirror for months, she called that one her 'ingenue'.

"Because you're fifteen and you're planning on taking one bag and moving all the way to California to be an actress. I picked you up on the side of the road, remember? What were you really doing out there by yourself, *Morgan*?" He asked looking her straight in the eye. Saying her name helped to remind him that he was not looking at his dead mother.

"Well, I think you're pretty lucky because my parent's never leave me alone." She said quietly and turned to face the books once again. She felt intimidated under his stare and thought she could have the conversation while feigning an interest in what he had to read.

"So, you ran away?" He said bitterly, he could still feel the sour film still in the back of his throat.

"It's more than that, you know? I didn't plan on running away but, last week when I got home from school all of my things were all over my floor. Well apparently my mother *thought she could smell marijuana* in my room when she was supposedly 'cleaning' it. She called my dad at work and told him, so he left early for the day and they both went through my room with a fine-toothed comb in order to find the source of the smell. I swear, if they could have borrowed dogs from the K9 unit at the local police station, they would have." Morgan said angrily, her voice shaking at the memory that was still very fresh, she could feel the tears forming in the corners of her eyes. And she still looked beautiful.

"Did they find anything?" Troy asked her.

"Of course they did... but they were more pissed because it took them so long to find it more than anything. And my father was super-pissed because he had to miss an "important work meeting", a.k.a., drinks with his friends, because they were so busy freaking out that their oldest child, me, is a suspected druggie. It was so not cool." She said and turned to see that Troy was smiling at her as he filled his glass once again with the whisky on the desk. He leaned in and waited for her to keep talking.

"And then what happened?" He said as he sipped his drink.

"Oh, well, it gets better. You know, my parents never liked my boyfriend, so it was perfect after they found the pot because they made me dump him. I had to cut off all communication with him because my father is convinced that he is the son of the devil.

But really, it was me who bought the bag of weed and I made my boyfriend smoke it. But that's not all, oh no, my father also did the most embarrassing thing I think a parent can ever do. Because even though I told my boyfriend, his name is Cash, which my father also hates, that we couldn't see each other anymore because of the drugs. He didn't believe me, so he kept calling my house, because of course, my parents took my phone away. So my stupid boyfriend calls the house one day and my little sister answered because she got there first. But because I wouldn't lend the little bitch my absolute favorite sweater for school, the little witch told my mother who told my father, who then went all the way down to my effing school during a basket-ball game and threatened my boyfriend. In front of everyone, while I stood there and watched." She said breathlessly then took a big sip of her drink. Troy got up and took the empty glass from her hand and before she had a chance to object, he filled it with more of the brown liquid.

"Holy shit, they did all that because of a little bag of pot?" Troy said.

"Uh huh." Morgan said, nodding her head.

"Wow, your parents must really care about you." He said, handing her back her drink and stepping back toward the desk where he stopped momentarily and took his jacket off, placing it folded on the corner of the desk. He resumed his leaning position and Morgan took another big swig of her drink, belched, then carried on talking.

"Yeah, whatever. They're going crazy trying to control everything in my life. I'm lucky I'm so pretty because when I do move to California, I won't ever have to talk to them again." She said defiantly and flicked her hair back as she walked further along the wall of books. He followed her with his eyes and did not move a muscle.

"You're not serious? Just because they care about you, you won't talk to them again?" He said in disbelief. He couldn't believe what he was hearing; before him stood a girl who didn't know it but, had everything that Troy had ever wanted in life. Morgan Dallas had every single thing he had ever dreamed of; two loving parents that cared about him so much that they wanted to know what he did all the time. He never knew what it was like to have someone care so deeply for him. He only ever imagined it.

"They are so controlling! That's why I left. They grounded me for two weeks. Not even allowed to leave the house except for school, which they drove me and picked me up. I had to quit my job because it was at the mall and everyone hung out at the mall, so they didn't want me working there because there was maybe a chance I could still see my friends. Do you see what I mean? My parents are obsessed with me." She said loudly, her hands shaking in rage, carelessly spilling some of her drink down the front of her t-shirt. She smiled shyly and attempted to clean it with her hand. "Um, not to change the subject but, you have a lot of books here, do you ever read any of them? Some of them I can even remember from when I was a kid. Who read the Nancy Drew books?" She asked Troy as she bent over to read the spines of the books closest to the floor.

"Those were my mother's when she was a kid, I think. So, what were you doing when I first saw you?" He said quickly, he was completely entranced by her story, a part of him felt as though she was an alien from another planet, the way she talked about her family.

"Well, I decided I couldn't take it anymore... so I snuck over to my friend, Dana's house and hid in her bedroom till we got busted. Boy, her mom was pissed. She didn't know I'd been crashing on Dana's floor for days till my mother called and begged her to check again to see if I was there. Dana overheard everything and I booked it before my mother got there." She said and laughed, proud of her own bravado and daring.

As Troy stood and listened to her, his mind drifted to his own family. His mother was being buried the next day because she had opted to take her own life rather than spend time with him. His father was still alive but no less absent than his mother who would be six feet under the ground, buried beside his grandfather. Then there was this girl he picked up on the side of the road; so angry and defiant because the people in her life that were supposed to care about her, actually did, and she was in his home whining about it. Morgan must have realized Troy had tuned her out because she stopped talking and turned to look at him. She smiled her million-dollar smile and it nearly took his breath away; he felt as if he was looking into the face of his dead mother. His face scrunched up and Morgan took it as a sign of agreement with what she was saying, so she turned back to the book-shelf and continued talking breathlessly.

Morgan continued to rant about her parents, and when she came to a place in the room where the wall space from floor to ceiling had been filled with dozens of framed photos. She zoomed in immediately to a photo of Troy's mother as a teenage girl dressed for a debutante ball. She whispered something and kept looking at the photos; sometimes bending over, other times straining her neck to look at the out of reach pictures. She was smiling and laughing and talking to herself as she got a glimpse into the privileged life of Troy Alexander Senior, and his family.

Troy watched her for one more moment before swallowing hard then putting his drink down on the desk. He walked silently over the plush carpet in Morgan's direction. She didn't hear him as he walked quickly up behind her and placed his strong arm around her neck. He smelled her hair briefly, then he lifted her two feet off the ground and watched as the glass she was holding dropped noiselessly to the carpet. He had stopped her from breathing and Morgan barely gave a struggle. Troy held tightly to her neck until he felt her tense muscles loosen, then he released her and watched as her fifteen-year-old body dropped quickly to the floor. Morgan's body didn't make a sound when it landed on the beautiful, plush carpet.

Parents of Murdered School Girl Asking the Publics Help in Finding Their Daughter's Killer
Lance Williamson

The parents of murdered schoolgirl, Morgan Dallas, 15, are asking members of the public to come forward in order to help catch their daughter's killer.

"She disappeared without a trace," Police Detective Cardosi told reporters. "And we are hoping that someone in the public can tell us anything regarding her disappearance and or whereabouts the night she went missing."

Morgan, 15, was last seen by one of her close friends before she left the girl's home to take public transportation to the local bus terminal, but Morgan never arrived at the terminal and was never seen alive again. When she did not arrive at school the next morning, her parents were informed by her teacher and shortly thereafter the police were called to file a missing persons' report. Only to have a parent's worse nightmare come true a few hours later, when the body of a teenage girl was discovered at J.M. Holeran City Park by a woman out for her morning jog. Morgan's body was identified by the student ID her parents say she always carried with her. She was 15.

Police have not yet released the cause of death but have let it be known that Morgan did not die of natural causes. If there is anyone that may know something about Morgan's last hours, they are asked to contact their local police station or call the Crime Tips Hotline at 1888-444-4444.

"Morgan's parents and her friends and family are all devastated by her tragic death at such a young age and the loss in the school community has been especially hard. They are looking for answers for their daughter and friend." Detective Cardosi has said.

Chapter Six

"Excuse me, Miss."

"Excuse me, Miss."

"Huh, what?" Celine said quickly then jumped in her seat away from the gentle touch of the flight attendant.

"Miss, I'm very sorry, but we are landing soon. You'll have to put your seat back up right and away, please." The young woman said with a warm smile. She wasn't surprised at Celine's reaction, and quickly pressed the chair release button and pushed up the seat back to its proper position. Celine smiled briefly at the woman who had already stepped away from her to another passenger and rubbed the sleep from her eyes. As Celine took a deep breath, a jolt of excitement ran through her entire body as she rolled up the tiny window screen and glanced at the scenery below. She held her breath at the picturesque view from high up in the clouds. Lush bright green vegetation as far as the eye could see and a rocky coastline dotted with uninhabited white sandy beaches made her crack a real smile for the first time since she left her home. Celine closed her eyes and said a silent prayer of gratitude and thought, maybe, just maybe, she had evaded capture and the police.

As the plane slowly descended, Celine quickly got out of her seat to stretch her legs and visited the lavatory. She surreptitiously glanced around the cabin of the plane, still on the look-out for anyone with the appearance of law enforcement who may have followed her but saw nothing but other travellers. After being in the air for thousands of miles over oceans and hustling herself through numerous airports and security gates, Celine felt as though she might finally be able to let her guard down by the time she got to a hotel and booked a room for a couple of nights. The country where she found herself was entirely new for Celine, but she did have time for some quick research before she packed her bags and said her final good-byes. She had consciously chosen to leave her lap-top and cell phone behind, knowing quite instinctively that she would find access to a computer and the internet at a café somewhere; a place catering to tourists in the beachside resort town she was headed to, and she couldn't care less about a phone. Celine didn't find her name in any on-line searches and she promised her mother before she left that she would use an alias when she did make contact the old fashioned way: the postal service.

Tears welled up in Celine's eyes as she thought about her future, so unknown, ahead of her. She wiped the tears away with her shirt sleeve and reminded herself that she was going to be fine, and that she was sort of on vacation for the first time in a long time and she always loved an adventure.

As the plane made its final descent, Celine looked around at all the other passengers. Some were still sleeping with their mouths wide open, others, like her, were looking out the window and pointing to things in the new foreign land they could see in the distance. Celine felt the thin, stiff money pack that was hidden discreetly across her abdomen in a travel pack and thought of her mother. Molly had surprised her daughter with her bravery and thoughtfulness, not to mention her loyalty, and Celine was especially grateful when her mother, in her time of need, handed her thousands of dollars and basically pushed her out the door to save her from being questioned by police and prison.

The shock from the events of the last few days and months had not worn off completely and Celine was hoping that a few days of island hopping and soaking up the rays on the beach would help her relax enough to sort through everything she had built up inside her. When she finally arrived at the hotel that her cab driver recommended. Celine paid cash for her room, took the elevator to her floor, found her door, unlocked it, dropped her bags, and passed out cold in her bed.

She awoke early the next morning, frightened at first by the unknown room, then remembered where she was and how she got there. She got out of bed, smiled at her reflection before taking off her clothes and jumping in the shower. After she brushed her teeth and found some clean clothes, Celine grabbed her room key, hung the 'do not disturb' sign on her door and went off in search of a restaurant for breakfast and coffee. The sign posted outside the elevator advertised breakfast on the second floor, so Celine pushed the number as soon as the door opened then stepped inside the mirrored cube. The elevator door opened to a bright lobby where Celine was greeted at the entrance of the restaurant by two young local women in matching uniforms. They both smiled broadly at her as one stepped away from the stand and led her to a table by the window.

Celine thanked the girl and smiled as she sat in her seat and looked around the large, bright dining room. There were some families with young children, some businessmen in suits and couples, lots of couples. They were eating and smiling, talking and looking at photos on their cameras. The room was noisy with the chatter of guests eating their meals, with glasses clinking and silverware clanking against plates. There were glass doors that led to an open patio and Celine made a mental note to go outside after she had eaten her breakfast to take in the view from above. She ate her meal quickly as the last meal she had was the one on the plane a few hours before they landed and she didn't realize until there was a plate of food in front of her just how famished she was.

The view of the small town from the patio indicated about a distance of about three blocks from her hotel to the jetty where she could take a boat to one of the outlying islands. Celine quickly returned to her room to throw a bikini on under her shorts. She slipped on some sandals, put on her hat, grabbed a towel and her bag. Then stopped at the front desk to put her passport and money in the hotel safe. She smiled as she took the key then said thanks to the doorman as she walked out of the cool air-conditioned lobby into the blazing hot sun.

The walk to the jetty took about ten minutes and the moment she walked in the doors Celine was accosted by an aggressive tour operator sitting at a desk. Celine was then told that she had the option of three islands to visit. After some exchange of information and ideas, Celine chose the furthest and most secluded island for the day. She walked to the back of the large building to a souvenir shop and bought herself some sun block and a beach mat, and when the woman behind the counter asked her what island she was going to visit, she also bought a bag of stale bread to feed the tropical fish that were known to live around there. She waited on a long, wooden bench with some other tourists in the big, humid room until the tour guide told her that the boat she was waiting for would be boarding soon. She followed another man in the same t-shirt to a small boat at the dock, showed him her ticket, and then hopped on board. Celine felt the first real sense of peace since her arrival as the boat, about half-full, slowly glided along the water out of the marina towards the open sea. She smiled as she took a photo for a young couple on their honeymoon and laughed as salt-water sprayed her face when the boat crashed through a big wave.

Chapter Seven

After about fifteen minutes the boat docked at a large bustling boardwalk that stretched out like a long finger from the tiny island. It was crawling with other tourists and tour operators, all milling about waiting for their boat or waiting for the other tourists. Celine stood, put her bag over her shoulder then took the first strong hand that was offered to her, then was lifted up onto the sandy, wooden dock. She looked down and immediately noticed schools of shiny silver-blue fish swimming in the clear water below. She followed the crowd of other visitors down the long boardwalk to the entrance of the island, paid her fee, and walked along the stone path under the huge palm trees that led to the beach and the rest of the island. She stopped briefly and took in the image of the sign in front of her. She was tickled as she read the clever message, 'Take nothing but photographs. Leave nothing but footprints.' As she walked along, Celine noticed tents set up in the distance, far from the beach area. They were close to a small thatched-roof hut that had smoke billowing from its chimney and signs for the daily menu specials. There were people in scuba gear down on the shore and Celine watched as they waded into the water and disappeared under the waves. Celine took off her sandals and walked onto the sand. She found a great spot far enough away from the other sunbathers then rolled out her mat and towel. Celine took off her shirt and shorts, took out her sunscreen and began applying it all over her face and body. She heard parts of conversations in foreign languages and could hardly wait to walk into the surf. She walked in slowly then dove head-first and swam until she could no longer hold her breath. She felt wonderful and free as she swam up for air and looked back at the coastline, her towel and mat a tiny dot in the distance.

Celine waded in the water for a bit, watching as schools of shimmery tropical fish swam around her and enjoyed picking up seaweed with her toes. It was a clear, beautiful day and in the early afternoon there were only about a dozen other sunbathers on the beach. The water was warm and calm, and she loved watching the brightly colored tropical fish swim around her legs and ankles. Small hand-made fishing boats floated far in the distance and Celine thought they looked lazy. She took in as much of the scenery as she could hoping to capture the beauty and serenity of her surroundings, and in turn, hoping to enjoy the moment she was in before any of the guilt and worry had a chance to reclaim her consciousness. And, she admitted to herself a bit self-consciously, that she looked like any other tourist out there enjoying the sun and taking in the beautiful surroundings.

Celine returned to the shoreline and the spot where she had left her belongings earlier. As she was drying off, Celine noticed a sign for coffee outside one of the little huts. She laid her towel on the sand and walked over to the counter carrying some money she had taken out of her bag. The local man served her a hot, dark coffee in a Styrofoam cup with a smile and she took it to a wooden picnic table and sat down. She sipped her coffee and listened to the birds in the trees high above and the waves lapping gently on the shore, simply enjoying the moment of peace. She stopped looking around as her attention was drawn to her hands. They were wrapped around her coffee cup and she felt a sudden chill travel up her spine. Celine thought about what she had trained her hands to do; the skill and steady precision she had relied on to perform surgeries on animals seemed like a lifetime ago. Instead, she thought, she used her very same hands to commit crimes, to inflict grievous injuries on men, some of them whose names she didn't even know. She had used her skill to hurt, not help, and she felt the pain. She picked up her coffee cup and swallowed the last of her coffee in three gulps.

As she walked away from the table she stared mindlessly into the distant horizon, not knowing where her future was going to take her. Completely lost in thought, Celine walked carelessly in the direction of her beach mat. As she continued to walk in a haze of deep thoughts, Celine didn't notice the enormous, beautiful, pale yellow butterfly that was flying in the same direction as her. The two collided and Celine let out a small scream as she jumped in the air. The butterfly was temporarily thrown off course but reoriented itself and carried on to its destined path. Celine stopped briefly and smiled as she watched it fly away. She felt warmed by the soft touch of the fluttering wings on her arm and decided at that exact moment that she could be like that butterfly; temporarily thrown off course, but willing and determined to get where she needed to go, wherever that may be.

Mom,

I can't believe what I've done. I packed some of my things and was out the door within hours. And now, as I sit here, I can't help wondering if I just messed up the rest of my life. I mean, what was I thinking? What little chance of being normal do I have left over from here? What am I supposed to do now? I'm sorry to burden you with these thoughts. It seems as if all I do now is burden you and it's just not fair. I wanted so badly to be normal after daddy died. I wanted to work hard and accomplish my goals, then live the life of a normal person. I wanted to fall in love and have children one day, but after I was raped that night, I felt that no man would ever love me because I was so damaged, let alone have children with me. But then I started to feel okay about everything, like maybe I could have hope again. But something happened, and it's like I just snapped. It's the only way I can figure out how to explain it. Something snapped and all I could think of was getting those men. I wanted to kill them, I'm sorry to say. I wanted them dead. But then, I decided that maybe if they had to live with scars like I do, that they would feel shame for what they did to me, every single day. And that they would never think of hurting another woman again.

Maybe that's why I did what I did. I can't even say it quite yet. I know what I did, I was there, but I can't put it into words. But maybe because of what I did, I saved some other innocent woman from a similar fate as mine.

I'm sorry again, Mom. I know you didn't raise me to be this person, but I'm all there is now. Tired and alone, on the other side of the world.

I hope that you will forgive me.

Love, CB

Chapter Eight

Molly Bower finally breathed a small sigh of relief when the phone rang and it was Tunisha calling, letting her know that she had just dropped Celine off at the airport.

"How did she seem when you said good-bye, Tunisha?" Molly said apprehensively, she dried her tears on the back of her hand as she peeked out the kitchen window.

"A little sad. But brave somehow. Tougher than I remember her being in school." Tunisha said, hoping to offer some kind of reassurance to Celine's mother, despite the circumstance they all found themselves in.

"Did she say anything about where she was going?" Molly said on the verge of tears.

"No." Tunisha said quietly. "And she told me you'd ask. I'm so sorry, I really don't have anything to tell you. She insisted I drop her off at the first departure gates and not turn back. So that's what I did. I stopped the car, helped her get her bags, hugged her goodbye, and then drove away. I never looked back." Tunisha said feeling the gravity of the situation for the first time since Celine called her for a ride to the airport. She felt weighted-down and sad, not knowing if or when she would ever see her friend again.

"Oh, I guess. Then it's probably for the best. I know it's what we talked about before she left but I didn't think it would be this hard, Tunisha." Molly said then let out a soft whimper before drying her tears.

"She told me to tell you not to worry about her. She told me that she will be fine, and she promises to send you a message as soon as she can. She asked me if I would keep in touch with you, and I will be happy to. I know you worry about Celine, Mrs. Bower…I" Tunisha said, sounding as deflated as she felt thinking on the ride home that nothing, no book or TV show, could have prepared her or any of them for being in the most unusual situation she had ever found herself. Tunisha was scared for Celine and sorry for Molly, her mother, the woman Celine cared most about in the world.

"You, you…you can just call me Molly." Celine's mother replied, choking back tears, feeling the desperation of her situation. Molly was comforted by the idea that Celine had such a loyal and trustworthy friend in Tunisha, but she also knew nothing, no relationship she could ever have, would ever take the place of the one she had with her daughter, her lost, beloved Celine.

"Okay, Molly. I know you worry about her… I do too. But she is so incredibly intelligent and brave. If anyone were going to survive out there alone in this world, my money would be on Celine. And if you and I are going to get through this, we have to trust her to make the right decisions." Tunisha said confidently, perhaps more bravely than she felt at that moment.

"I know, you're right, but… we didn't really even get a chance to say goodbye and now I don't know when I'll see her again, Tunisha. I don't know where she went or what she's going to do when she gets there. That money can't last forever. What will I do if and when the police show up at my door? When will I see my daughter again? What do I tell our family?" Molly said, losing control and crying loudly into the phone. The more she spoke to Celine's best friend, the more worries and fears bubbled to the surface. And it was the moment she realised she would have to face it alone.

"I'm so sorry to have all this happen to you… but Celine told me to tell you not to worry about her, as impossible as that sounds.

She said she will be fine. She seemed… strong and confident and even a little relieved when we arrived at the airport." Tunisha said slowly, looking for the right words to say, thinking about her own mother and what would possibly bring her an iota of comfort in a situation like this. "She's worried about getting caught and what that would mean for the two of you. She asked me if I would keep an eye on you…" Tunisha said shyly. It wasn't the way she was raised, to speak to someone's parent like that, but she wanted Molly Bower to know just how much Celine really cared about her. Tunisha felt she owed that to Celine, and she promised to help her friend's mother in any way she could.

"Keep an eye on me, whatever for?" Molly said, a bit taken aback by Tunisha's confession. She almost giggled at the thought of Celine insisting one of her friends watch over her. But then she remembered why the three of them were in this position to begin with and she smiled.

"Because she doesn't want you to get…" Tunisha said quietly, not really knowing what was acceptable to say, she didn't want to hurt Celine's mother anymore on such a dark day.

"What?" Molly said, curious.

"Celine told me she worries about you being alone and about it being her fault. She asked me if I would keep in touch with you… considering I'm the only other person who knows what's really going on with you guys. I love Celine. I hope you don't mind if I call every once in a while… just to chat?" Tunisha said, exhaling loudly into the phone, not even realizing that she had been holding her breath.

"Of course… I don't mind, Tunisha. You're the next best thing to my own girl. But I don't want to put you out though." Molly Bower said quietly, then began to cry silent tears. "I just don't know when we'll ever be able to see her again.' She said as her voice cracked, and the heavy tears rolled quickly down her face.

“One more thing,” Tunisha said apprehensively. “Celine had me worried and thinking about this when we were in the car… what about the police? Have you heard anything? Have they come by your place, or the clinic?”

“I haven’t heard anything… I don’t know anything, Tunisha.” Molly said in a panic.

“I’m sorry. I’m so sorry. Please, we can’t get ahead of ourselves…” Tunisha said calmly, hoping that she didn’t give Celine’s mother a heart attack.

“You’re right… we’ve got to hold it together. We’ve got to believe. We can’t go out borrowing trouble, as my mother used to say.” Molly said slowly then took a deep breath to steady herself and her nerves.

“I didn’t mean to scare you, Mrs. Bower. Uh, Molly. I’m so sorry.” Tunisha said quietly.

“Its okay, Tunisha, it really is. I have already thought about this a thousand times myself. I’ve been looking out the front window so much since you girls left that I’m afraid I might be scaring the neighbors. And I don’t want them to think anything suspicious.” Molly said with a giggle, hoping to cover how she really felt about the situation; unmitigated fear that she and Tunisha were right, that the police were going to discover that it was Celine who carried out the attacks and come banging on her door in the middle of the night, demanding her only child be arrested and thrown in the back of a police car, never to be seen, or held, or hugged, again.

“Well, this ought to make us feel better…I dropped Celine off at the first departure doors and although we don’t know exactly where she is going, we know that she’s going somewhere. No one followed us and no one has showed up at your house. I think the timing was perfect and I know myself, that I will never say a word about this, about tonight, to anyone. You and Celine have my word." Tunisha said bravely, hoping her words, that sounded so strange coming from her mouth, were worthy.

"Thank you, Tunisha. That means the world to me. That is the bright side to this whole situation. My brave girl got away… and I won't say anything either because I will do as I have always done; my very best to protect her. I feel that she needs it now more than ever, so she, and you as well, will be in my prayers tonight. And another thing, I wouldn't be lying if the cops came to my house and asked me where she was anyway. Because I have absolutely no idea. Oh gosh, Tunisha, I hope this works out." Molly said, holding tightly to the phone, whispering a silent prayer right there where she stood in her kitchen.

"It will, Molly. Celine is clever, she has her intelligence on her side. And she's brave, braver than I could ever be, especially in a situation like this. For as long as I've known her, she has always done the right thing, and I doubt she'll stop now."

"Amen to that. I'm trying not to be scared. Sometimes I can't believe how brave Celine really is." Molly said cautiously, thinking of her daughter, and missing her already.

"Yes, and thank God for that…I know, it sucks, all of it. But don't worry, Molly. We'll get through this, all of us. You'll see, it won't be long before you hear from her." Tunisha said bravely, holding in her own tears.

"I hope so. Thank you, you are very kind. I know why my daughter loves you so much." Molly said breathlessly.

"Thank you, and don't worry…everything will be fine." Tunisha said quietly.

"Keep in touch." Molly said before hanging up the phone.

Molly cried that night in her bed. She cried because she was alone, she cried because one fateful night cost her only child so much that she could barely stand it. And she cried because she didn't know what else to do.

Tunisha put her worries for her friend in their own compartment in the corner of her mind. As terrible as she felt deep inside for everything that Celine had been through since that fateful night at the hands of her rapists, and her now being gone to who-knows-where, living her life on the run from the law. Tunisha could read the writing on the wall: she was on the cusp of a very important stage in her life, and she knew she had to use all her focus in order to successfully move forward with her life.

Chapter Nine

After waking up from another horrifying nightmare, and receiving that nasty, terrifying visit from John Scott, Frankie decided the best thing he could do for himself was to lay low and keep his nose out of trouble. He still had so many goals that he wanted to achieve in his life and he still had his own baggage that he carried around with him from his other life, his own not-so-distant past. Frankie Angel knew that he never again wanted to be any part of what he'd almost been involved in that night down at the creek. Frankie tried to make sense of his choices, mainly that he had even accepted the invitation to go out that night; he knew those guys were bad news to begin with, but he never thought in his wildest dreams, that he could ever even imagine them to be such lowlife abusers. Frankie was genuinely living in fear for his life, until that one day when he read what had happened to John Scott in the newspaper. Well, he didn't know it was John Scott until a few weeks later when the two other guys ended up in the hospital, and it was only then that he started seeing the vision.

One of Frankie's co-workers knew of an older gentleman in his neighborhood who was trying to sell a second-hand car that wasn't needed anymore, and for a steal. The guys wife had gotten very ill, very suddenly and the man didn't think she would drive on her own again, so selling the car became more important than holding out for a good price. Frankie happened to be in the right place at the right time and was ecstatic to learn that he had just enough money saved to get his hands on his very first car. It was in excellent condition; the wife didn't drive very much outside of their city and the husband did his best to maintain the exterior of the car as a hobby. Frankie was beside himself with pride when he handed over all the cash he had saved and was given the two sets of keys. After insurance and whatnot, he was completely psyched to drive himself to work for the first time in his life, he even offered to pick up the guy who had been driving him on and off for months. The guy declined, but Frankie was in his element nonetheless. For the first time since the night in the van, Frankie thought things were finally turning around for him. He had even considered finding himself a girlfriend, maybe that cute girl down at the grocery store that had always smiled at him, since he could be the one to take them places for dates.

The excitement he felt however, was short lived because Frankie started seeing a vision of a woman silently weeping when he would look in his rear-view mirror when he was out driving in his car. It didn't happen every time he went out for a drive but the first time he saw 'her' it nearly caused an accident. Frankie was so shocked to see this pale, lifeless blonde woman in his reflection that he came pretty close to totaling his car one day while he was out running errands. He swerved and braked and almost ended up on the curb but straightened his wheel at the last second and avoided a collision. Frankie Angel had to pull over and stop to get his bearings and gather his thoughts before he could continue to his destination. At first, Frankie thought that he might have been hallucinating, so he went home and promptly flushed the last of the marijuana that he had lying around down the toilet, but even after a few days of being clean it did not stop the woman from appearing at the most inconvenient of times. Once, it happened when he was getting ready to go on a date. The first real date that he had ever had. Frankie had dreamt about it for as long as he could remember. And it was finally going to happen. There was a guy he knew from work that was setting Frankie up with his younger, sister as soon as possible. Frankie was going to great lengths to ensure that he would look and smell his best for when he met the prospective love-interest for the first time. Frankie got out of the shower, got dressed and was putting gel in his hair when he thought he saw the same weeping woman behind him in his small bathroom. He nearly crapped his pants but when he turned to look, she had disappeared. And even though he knew it to be impossible, he walked around his tiny apartment to see if any blonde woman had snuck in and was hiding from him under his bed or in the tiny closet in his bedroom. Frankie once again gathered his thoughts and focused on being excited for his date for that night. But still, he couldn't help thinking something beyond his everyday comprehension was happening to him. He felt intuitively that it had everything to do with Celine and the night that he left her there with those animals to save his own ass. And the fact that he had done absolutely nothing about it since. Frankie knew what he needed to do but he wasn't sure he was willing to give everything up, including a budding relationship with a great catch, to do it. It was a few more days of torment by the pale, blonde, ghostly vision that forced his hand so better judgment could take a hold of him. Frankie left his apartment alone one night on foot and went to the only place he could think of to find answers.

Chapter Ten

Frankie Angel walked into the sports bar with his head down, not knowing who or what to expect, but determined to get some answers, and hopefully find some peace. Frankie quickly looked around and saw a few faces he thought he might recognize. He didn't see any of the guys who were there that night Celine was raped and left for dead, so he slowly walked up to the bar and sat down on a stool. Trying his best to act casual, Frankie looked up at a television playing sports just as the bartender walked over and said 'hello'. They made some small talk, then she walked away to fill Frankie's order. He looked around briefly and smiled at some of the regulars he remembered that he liked talking to. The bartender returned with his drink and Frankie pulled out his wallet and paid. He felt a sense of relief and relaxed a little bit once he saw that none of the guys were there. He began talking to some other people and learned very quickly the fate of those no-good sons-of-bitches that he deemed the cause of his unrelenting stress and anxiety. Frankie Angel heard it from the grapevine that John Scott never showed his face again in the bar since that night when he was last spotted leaving with the mysterious brunette woman and was later found tied up with his testicles in a jar. And it was no surprise to Frankie that Tweedle and Dumber were two guys that no one missed or even talked about other than that one time after they were castrated at the strip club. Frankie wanted to ask about Adam Johnson, but felt too insecure, as if someone might put together that he really was a part of their gang of criminals. Frankie didn't have to worry though because one of the waitresses that was actually the person to have given him his nickname, spotted him from across the room and went over to talk to him. She asked where he had been hiding, then spent the next five minutes telling him all that had happened in the sports bar in his absence. If Frankie had been more perceptive from the very beginning, he would have known that that waitress in particular had had a big crush on him for some time. Frankie cut it short then thanked her for her time; he could tell she was busy with a table of what looked to be a big group of co-workers out for beer and chicken wings standing a few tables over. She saw him looking and told him it was a sports team of cops and firefighters the bar sponsored every year and she recommended quite insistently that he not drive home or smoke marijuana anywhere near the bar that night. Frankie thanked her again and smiled as he took a swig of his beer.

Frankie sat hunched over the bar with a beer in his hand and a look on his face that suggested he had more to think about than whatever team was winning whatever game was on the wall-mounted TV in front of him. He hadn't been by in his old hangout in a while, a few months, and he felt as though he looked out of place sitting on a barstool in his usual white t-shirt and jeans. Frankie forced himself to loosen up, he wasn't doing anything suspicious, in fact, Frankie thought, he did have a few legitimate reasons as to why he hadn't been seen around the past few weeks. There was the fact that he had finally saved enough for a car and after he paid for the insurance and licensing fees, he didn't have two coins to rub together, let alone the cash for a few beers down at the old sports bar. Plus, Frankie was no idiot, he had seen the news and read the papers. He knew all too well what had happened to those other guys because it was in every paper and news program for miles around, and in the back of Frankie's mind, he couldn't help thinking that he might be the next one to suffer that unforgiving fate. He tried to make peace with the voices in the back of his mind; his conscience having woken him in the middle of the night on more than one occasion, the one that demanded he waltz himself down to the nearest police station and reveal all he knew, but another voice in Frankie's mind always stopped him. The 'One', the loud one, the one that stemmed from years of always being the 'little guy', the loner, the invisible one that people always seemed to ignore, or step on, or forget. The one that told him that John's words were true: that no cop in their town was ever going to believe a little half-breed punk like him, no matter what he said, so he better not even try to tell his side of the story. That was the voice that always won.

Frankie hadn't seen John or the other guys around after that night, when he decided it would be safer to do his own thing, and he was grateful for that small mercy. A few times some of the staff in the mini-mall and the coffee shop, it was usually a female or a group of them asked Frankie if he knew anything about what happened, but he just smiled and shook his head, 'no'. He secretly hoped they couldn't tell he was lying. That's when he began to search for a car he could afford and focused on putting that terrible business behind him. But the voices would not be ignored. He tried to write down his thoughts to get them out, like a confession, but Frankie thought it looked stupid on paper, and fake. Then he tried something he hadn't done in months; he tried to contact his sister, in the desperate hope that she could tell him what to do. But all he got when he dialed the last telephone number that she had given to him was a recorded message telling him the number was no longer in service. Frankie gave up hope after multiple tries and cursed loudly at his own company, stuck in a mindset that no one ever wanted to be in.

After speaking to the bartender and slowly looking through the crowd, Frankie noticed a younger-looking guy in a grey suit, hanging around one of the baseball teams. The second their eyes met, Frankie could tell this wasn't just any 'regular guy' enjoying a few beers. The guy looked too slick and alert to have just finished playing, not to mention what he was wearing happened to be a nice suit with some decent-looking shoes. But the guy smiled and laughed and drank his beer with his friends on the sports team.

Frankie was glad he felt comfortable at that moment and truly thankful that he wasn't carrying any of the marijuana he might have been tempted to bring with him before. He still hadn't bought anymore since the visions started and he flushed the last of his stash down the toilet. He also reminded himself that he didn't want his new love interest to end things with him because of the drugs he used to smoke. Frankie sat alone and slowly peeled the label from his bottle of beer. He was really confused as to why he was there with the last bit of petty cash he had till payday. It was irresponsible of him to be seated there because he should have used it to buy food. Caught up in his own thoughts, Frankie forgot to act naturally, and after a few minutes, he could feel someone staring at him. When Frankie looked up, he noticed a tall man from the other table looking in his direction. Frankie was sure he had never seen the guy before, so he shook off the feeling and made a half-hearted attempt to get the bartenders attention. He ordered his beer and engaged in conversation with some of the other regulars. Frankie knew he had to be there for some reason; it was the vision of the crying woman that sent him out of his apartment seeking answers, only to end up at the one place that he had been afraid to enter since that fateful fucking night, but he didn't know if he just had to sit around drinking and wait for something to happen. As the night wore on and Frankie got more and more drunk, he noticed the guy at the table of cops and firefighters staring at him more often. The staring piqued Frankie's interest and in turn he began to stare at the man thinking that maybe between the two of them they would figure out what it was the other wanted. The guy was probably a firefighter, he looked pretty well built and had a different kind of confidence than a cop. The cops that Frankie had seen while he was growing up on the reservation had a seething arrogance about them that Frankie could never forget. Even as a young child he felt they were looking down their noses at him and his family, and even if his father was a raging drunk who used to toss his mother around by her hair, he didn't feel their attitude was justified at all. So when Frankie watched this tall dude in the grey jacket from across the bar, he was sure he was just a firefighter who had a bit too much to drink and probably thought he was someone else, after all, Frankie had not gotten into one lick of trouble with the law since he moved to Norfolk Falls, and he wasn't about to change that.

Frankie got up from his bar stool and slowly made for the direction of the washrooms at the back of the building. He was minding his own business and was a little drunk, so he didn't notice the guy in the grey jacket slowly and inconspicuously follow him toward the bathroom. A man was walking out the bathroom door at the same time and held it open for Frankie as he walked in. Frankie thanked the guy and walked into the nearest stall and shut the door behind him. He heard the door open moments later and was finishing his business when he heard the stall door next to him open, then the lock closed. Frankie zipped up his trousers and flushed the toilet. He opened the door and walked to the counter to wash his hands at the sink. He looked up at the mirror at his reflection, hoping he wouldn't see 'her' while he was out drinking, and it was a few seconds before he realized he was holding his breath. As he reached down to turn on the tap, Frankie noticed a white business card sitting on the counter, leaning up against the mirror, and sitting in such a way that it appeared to be waiting for him. He looked around the small bathroom knowing he wouldn't see anything, and he could still hear the man in the other stall urinating loudly. Frankie Angel ran his fingers under the cold tap water, then ran them through his hair. He looked again at the card and decided that it must be the sign he had been looking for. Frankie picked up the card and turned quickly toward the door and opened it, he heard the toilet flush and knew whatever man had left the card was the one in the stall. Frankie walked quickly through the bar and out the front door. He turned quickly to the right and bent down in front of the big glass window. The green blinds were down inside but Frankie had a clear view through the glass at the bottom of the window, directly into the restaurant side of the sports bar. He watched as the man in the grey jacket walked slowly from the men's bathroom back toward the big table of guys at the front. Frankie quickly walked away from the bar in the direction of his apartment, and after about twenty feet, he felt comfortable enough to take a closer look at the card. On it he saw the decal for the local police station and the name of the officer who the card belonged to, 'Lee James Morrison, Sex Crimes Division', and his phone number. When Frankie turned the card over, he saw that the officer had written something on it, 'Call me', was all it said.

Frankie Angel tossed and turned the night he found the card. He dreamt that he was excited while waiting for someone to visit him. He looked down and saw that he was wearing a bright orange jumpsuit and when he tried to move, he saw that his leg was chained to a table. He saw the blonde woman walk by him several times, and when she tried to call his name there was no sound when she opened her mouth. Frankie tried to run to help her but when he did, he could feel something grabbing at his legs. Frankie looked down and saw blood pouring out of his pantlegs from a deep gash on his calf and a growing pack of mangy wolves surrounding him. They were snarling and snapping their vicious jaws, their mouths bloodied as they continued to tear away at him as he sat chained at his feet trying to fight them off.

Chapter Eleven

'She had the most beautiful blue eyes,' He remembered thoughtfully, thinking back to that night in the rain. The mist that had landed on her face and sat gently on the fine peach fuzz that coated her cheeks and illuminated her skin so much so that she looked almost alien. He noticed her hair first; the long, thick, pony-tail flying loosely behind her then falling in soft, sexy curls when she approached his car.

Troy was most surprised at the pin-point accuracy of his vision; he was driving at a near crawl though the busy 'university circle' after finishing up one of his assignments. He was heading in the direction of home, when he spotted a girl far in the distance sprinting as fast as she could in his direction. Traffic was at a stand-still because the city buses that circled the university on their routes were stopped and filling up with students not fortunate enough to have their own cars and who were desperate to get out of the rain in one of the last buses of the evening. Students all around the area were prepping for their midterm exams and most had camped out in the library for the evening or met on campus for study groups and were now eagerly piling onto buses. Troy Alexander's car sat idle in a long line of vehicles and he saw as he watched her run that the bag that she was carrying over her shoulder could no longer support the weight of what he could only imagine were numerous heavy textbooks. Troy kept his foot on the brake as he became entranced by her mission to arrive in enough time to catch the bus;

he was so consumed with her struggle that he heard himself rooting her on, quietly chanting, 'go, go, go'. Then her heavy bag fell to the ground mid-run and it took her a few steps to realize that it was no longer on her shoulder and she would have to stop to go back and pick up her things. Which she did with amazing speed, and once she had bundled all her belongings together again, she picked up her pace and sprinted directly toward the bus stop.

Troy watched her out of the corner of his eye as he kept up with the flow of traffic in front of him. It was still raining and the air outside was damp enough to penetrate bones. Troy had the heat on low in his car and the windshield wipers on the intermittent setting. He looked into his rear-view mirror, noticed a few cars behind him and slowly decided he wanted to see if she would make her bus. He put on his indicator signal and crept slowly over to the curb, a few cars passed him, then stalled to a slow crawl as the massive fleet of city buses signaled brightly then pulled away from the curb in sequence, like a military convoy. Troy caught the girl in his sights again, he noticed that she was almost to the point of reaching her destination, and he figured, with a smile on his face that if her bag hadn't broken mid-sprint, that she would have gotten to the stop in time to catch her ride. And perhaps, if the buses weren't so crammed or the drivers so callous, she might have had even better luck. Instead, when she got to the concrete area that housed the glass shelters that were covered in signs and graffiti and bus schedules and numbers, all she encountered was the toxic smell of the buses' exhaust with everything else completely empty because every other passenger that had been standing there waiting got on their specific bus and were now heading in their desired direction and out of the rain.

He sat in his car twenty feet away from the stop and watched her quietly; he had rolled down the passenger window a crack and was particularly grateful for the bright street-lamps placed around the area. He could see and hear her quite clearly, the moment she arrived at the stop and realized her bus had driven away without her on it, he could see her angrily stomping her feet and saying the words, 'shit, shit, shit', over and over again. He chuckled to himself in his warm car as he watched her struggle to control her anger. It was her own fault the bus drove away without her on it; she wasn't paying attention to the time in her lab because out of sheer laziness and neglect, she had fallen behind on her course work and then as midterms began to loom, she discovered that she was so far behind that she could do nothing but devote every waking minute to catching up or be forced to drop the class. She didn't really like the class all that much, but she was only in her second year of a four-year program and was still learning the ins and outs of a university education. And she felt, she was even farther away from knowing exactly what she wanted to do with her life than before she started her post-secondary education. Lindsey Sparkes was studying for a career path she didn't really know she wanted with her whole heart and after one year of student loans already accumulating in her name, she was seriously considering alternate paths for her future. And when she missed the bus because the strap of her favorite bag broke mid-hustle, she couldn't help herself, she stomped her feet as loud as she could because it stopped her from crying tears of frustration for a day that didn't seem to be getting any better. She was stomping around, cursing her miserable luck; contemplating returning to the warmth inside of one of the school's buildings or desperately calling one of her friends for a ride when she heard a car pull up slowly behind her. Her mind didn't register that it might be for her at first, then when she noticed, gratefully, that there was no one else around and she could still hear the car, she slowly turned in the direction of the sound.

Troy watched her turn to look in his direction as she became aware of his presence. The girl turned toward the sound of the purring engine and slowly smiled, all of her anger forgotten. His first impression of her upon closer inspection was that he could not believe his luck. He just couldn't believe it, and even though he knew before that moment, he felt after seeing her that first time on that rainy night, that he was never going to get through the gates of Heaven, he didn't care. Troy Alexander stopped his car just as he pulled directly beside her and rolled the passenger window down three quarters of the way and smiled at the cute blonde who just so happened to miss her bus and was desperate for a ride home. The excruciating guilt he experienced months earlier no longer had a strangle hold on him or his thought processes. As he studied her with the one window open, he reached over and turned down the radio, bent his head and looked out the window and smiled.

Chapter Twelve

Lindsey walked right into his world. His smile was warm and attractive, and he looked genuinely happy to see her. She smiled back, and scrunched her brow, thinking she might have known him from before, either from a class lecture, or from one of the pubs on campus, the latter being the most likely. Lindsey pushed her hair back off her face and smiled at Troy for the first time.

"Hey." Troy said casually. "How's it going?"

"Hey," Lindsey Sparkes said in her girlish voice. "It's kinda shit, actually. I just missed my bus and it's about twenty minutes till the next one comes." She said as she laughed then leaned into his car; she got a good whiff of his expensive cologne and imagined herself riding next to him as he drove her to the apartment she shared with one of her girlfriends.

"Twenty minutes?" He said incredulously, looking at her eyes and hoping to smell her long brown hair. "Where are you going?" He asked casually, hoping she would take a ride from him. He had been on campus studying too and had not planned this encounter. He was dying inside to feel the way he felt the very first time he picked up a stranger in his car.

"Perry Street, that big apartment building across from the hospital." She said, hoping he would offer her a ride. He was really nice looking and well put together for a university student and she imagined that his parents had a lot of money and weren't shy about providing for their son.

"Across from the hospital? That's pretty close to my place. Any chance I can give you a ride?" He said, looking from her to the campus, then back to her.

"Um, well." Lindsey said as she let out a deep breath. She didn't want to seem too eager and she wanted a moment to consider her predicament. It was going to be another twenty minutes before the next bus came and she had been on campus all day and having had just about enough of it considering she would be going back to the lab early the next morning. Her feet were soaking wet from running across the field instead of walking on the sidewalk. She bent down further into Troy's car to get a better look at him; he was clean-cut and attractive and the way he bent down to speak to her she found flattering, but still, she couldn't remember if she had seen his face before. Then, she thought, she wasn't getting any warmer or going anywhere standing in the rain, and his car looked clean and dry, and very expensive. Lindsey threw caution to the wind and reached for the passenger side door, that moments earlier, Troy had unlocked for her with the press on a button.

There were only a few lowly students making their way over to the bus stop. None paid any mind to the sleek, dark sports car in the distance as it slowly pulled away from the curb after picking up a passenger. Incidents like that happened all the time around a university campus, and those students who were walking in the rain to stand in the rain and wait for a bus were usually green with envy that they weren't the ones being picked up instead of waiting for public transportation. It was not unheard of for a student to accept a ride from a fellow student, even if the students had never properly met. That type of reckless behavior happened more than most students, usually on their own for the first time in their lives experiencing unlimited freedom, would ever care to admit.

It wasn't until two days later when Lindsey's roommate, a girl with her own busy course load and jam-packed social life began to suspect something was amiss when her friend still hadn't responded to any of her text messages. The room-mate frantically banged on her door, only to discover that Lindsey was nowhere to be found and her bed had not been slept in. In a statement given to police, Lindsey's roommate cried as she told them how sorry she was for not suspecting something sooner, stating that she figured her and Lindsey, "were really busy and just kept missing each other."

It wasn't until two days after that when a young mother, out walking with her three-month old baby in a stroller stopped mid-step because something yellow in the underbrush of her favorite local park had caught her eye. The woman discovered upon closer inspection that the 'something yellow' was in fact a bracelet attached to a stiff, bluish purple arm belonging to the missing university student, Lindsey Sparkes. The woman cried out then vomited on one of her shoes, before she stumbled away as fast as she could and called the police. The investigation that followed revealed that Lindsey had been strangled to death and when her room-mate went to the morgue to help police identify the body, she informed them quite sadly that that clothes her friend was wearing when her body was found were the same clothes she wore when she said good bye the last morning she saw her alive, leaving their apartment for the bus stop, eager to get to school because she had weeks' worth of labs to catch up on.

Troy had not made any concrete plans when he pulled out of his registered parking space on the university campus that night, although it was his intention to get home early and get some rest in order to do well on his exams. He was pleasantly surprised when Lindsey (he found out her name within seconds of her taking a seat in his car as the introductions were quick and flirtatious), agreed to go back to his apartment with him for, 'one quick drink', seeing as they both had work to do the next day. But Troy's evil feelings took over and Lindsey, he decided, after seeing her drinking a wine cooler on his sofa, was never going to see the next day. She reminded him too much of his mother and he was convinced that she, like his mother, needed to die. He strangled Lindsey quite quickly. She wasn't expecting his violence as she stood and looked at the view of the river from the window in the living room of his apartment. She barely struggled as he squeezed the life out of her, blocking off the air flow from her throat, then letting her body fall to the floor. Troy enjoyed his moment of release, then felt a surge of panic rise up through his body as he looked down at the lifeless corpse of a girl, a fellow student, that he had only just met ninety minutes earlier. It wasn't really convenient for him to move the body of a dead girl from the 5th floor of his apartment to his car in the underground garage. Troy paced in his place seemingly at a loss for a way to remove the body. He tried lifting her but quickly discovered it would be ridiculous for him to think that he could simply lift her up and carry her out of his place with no one seeing him in the hallways or elevator. Troy went to the closet in his spare bedroom where he found a large duffle bag that he had used in the past for carrying sports equipment. He brought the bag over to Lindsey's body and quickly shoved her in. Troy calmly locked the door to his apartment and went down into the utility room where tenants could borrow equipment for moving heavier items. He found then used a roller dolly to move her corpse from his apartment on the 5th floor to the trunk of his car unnoticed. Troy then drove three miles to a city park that he had driven by a thousand times in his life and after looking around on that dark and rainy night, he carried the duffle bag to a large patch of bushes, unzipped the bag and threw Lindsey's body in.

When the news of her disappearance and then the subsequent discovery of her body hit the school, both staff and students planned a candlelit vigil in her honor. Troy was sympathetic to the countless friends and mourners that sat in circles and burned candles and sang songs in her memory. In his memory, Troy recounted the smell of her hair and the light in her eyes in the moments leading up to her death. And when he was alone at night in his bed or in his shower, he loved remembering her and the other one he took so cruelly from the world.

Friends had said when interviewed, 'for as wild as she was sometimes, she would never have gotten into a car with someone she didn't know or someone that made her feel uncomfortable.' No witnesses came forward to report anything. Police give two reasons for this: the first being that the weather made it hard for anything to stand out that night; the usual amount of foot traffic, the number of students traveling across campus, the buses, and larger-than-normal crowds at the university circle because of mid-term exam preparation, leaving most students so consumed by their studies on that evening that they didn't pay attention to things other than themselves anyway. And the weather was perfect for murder; forensics concluded that she had probably been out in the rain all night, based on the amount of decomposition on the body.

Local University Student Has Been Found Dead
Lance Williamson

A local university student, Lindsey Sparkes, 20, has been found dead, it has been reported. Lindsey, a young woman from out of town, but studying full-time at the local university was found dead 2 days ago. The gruesome discovery was made by a young mother walking with her children down a trail by a local ravine. Neighbors in the tight-knit community where Lindsey was found reported no unusual sightings or disturbances in the area.

"Her body was discovered in a thick brush and it appeared as though Lindsey's cause of death was strangulation," Police Detective Cardosi said while speaking to reporters outside of the police station. "Lindsey was not a local student, from the area, but we are determined to find her killer nonetheless."

Lindsey, 20, had been studying at the university for the last two years and was well on her way to graduating with a degree in Social Work. Her roommate for the last 2 years said that Lindsey was well-liked and extremely intelligent and hardworking, in fact, the roommate, who wished to keep her identity a secret, claimed that she hadn't seen Lindsey "for days because she was always busy studying on campus. Lindsey was getting ready for exams, and she took her work very seriously." The roommate told reporters.

Local and Campus police are asking anyone with knowledge of Lindsey's final hours to contact their local police or to call the Crime Tips Hotline at: 1-888 -444 -4444.

Chapter Thirteen

Frankie Angel didn't know it at the time but, Lee James knew exactly who Frankie was when he put his card down on the bathroom counter at the sports bar that night. But it was sheer luck, or maybe coincidence that both men were in the bar at the same time. Lee James always relied on his own perseverance when he had a job to do because it seemed to pay off, more often than not. He discovered Frankie's existence on his own time; he was investigating the castration attacks and his search led him to the sports bar where it all began. Lee James discovered from a few different sources that John Scott and the two unfortunate lowlifes at the strip club all had one place where they spent their time together after work. The waitresses and bartenders had no qualms about informing Lee James of exactly what type of customers they were: cheap, rude, and completely void of any social graces. Lee James also carried with him a secret hope that no one would be able to properly identify the woman that John Scott left with on that fateful first night after questioning about the other patrons. Lee James asked around even though the other officers in his precinct had already done the job weeks before. He was met with some strange looks when he flashed his badge and explained what he was doing there so long after the fact because most of the ruckus had already died down. But Lee James had something to prove, not only to himself and his partner Rick, but to the many innocent victims of violent crimes that he had personally encountered along the way or that he knew existed in the world. Lee James wanted to show people that he was more than a cop with a badge and a gun; he wanted to demonstrate that he was a man, a human being, with a conscience and compassion, and one who cared that justice be served to all who deserved it no matter how long it took. So, as he sat at his desk and waited patiently for Frankie's phone call after the night in the bar because he was sure it was Frankie that took the bait because he even left shortly thereafter. It didn't come the day after Lee James saw him at the sports bar, or even the day after that. It came five days later when Lee was just about to give up on hearing from him. The conversation was short and to the point and Lee James had questioned immediately if Frankie would gather up the nerve to show up at all for the meeting that they had arranged.

Chapter Fourteen

Frankie Angel pulled his car into the parking space that he had scoped out earlier. He knew of this meeting spot and had chosen it very specifically; it was twenty minutes out of Norfolk Falls, and he knew he wouldn't see anyone he knew there. He came to know about the spot one day when he was doing some work on an older home and needed to find a place to have a coffee break. The owner of the home, a kindly older gentleman, told Frankie he could find an endless supply of park benches if he just walked down his street to the end of the block and crossed the road. Frankie went back during his break every day that he worked at that home and felt comfortable enough to meet with the cop there. Frankie Angel looked at his reflection in the rear-view mirror after he pulled into a parking spot; he was hoping he didn't appear as nervous or as guilty as he felt. And he prayed that she wouldn't be there anymore looking back at him, crying her silent tears and scaring him senseless. Ever since the night he was in the van with Celine he felt a heavy, suffocating, and cruelly unrelenting guilt. An insidious choking sensation that he couldn't escape. Never before in his life, throughout all he had seen and done, was there anything that he was dying to take back more than his decision to go out *that night.* For days on end he just imagined walking up to the van as it sat in his parking lot full of those guys with their horrible plans and telling them that he wouldn't be joining them. To go on without him. Frankie wished so desperately that he had just rejected John's invite from the beginning. Every once in a while, Frankie would catch himself fantasizing that instead he would have brought a baseball bat with him and when he stepped into the van, he would have bashed in all their faces the minute he learned of their plans. Frankie still could not wrap his head around why John had invited him to go in the first place. It left him deeply ashamed, and he found himself questioning his own judgment on more than one occasion since that terrible night. Frankie would beat himself up in his mind, thinking of every second, every sound, every word that was exchanged in every instant he had ever spoken to that guy. Always questioning if there was a single thing that would have made John think that Frankie was anything like him or his friends. He would become insulted then indignant at the thought of John's assumption that Frankie would ever do something as incredibly inhumane and disgusting as rape a woman just because he was presented with the opportunity to do so. Frankie had his own dark and painful experiences at the hands of an abuser; he was still unable to deal with his own demons, let alone make someone else a victim at his hand.

Frankie looked up and noticed the beads of sweat that had appeared on his forehead, and when he raised his arm from the steering wheel to wipe his face, he noticed his hands were shaking uncontrollably. Frankie had to admit that his feelings about the circumstances that he had been a part of were getting worse. He didn't think he could go on much longer with the vision of a woman showing up at any time and scaring him half to death or with the almost-nightly terrors he experienced in his sleep. It all started with nightmares of her suffering and crying out to him, and then when the news reported that certain local men were being castrated by an unidentified woman, Frankie knew he had better do something to change his role in everything that had happened on that night or he might end up paying a very dear price for the decision he had made. And Frankie thought, optimistically, if he told a cop what he knew, that maybe he could move on with his life with a clear conscience and be released from the grey and crumbling prison that had infiltrated his mind. The news that the woman still remained at large after committing the crimes was to sensationalize the story and sell papers, but Frankie couldn't look at all that was happening to him as mere coincidence. Even if people in town were still talking about the events months after they happened, people probably weren't thinking about it the same way he was, especially knowing what he knew.

As Frankie sat in his car, bracing himself for his meeting with the detective, he realized that he had not told a single person about what he saw that night or what he did to save his own ass. He couldn't admit out loud at how cowardly he felt; how he left her there, utterly defenseless at the hands of those goons. Insomnia had become a nightly burden, an uninvited guest that he couldn't shake, and he knew he couldn't keep it up much longer. At least that's what he planned on telling Lee James. He was going to tell the cop that as recently as the night before he had been awoken in his bed, covered in sweat and breathing heavily because of another nightmare. The wolves were the usual suspects but the night before he dreamt again of Celine. She was naked and crying, begging him for help. As hard as he struggled, he just couldn't reach her to take her hand or cover her with a blanket. She was always being pulled by an invisible force just out of his reach. Frankie was angry and frustrated every time he woke from one of the nightmares. He could never fall back asleep. He lay in his bed wondering how long he was meant to suffer for what he had done, or in his case, hadn't done, to Celine. Frankie never forgave himself for leaving her there that night and he could never quite convince himself that he wasn't given a choice.

Frankie exhaled deeply before he took one last look at his face in the mirror. He took another deep breath then turned off the engine and got out of his car. He locked the door then stepped away from his car and looked at the water in the distance. He could not yet see the bench in the distance where Frankie had told the police officer they would meet, and he was in no hurry to get there. His legs shook uncontrollably but his feet felt heavy, as if he were wearing blocks of cement. He looked up at a few seagulls that screeched over his head, then quietly watched as a car full of people was pulling into the parking lot. He imagined they felt so carefree as he watched them choose a spot, just a regular day with a picnic lunch. Frankie ran his fingers through his hair, flipped up the collar of his jacket and headed in the direction of the lakeside benches. As he strolled along, he noticed all the people that were also enjoying the area. It wasn't very often that Frankie had been down there and not seen another person, and this time he felt he would be grateful for the distraction. People watching was a past-time Frankie had picked up since he moved to the small, busy tourist area; he was surprised to learn that these benches provided the best view of anywhere around. People from all over the world were taking pictures of the beautiful scenery, or he could see them watching the ducks float lazily along the current, while other people picked up stones to throw in the water. It was a peaceful place and Frankie was hoping it would help keep him calm. He was scared to death because he could still hear a voice in his head telling him that he was an accessory. As he walked along the stone path and got closer to the row of benches, Frankie saw him. The officer that had left his card in the bar. As Frankie casually approached the bench from behind, he noticed the officer had a take-out tray with coffee in it from a local coffee shop, and he was grateful because up until that very moment, he realized he didn't bring anything with him except for his car keys and a pack of smokes. He walked a few steps closer then cleared his throat before speaking because it didn't seem like a good idea to be sneaking up on a cop.

Chapter Fifteen

"Are you Lee James?" Frankie said quietly stepping closer to the bench.

"Yes, that's me." Lee James said and stood up to shake Frankie's hand. "And you are Francis Willow Tree, I assume?"

"Yes." Frankie said and held out his hand to shake with Lee James. "Everyone calls me Frankie."

"Thanks a lot for meeting me here, Frankie." Lee James said as he shook Frankie's hand then motioned for him to sit on the bench. Frankie sat down and looked out at the water. A giant goose was flying in and made a superior landing, gliding expertly across the top of the water then coming to a stop in a gaggle of other geese. Frankie turned sideways just as Lee James spoke.

"No problem. I really like this spot." Frankie said and turned back to the water.

"Me too. Actually, I almost forgot about this place until you mentioned it. I used to come here all the time when I was a kid. Shit… I probably haven't come here since before I got married." Lee James said as he smiled fondly at the memory.

"Are you from the area?" Frankie asked shyly. He had a good feeling about the cop so far, he was hoping it wasn't going to be as bad as he had led himself to believe up to the moment he sat down.

"Not here exactly. I grew up in the next town over. But my grandmother used to pack up me and my cousins, shove us in the old station wagon and take us for picnics here when we were children. She loved the water and she loved to drive through this beautiful area. I guess I stopped coming here after she died." Lee James said and picked up the tray of coffee. He offered one to Frankie who took it gratefully and smiled. "They're both with cream and sugar, I didn't know what you liked."

"Thank you." Frankie said. "You were lucky to grow up somewhere so nice." Frankie said as he and Lee James both watched a young family walk by, the two young children holding hands in between their parents.

"It was nice… except for the geese." Lee James said and crinkled his nose.

"The geese?" Frankie said, confused.

"Yeah, the geese. Man, I liked everything about the area when I was growing up. They used to have this little stand right over there. I guess they got rid of it. And then there were… the geese. You know, they look harmless and pretty, but man, those suckers are as mean as snakes." Lee James said. "My grandmother always warned us kids to stay far away from them, especially when they were around their young. But do you think I would listen to my grandmother? No, not this boy. And let me tell you, I learned pretty quickly… that I hate them."

"What happened?" Frankie asked.

"We came here one weekend when it was really hot… at the end of the summer. Right before school starts. My grandmother packed us a really nice lunch, kinda as our 'going away' party, or something. I remember I had these wicked new shoes on. I wasn't supposed to be wearing them because they were for the new school year that was starting, but I snuck them outta my house anyway. It was packed… not like this, it was rammed, there were people everywhere. So, I got my new shoes on and I guess I just want to show them off, but my grandma's like, 'Lee, be careful of those geese over there.' And I'm just like, 'Yeah, whatever, Grandma, the geese can be careful of me'. Because I'm running around, just being a little shit disturber, chasing my cousin. Running as fast as I can through all these crowds and around these people and when I look up, I can't find my cousin anywhere…and I've stopped right in the middle of a flock of geese." He said, laughing and wiping his eyes. "All of a sudden there's this huge, mean prick standing right in front of me and we lock eyes. He takes one step forward, opens his huge wings and just guns it for me. All the other geese just start honking like mad, and I run as fast as I can, screaming, and looking for my grandmother. Everyone was watching, laughing, pointing at me and the geese are honking like crazy… and I was crying. Ran right into my grandmother's arms. I fucking cried…those damn geese. And ruined my new shoes too. My mother was so pissed. I will NEVER forget it. Those damn geese."

"That's hilarious." Frankie said laughing. "I'm guessing you don't share that story with too many people."

"Nah," Lee James said and laughed. "Probably wouldn't be too good for my image." Lee James said and ran his fingers through his hair with a smile on his face.

"Probably not. I don't know how much respect you'd get if all the crooks in town knew you screamed like a girl because you were afraid of big, bad birds." Frankie said, laughing even harder.

"Hey, I was just a kid…" Lee James said in mock offense.

"Yeah, sure, man. Probably best to keep that story to yourself." Frankie said still laughing as he wiped a tear away from the corner of his eye.

"Yeah, you're probably right about that. Can I trust it will never leave this bench then? I don't even think my wife knows that story." Lee James said slowly, smiling and looking at Frankie Angel.

"Your secret is safe with me. I'll take it to the grave." Frankie said.

"Thanks, appreciate it. So, were there any vicious, man-eating geese where you grew up?" Lee James said as he opened the lid and took a sip of his coffee.

"No, not a lot of geese. Or maybe it was because we didn't go on a lot of picnics when I was a kid. But I've seen a lot of deer and bears and a moose once. That was pretty cool, those things are huge." Frankie said proudly. He didn't talk about his childhood much to anyone, but he did have a few pleasant memories to share.

"Cool. So, what brought you to Norfolk Falls?" Lee James said, sipping his coffee.

"I knew a guy that moved out here after high school, so I thought I'd give it a try myself. It's been alright so far… except for…" Frankie said slowly, his voice trailing off.

"Except for? What?" Lee James asked hopefully.

"Everything was fine until that night I met that woman." Frankie said sadly, bitterly.

"I think I know what woman you're talking about." Lee James said.

"I only ever knew her first name." Frankie said cautiously. He was ignorant when it came to the law and although he considered himself a law-abiding citizen, he wasn't sure if he could get in serious trouble because of what happened to Celine. He was still insecure about his Native heritage and worried deeply that what John said could be true; that the police in Norfolk Falls would never believe a word out of his mouth.

"What was her first name, Frankie?" Lee James asked carefully, sounding more like a friend, or school guidance counselor than a cop.

"Her name was Celine." Frankie said as a tear rolled down his cheek. He wiped it away with his hand and stared blankly out at the water.

"Can you tell me what else you know, Frankie?" Lee James asked quietly.

"I don't know much about what happened, only what I read about when they found her in the paper. I know that they drugged her, that John slipped something in her drink. We drove to her work and John gave it to her; she never stood a chance. I know she didn't know anyone that was there except for John. And I *know* all those guys, except for me, knew exactly what they were going to do to her... so I didn't think it would be hard to guess what those guys did to her that night." Frankie said, suddenly dry-heaving, his body trembling at the thought. Lee James watched as the color drained from his cheeks. Up until that very moment he had not spoken one word aloud about the events of that dark and rainy night to anyone. And Frankie never imagined he'd be having the conversation for the first time with a cop.

"All I can say for myself is I never wanted anything to do with it from the start. If I had known anything before… I had even gotten into that van with them, I would never have gone. And I wish with all my heart that I could take it back…" Frankie said, crying, trying to hold back his tears. "I wish that I could have been stronger or braver, or… I don't know…" Frankie said, wiping his face, taking a deep breath. "Maybe I wish I could have saved her from those guys. Those fucking guys who tricked me into going with them and made me feel like a piece of shit for even being there. Do you know I walked home that night by myself in the rain?" Frankie said bitterly, staring into the distance, his spine stiffened as he took a quick swipe at his eyes, his emotions turning on a dime.

"No, I didn't know that." Lee James said softly, almost putting his arm out and reaching for the man that sat beside him.

"That wasn't the worst of it. I don't care that I walked, I probably deserved worse, you know, for leaving her there and not doing a single thing about it." Frankie said and wiped more tears from his eyes. Lee James was quiet as Frankie continued. "But those guys didn't care about me. They were going to hurt that woman no matter what I said. And they told me that. Do you know I have a sister?" Frankie said wiping his face and trying to maintain his composure. Lee James shook his head gently.

"I have a younger sister named Celia and I haven't seen her in a really long time. The whole time I walked home all I could think of was if anyone had done to my sister what those guys did to Celine, I think I would probably kill them. That's all I could think for so long. That I knew what was going to happen, and I did nothing about it. I felt like I let down my sister, and every woman I ever knew. Ever since that night, I have hated looking at myself in the mirror. Hated myself because I feel so ashamed by what I *didn't* do. For walking out on her. For listening to them. I fucking hate them. It has haunted me for so long that I have started to think I am going to go crazy…like I should throw myself over a bridge, or something." Frankie said quietly as he wiped the tears from his eyes and looked over to Lee James.

"I know this might sound stupid but, why didn't you call the police? You could have left an anonymous tip. At least you would have gotten it off your chest." Lee James said sympathetically, feeling so much compassion for the poor soul.

"Well, this might sound stupid too," Frankie said and paused to take a deep breath. "But John told me two things that night and I believed both of them. The first thing he said when I told him I didn't want to…" Frankie said in a whisper, then stopped to catch his breath and wipe his eyes. "Have sex with that girl was that if I said one word to anyone, he would come to my house and burn it down with me in it. He said he would kill me, and I believed him. Part of me still does. Part of me is still afraid of that piece of shit." Frankie said angrily, thinking bitterly that his own fear of John and the situation that he had gotten him in was the worst of it all.

"Well, I don't think you have to worry about John Scott anymore…" Lee James said quietly.

'Yeah, I guess not." Frankie said with a small smile in the corner of his mouth. "I heard about him from that papers and the people at the sports bar. Fuck him. He got what he deserved."

"What else did he say to you that night?" Lee James said as a warm breeze blew in off the water.

"Huh?" Frankie said quickly, his mind was racing with memories of the night he had tried to block out for so long.

"You said John told you two things that night. What was the other thing he told you?" Lee James said.

Frankie sat straight up on the bench and turned to Lee James. "John Scott told me that even if I did tell the police about what happened or who was involved, that no one would believe a stupid, wino, spear-chucker like me anyway." He said bravely, then wiped the tears that had rolled down his cheeks.

"Wow, he actually said that to you?" Lee James said incredulously. Frankie nodded slowly. "I didn't even realize people still talked like that to other people."

"He was in my place when he said that to me. I'll never forget it for the rest of my life… any of it." Frankie said sadly, drying his eyes then looking out to the water and further to the horizon. He looked down at his coffee for the first time since Lee James handed it to him, opened the lid and took a sip. He reached into his pocket and pulled out his cigarettes, lit one and blew out the smoke. "I'm pretty sure he didn't even know what he was talking about. Most people my age don't even know about Native Peoples anymore but I was so scared that he was telling the truth about everything that I never thought to question it. Tell me…" Frankie said slowly, taking a deep breath, so afraid of the answer. "Is that woman, Celine… is she ever going to be okay?"

"That's what I'm trying to figure out, Frankie. I just wanted to know what happened to her because she couldn't remember anything from that night, and we had no evidence against anyone that was there. At least not until a few of those guys started showing up in the emergency room without their testicles."

"Do you really think it was her who was doing that? I mean, I know for a fact that those guys put drugs in her drink so she wouldn't remember anything. But how could she suddenly remember their faces?" Frankie said quickly.

'I don't know the answer to that myself. And between me, you and those geese over there…I agree with you a hundred percent… *those guys got exactly what they deserved.*" Lee James said and took a sip of his coffee, then looked away.

Chapter Sixteen

"Hi, Mrs. Bower." Lee James said as he stepped out of his car, onto her driveway in the bright sun. When he pulled down the quiet street, he noticed that the door to Celine's mother's townhouse was open a crack and as he pulled into the driveway, he saw her step out the front onto the steps, then turn to lock the door behind her. He noticed immediately that she had her car keys in hand and was dressed to be out for the day. She looked very ready to leave.

Lee James' first instinct after speaking to Frankie Angel was to rush over to the Bower residence and tell them everything he knew. Although being armed with that type of information, and based on past experience, especially considering the severity of the abuse Celine had suffered, Lee James felt as though there might be a way to offer Celine and her mother some peace that he was sure they could use in their lives. Lee James was an honest man, and he never had one single intention of alerting Celine or her mother to the fact that he, and his partner, Rick, believed with good reason, that Celine was responsible for the spate of castration attacks in their town. When Lee James left Frankie Angel, who himself breathed freely for the first time in a really long time, he went directly to the station so he and Rick could discuss what he had just learned. It took a while and they were careful to be exceptionally discreet so as not to draw any attention to themselves, but, Rick and Lee James discovered the truth about what happened the night Celine was kidnapped and raped so many months ago. Armed with Frankie's account of what happened, together, the detectives checked the names Frankie provided and cross-referenced them with the men that were castrated in the months following Celine's attack. There was one name on their list that belonged to Adam Johnson, and after a phone call to an old buddy that worked at the courthouse, Rick learned that Adam was still serving his sentence in a medium-security penitentiary for assault and battery on his girlfriend and assaulting a police officer one night not long after the attacks started. The detectives couldn't be sure, but they felt it was safe to assume that Adam had met Celine at some point after the night he raped her but had somehow gotten away. Both detectives admired Celine's tenacity, thinking that one day there might be a book or movie about her, but they had to keep the information to themselves. And considering castration was not a viable punishment for rape, they kept a tight lid on their discovery, believing that the men who raped Celine had truly gotten their justice served.

When Lee James pulled into Molly's driveway, he had a smile on his face; it wasn't very often, or at least, not often enough that the men in Rick and Lee James profession got an opportunity to offer such comforting news. Lee James knew there was no such thing as 'closure',(Rick had taught him that the first week they were partnered),but he thought relief could come with certain types of information. The exact kind he was about to give to Molly and especially, Celine Bower.

Molly turned quickly at the sound of another car in her driveway. The color drained from her cheeks when she saw who she thought to be one of the detectives that had worked Celine's case so long ago. She froze as she felt the fear creep down into the core of her being. Molly stopped for a moment to steady herself then put her hand against the garage door just as Lee James had stepped out of his car.

“Woah, woah, are you alright?” Lee James asked as he walked quickly towards Molly Bower. He reached for her arm to steady her, but she had already stepped away from the garage door and straightened her jacket. Not knowing what this encounter meant for her and her daughter but hoping she had prayed enough to save them from any further trauma.

“Oh, I’m fine, Detective. Don’t mind me, ha ha. Whew, I thought I saw something in the neighbor’s yard… a giant bug flying around, or something. Ha ha. I don’t like to talk about it but, I mean it’s a bit embarrassing but… I am so scared of bugs. It’s so funny, we are so much bigger than they are but oh, they can just stop me in my tracks. I can’t help it. I’ve just always been that way. Celine makes so much fun of me when I freak out.” Molly said with a smile as she regained her composure and felt the blood slowly return to her cheeks. She was petrified that her worst nightmare was coming true, but Molly Bower was an extremely intelligent woman and not playing games; she did a little research on her own since Celine’s escape, and knew she did not have to say anything to the police unless they came to her house with a warrant, and she had already picked a lawyer out of the phone book, should the need arise.

“Oh okay, just checking…” Lee James said slowly, sounding a little confused. “You looked a little pale there for a minute. Are you sure you don’t want to sit down? Maybe just rest on the stairs for a minute?” Lee James said with obvious concern in his voice.

“No, no, no thank you. I’m absolutely fine, Detective. Actually, I’m running a bit late for an appointment. Is there something I can help you with?” Molly said as she walked past Lee James towards her car in the driveway. She pressed a button in her hand and heard the doors unlock. She was doing her best not to seem like she was acting standoffish or hiding something and crossed her fingers that he didn’t know enough about her to tell that she was acting anything out of the ordinary. But Molly Bower had a poker face and it was a skill earned from years of marriage.

"Oh, well, it turns out that we've made some strides with Celine's case and I was wondering if she's here and there's a chance I could speak to her… to both of you, actually. I think it is news that you'll want to hear as well." Lee James said hopefully, exhaling a deep breath, hiding his excitement.

"Well, I'm sorry, Detective, not only am I late for an appointment but, Celine isn't here right now. She… well, she wasn't doing too well after everything that happened to her, you know, on that terrible night, so we, or she, decided to take a leave of absence from her job, and… we've got family in Florida, so Celine decided to take a drive down there to stay with them for a little while." Molly said, stopping to catch her breath, raising her arm to shield her eyes from the sun. No matter what she was meant to be hiding, Molly could never truly disguise her emotional heartbreak that she felt with what happened to her Celine on that fateful night. "I can pass a message along, if you like, Detective, but she and I both agreed that it was in her best interest if she didn't have any contact, or reminders about the night she was attacked." Molly said quietly to Lee James. She suddenly became aware that she may have said too much, although deep down she knew she really didn't say anything at all. Molly Bower knew her daughter so well that when she was formulating a story to give to the police, should they ever show up at her house, that she would pick somewhere that Celine had only ever mentioned going to. And Florida was somewhere Celine wanted to visit when she was a teenager. She and her father were supposed to go together as a trip to see the manatees but after he died, she never mentioned it again. Molly thought it was a clever way to keep both of their memories alive.

"I'm so sorry, I really have to go," Molly Bower said as she stretched out her arm in order to see her watch. "I'm late for my appointment as it is. When I talk to Celine, I will pass your message along. If she wants to hear from you, I will have her call you at the police station. I really must be going, Detective. Sorry you went to all this trouble and thank you for stopping by." Molly Bower said as she opened her car door and sat down inside. She put her keys in the ignition and was about to start the engine when Lee James leaned toward her.

"I didn't come here to trouble you, or Celine." He said quietly as he stepped closer toward her open door. "I just thought it would be helpful for both of you… but especially Celine. I thought maybe if she had a better understanding of what happened to her the night she was attacked. I didn't come here for any other reason, anything at all. Only to tell Celine that there was someone else there that night, someone else that saw some of what happened to her. That is the *only* reason I came here today. I'm sorry to have troubled you, Mrs. Bower. and I won't keep you any longer. Take care, Mrs. Bower." Lee James said as he closed her car door and walked back down the driveway to his own car. He got in, turned on the engine, pulled down her driveway and drove away.

Molly sat in her driveway, frozen in place. Her body felt like it was made of iron and she could feel her heart thumping in her chest. Her pulse quickened and she fought the urge to vomit all over. Molly switched off the engine, got out of her car and ran inside. When she was sure no one was watching, Molly Bower walked into her kitchen took the phone off the wall and called Tunisha.

Lee James made it to the corner of Molly's street before he realised that he had probably been duped. He couldn't say for certain, but he felt deep inside that she was not entirely truthful with him; that she had something to hide and maybe it would be up to him to figure it out. He switched on his turn signal, drove to the next block, then turned down a street and come to a stop sign. He made a right turn and drove back down the Bower's street.

He was stunned to see her car was still in the driveway, and that she was nowhere to be found.

"Tunisha, this is Molly Bower. Celine's mother… oh gosh, you know that. I'm a little frazzled right now but I don't know what else to do. I just wanted you to know that what we talked about actually happened. The police came to my house today, *a detective*," Molly said breathlessly, holding in her tears. "But I didn't tell him a thing. You don't have to respond to this message, in fact, it's probably better that you don't. I just wanted someone to know what happened… I really miss her, Tunisha. I hope she's okay. Let me know if you hear from her, okay, Tunisha? Okay?" Tunisha listened carefully to the message and was about call Molly when she heard there was another recording that came in less than a minute later.

"Tunisha… this might make me sound crazy but, *I think they know something.*" Molly Bower said breathlessly before she hung up.

Chapter Seventeen

After getting her fill of sand and sun, and especially once her internal clock renegotiated some of the problems associated with jet-lag, she had passed out cold on a lounger with a cup of coffee in her hand after breakfast and woke up in a pile of her own drool, her cheeks pink and her hair plastered to the side of her face. Celine filled her days with walking to the jetty near her hotel, then down the long board walk, where she waited and watched the vibrant schools of tropical fish, then got on her particular boat to cruise over the ocean and visit an island she had never even heard of. Celine loved the beach and swam like a fish once she solidified the idea in her head that no one there had any idea what she was hiding and that she could blend in with the rest of the tourists out for an island getaway. Celine took the same boat back to her hotel with every intention of returning to the island the next day. She knew there was more to see and explore, and she felt herself becoming addicted to the exotic wildlife and locale. Although she had only been there a day, Celine already loved the freedom and anonymity being so far away from home gave her. Slowly she began to enjoy herself more and more and the more time she spent among people she didn't know, or even better, people that didn't know her, the better she felt about herself. Celine still struggled with every breath to leave behind the girl she once was and the one she ever really knew, only to embrace the woman her choices had forced her to become.

It was easy for her to remember 'the old Celine', she just had to think of her father, the one person she loved that would never 'know' her as the person she had become. She thought of her father and missed him dearly as she pressed the button on the elevator in the bright lobby of her hotel. When she got to her room, Celine sat down on her bed and cried. In the madness and chaos of packing to leave the country, Celine almost forgot to think of her father and properly miss him, the way she had every single day since his untimely death, and it almost felt like a betrayal to his loving memory. She was still convinced (although the strength of her conviction was fading slightly), that the night she had been raped could have been altered somehow if her father had still been with her. Celine knew it was hopeless to think such heart-breaking thoughts, but in her moment of utter loneliness, her exhaustion and irrationality won out and she cried. She sat on the edge of her bed and balled her eyes out. Tears streamed down her face and her sobs rocked the bed. She cried until she could cry no longer. When she stopped crying, Celine looked up at her reflection in the mirror on the wall across from where she sat. Her cheeks were pink from the sun and her hair looked sexy and windblown, and her eyes, normally so clear and bright, were puffy and red. But she noticed something she hadn't noticed in a really long time; she saw herself. The person that her father had loved so deeply and the person her mother still loved. The funny girl her friends always had a good giggle with and who they loved to be around. The young woman who studied hard and earned grades good enough to be accepted and graduate from veterinary college. She looked down at her hands and saw the doctor that had every intention of devoting her life to rescuing abandoned animals. And that was who she forgot so easily when she looked in the mirror. Celine was sad that her only connection to that person she once was could be found in the girl she still carried around with her after losing her beloved father, somehow lost in time and space but knowing she could always return to that grief and loss and remember who she once was.

Celine shook off her sadness, wiped her eyes, whispered a silent prayer to her father then got up and took a shower. She was practically starving by the time she got dressed, slicked her hair back in a ponytail and made for the elevator. All Celine knew was that she didn't want to feel like a victim anymore; she didn't want to go back and be that person who cried all day and lived under a dark, stormy cloud. She wasn't sure how easily she was going to accept the new part of her, and she had no idea if the new and old parts of her could figure out a way to mesh somehow, to co-exist together in the same body. Her brow furrowed deeply at the thought as she walked alone into the lobby. The front desk clerk at Celine's hotel kindly informed her that if she exited through the double doors and made a left, she would be able to find everything she was looking for, when she stopped to ask about a place to eat for dinner before going out. Celine thanked the man then walked out the doors and down the crowded main road. She was wearing cut-off jean shorts, sandals and a tank-top, with a sweater tied around her waist. The weather was incredibly balmy, hot and sticky, but the sun was just beginning to set over the bay. Other tourists had started piling out of their hotels, heading in the same direction down the busy street. As she walked along the road, Celine began to sweat after only walking one block and she was careful not to stumble on the uneven sidewalk while taking in as many sights as she could without falling flat on her face. The little seaside town was the first of its kind that she had ever been to and she was trying to make the most of a journey that had only just begun. The one where she couldn't see the end.

Cars on both sides of the road were old, loud and most had dying exhausts that blew black, acrid smoke out of their behinds. Other tourists were the only people walking leisurely down the cracked sidewalk. Some were couples that walked hand-in-hand while others had arms around their partner's waists and hands in opposite pockets. When Celine came to a one-story building on the side of the road she had been walking on, she stopped and poked her head in one of the open doors, where she discovered a handicrafts market. She smiled at one of the proprietors who was standing in front of shelves packed with different kinds of hand-carved trinkets and masks, keychains and bracelets, and promised the woman that she would be back after dinner. Celine smiled as she walked back gracefully from the entrance way and carried on down the street. She could see streetlight ahead and lots of foot traffic heading in the direction of two massive shiny buildings about a block over, which she assumed to be the ones the concierge at her hotel had recommended she try. The street was alive with bright lights and loud music pumping from speakers on outdoor patios. She could smell smoke from food stalls that were set up on every street corner and the smog from the pollution would rear its ugly head to mix in with the delicacies every few feet. Celine was overwhelmed with the amount of choices available on one street. She stopped mid-walk to take stock and decide which restaurant she would try. The loudest restaurant was attached to a large modern-looking hotel and most of the seats at the front of the patio were taken by a large group of foreign men. She looked further down the strip and noticed the usual Western fast-food joints and when she turned to look, she noticed she was standing in front of a little Italian bistro that had votive candles lit on the tables and played soft violin music. It looked to be full of couples gazing into each other's eyes over their shrimp linguini and chicken parmigiana. Up ahead on the right, Celine was drawn to a funky-looking chicken painted over the door of a small restaurant. There were tables and chairs out front and a menu on a poster-board that displayed all the restaurants specialities.

A waiter spotted her as she stepped closer to the patio to read the sign and greeted her with a warm 'hello' before she had a chance to change her mind and walk away. He smiled pleasantly and stretched open his arms to indicate that she should enter. And she did.

"Welcome, welcome." The waiter said with a warm smile in heavily accented English.

"Thank you." Celine said shyly as she stepped onto the patio and smiled.

"Oh… just for one?" The waiter said as he looked past Celine's head towards the sidewalk to see if there was anyone that would be joining her.

"Yup, just me!" Celine said, a little too loudly, suddenly self-conscious at the thought of dining alone. She hadn't had too many opportunities to eat alone, other than in university and while traveling, but she didn't mind it, although she did have to admit to herself that she had not seen one other female traveller vacationing solo since her journey began.

"Oh, that's okay." The waiter said quickly, he was smiling and doing his best to offer her encouragement. "We have the best seat in the house reserved for you right here." He said as he giggled, then pointed to a table that was smack-dab in the center of the outdoor patio.

"Oh," Celine said, smiling and walking slowly over to the table he'd indicated, all the while looking behind him to the interior of the restaurant, hoping for a seat a little less conspicuous. "Do you have anything inside?" Celine asked politely.

"Inside? No, you should sit out here." He said, pulling a heavy metal chair away from the table and motioning with his hand for her to sit down. "It's the best seat in the house. You can see everything that's going on out here." He said flagging her over with his hand. Celine walked somewhat reluctantly to the table.

'Yeah, and everyone can see me…' She thought to herself with a laugh as she gave in and made herself comfortable on the chair. She didn't know it at the time but figured it out later in her journey that for a restaurant to have an attractive foreign woman enjoying a meal at their establishment for everyone to see was the best free advertising available.

"You just sit here, and I'll get you a menu." The waiter said with a smile, then turned and walked into the restaurant. When he returned moments later, he handed Celine a menu and lit the votive candle on her table.

'Better for people to see me with…' Celine thought dryly as she accepted the menu with a smile and nodded 'thanks'.

"Take your time. Would you like something to drink?" He said and smiled a big smile.

"Thank you. I'll have an iced tea, please." She said smiling as she quickly opened the menu and looked for a drink list.

"Okay," He said and happily returned to the restaurant while Celine looked through the menu. By the time the waiter had returned with her iced tea, Celine had narrowed down her choices to two and asked her waiter for advice on which to order.

"Oh, I would try the Santa Fe Chicken." The waiter said and pointed to the photo on the poster board behind Celine.

"Okay, I'll try that then." Celine said and closed the menu. She handed it to the waiter who took it from her and smiled.

"You know, you are very pretty." He said as he batted his eye lashes at her.

"Thank you." She said and smiled. "You are too." Celine said and laughed as the waiter squealed with delight and did a small curtsey before turning around and walking quickly towards the door that led to the kitchen inside to place her order. She could hear him behind her speaking quickly in a foreign language as he finished telling his story. He returned briefly to Celine's table with another member of the restaurant staff, smiled warmly as he pointed to Celine, and spoke to his co-worker as they both walked away. Celine smiled and chuckled to herself, then turned her attention to the road in front of her. She realised instantly that he was right, that she did in fact, have the best seat in the house. The patio was set a few feet off the sidewalk and her high-back chair was more than likely meant as a bar stool. But, Celine thought, even with the candle lit, she was seated in the shadows of the buildings and no one even noticed she was there. She didn't notice the heat so much earlier in the day, she had been in and out of the ocean too many times to count, but as she sat at the table sipping her iced tea, she could feel beads of sweat rolling down her back and chest. She used a napkin to wipe off her upper lip, then lifted her hair and dried the nape of her neck.

While waiting for her dinner, Celine watched as one couple after another walked down the sidewalk in front of her. She watched as groups of young, local girls, with their long, shiny hair, high heels, and short skirts walked by smoking cigarettes, talking and laughing, and she watched as the teenage boys chased the girls, only to be swatted away then laughed at. Celine wondered, as she sat there, how long it would be before she felt normal again, like her old self. And she wanted so badly to contact her mother. Celine wiped a tear from her eye and reached into her purse for her little journal.

Dear Mom,

Some bored children, or possibly teenagers, were running the hallways and ringing doorbells of random rooms today. I nearly jumped out of my towel the first time it happened to me. But I was too scared to open the door and look outside in the hallway. It took about five minutes for my heart rate to return to normal so I could walk over to the door and look out the peephole.

I have got to get it together.

No one knows I'm here. No one is looking for me here. I have to keep telling myself that.

Nobody knows where I am. Breathe. Nobody knows I'm here.

Oops, my dinner just arrived. I don't remember what I ordered but it smells great and looks like chicken.

I love you, CB

p.s. tomorrow I'm taking a boat to an island to catch another glimpse of the local wildlife. And this time I will be more prepared. I'm so excited!

"Here is your chicken, missy." The waiter said brightly as he carried a steaming plate of food to Celine's table. She moved her journal quickly as he set the plate down, then pulled some silverware and a napkin out of his apron.

"Wow, thanks. It looks really good." Celine said as she looked down at the colorful plate of food in front of her. She wasn't ever known as the 'bravest' of eaters and her dinner choice proved that. Her plate consisted of a fat, juicy chicken breast stuffed with fresh salsa, melted cheese and avocado. And she didn't realise how hungry she was until the smell hit her nostrils. She smiled at the waiter and dug in. After a few bites, the waiter returned to her table with a fresh iced tea to which she responded with a grateful thumbs-up.

He returned sometime later to an empty plate and offered Celine a dessert menu. As she leafed through it, he plucked up the courage to ask her some questions.

"So… how come you don't have a boyfriend?" he asked shyly.

Celine responded by smiling and shrugging her shoulders. He smiled a knowing smile.

"Are you here all by yourself?" He asked her as he reached for her empty plate.

"Yes, I am. It's very beautiful and relaxing. It's my first time here." Celine said and smiled.

"Wow, you are so brave." He said. "How old are you?"

"I'm twenty-six… and thank you." Celine said.

"You're really pretty… can I touch your hair?" He said and reached out shyly. When Celine relaxed her shoulders and opened the space between them, he gently ran his fingers through her long blonde hair.

"Wow, it's so soft." He said and nodded approvingly. "What's your name? I'm Micah."

"Hi, Micah. I'm Celine." She said and smiled at him.

"Nice to meet you, Celine," he said. "Are you just here on vacation? What kind of job do you have? You are so pretty." He said and smiled at her. He was cute and handsome at the same time. But gentle and calming too.

"I'm a teacher, I'm just taking some time off to travel. It's really nice to get away sometimes. And… thank you." Celine said gratefully and smiled.

Celine couldn't remember the last time she smiled so freely in the company of a man. He was only her waiter, meant to serve her food and drinks, but at that moment, in that funky chicken restaurant, he served as a distinct reminder that not all men were vile, evil creatures, destined to destroy the spirit of women. As she sat there and answered his questions about her life and laughed at his jokes, Celine felt herself feeling comfortable and opening up to a stranger on the other side of the world, being at peace with it and being grateful.

They both felt a twinge of sadness when Celine eventually asked for her bill, but after many 'goodbyes' and a hefty tip, Celine promised to return again to see her new friend. She had a spring in her step and a confidence in her choice; she felt as though she was exactly where she was supposed to be in her life. As she pushed in her chair and walked toward the front steps, Celine noticed the sun had set and she completely missed it. She had been so caught up in enjoying the moment that she didn't notice her surroundings had changed dramatically around her. The waiter in the restaurant didn't know who Celine was before she stepped foot on the wooden patio, but he treated her with kindness and respect, and she enjoyed every minute of their time together. That comfort left her with the feeling that she was still attractive in other's eyes and she was someone that strangers might be interested in knowing more about, even if their encounter was brief and fleeting.

She was smiling, feeling full from dinner, and believing for the first time (if only slightly), what her mother, and therapy and Tunisha had been trying to tell her all along; what a wonderful person she truly was, and how no amount of abuse inflicted on her by another person could change that. As she walked along the busy main road, Celine stumbled slightly over an uneven part of the sidewalk. She laughed to herself, checked her toes, and kept going. Celine walked down the busy road in the direction of her hotel. She stopped occasionally as she was walking to take in the sights around her; women on the sidewalk with baskets of dried fruit and small trinkets for sale, the open door of the market she passed on her way to the restaurant still called to her. She went inside and found herself drawn to each stall individually. They all had something interesting and unique to offer and the shopkeepers greeted her loudly and with enthusiasm. Celine enjoyed looking but was saddened by the thought that she would not be able to buy any souvenirs; without knowing anything about the police and her situation back home, she thought it too risky to send a parcel with a foreign stamp on it to her mother's address. But she smiled and thanked each shopkeeper as she walked away empty handed from their stalls. Celine found a side exit door and walked out into a busy parking lot that had come to life when the sun went down.

There were stalls serving food down a long line in the middle of the parking lot. Huge, steaming silver pots of local fare, charcoal grills covered with meat on sticks and large silver griddles the length of a car with steaming piles of food on them, eagerly anticipated by the waiting customers seated at plastic dining tables only a few feet away. The people, mostly locals, ignored Celine as she walked by and took in the sights. The smell was incredibly enticing but she already had her dinner at the chicken restaurant. She continued on her walk back to the hotel at a leisurely pace, she was really beginning to enjoy her new surroundings. She felt more comfortable in the balmy air and she loved to watch the different types of people that were around the area. She could have lived without the cockroaches though, and the giant rat that poked its head up from the sewer grate just as she was walking by. She screamed and jumped onto the sidewalk and instantly felt her cheeks flush when she realised what she had done. She wasn't the only one who noticed what she did, and when she heard laughter at her over-reaction, she turned quickly to the sound. Not more than ten feet behind her, Celine noticed a group of about three younger local men watching her every move as she walked back to her hotel. They had been leaning up against a side of a building and as Celine got closer, she noticed they began to focus an unhealthy amount of attention on her. But Celine was minutes from her hotel and nowhere near a convenience store, and she was looking to get something from one of the stands in the parking lot to take up to her room for the night. She slowly walked over to a truck-bed that had been cleverly converted into a fruit stand selling fresh juice. She could hear the boys getting louder behind her, but she tried not to react to the sound, instead she smiled at the woman behind the counter as she walked up to Celine. The woman, probably in her late 50's, had her hair tied back in a loose bun and she had a beautiful smile with perfectly straight, white teeth. She had a generous bosom and was chubby in the hips. She wore a long, tiered skirt and a loose-fitting cotton shirt.

Celine took a quick look at the fruit that appeared on offer and when she pointed to a giant container with orange liquid in it, she smiled at the woman and hoped for the best. The young men that had gathered behind her would not let up, in fact, they had gotten louder and bolder with what they were saying. Celine could feel her blood pressure begin to rise, but she had promised herself, made an iron-clad deal with herself, that as a foreigner in a foreign country, she would not act in any way that would draw attention to herself. She knew why she was on the run in the first place, something that happened to her had driven her to react in a way that wasn't necessarily acceptable or legal behaviour, and she knew how fortunate she was to be standing free at a juice bar in an exotic location on the other side of the world.

The woman had filled Celine's order and was slowly walking back to where Celine stood with a drink in her hand and a smile on her face. Celine smiled in return at the woman, then took the drink she had ordered and handed the woman a bill from her back pocket. She smiled again and took a sip of her drink while she waited for the woman to make change. All the while, the whistles and cat-calling continued loudly behind her. When she glanced briefly over her shoulder toward the sound, Celine noticed that at least two more had joined the group of harassers. Celine thanked the woman again, rolled her eyes at the sounds of the group behind her, and then watched as the woman looked at Celine with a knowing glance before handing Celine her change and smiling a good-bye.

"Ooh, sexy lady. Oh, baby. Sex me, baby." Seemed to be the only fitting English words the pack had in their vocabulary. And they said those words repeatedly, along with, 'Missy, Missy," every couple of steps before saying something in their native language then laughing hysterically. Celine didn't need a translator to understand the words they were saying amongst themselves, or to figure out what the topic of conversation was. They were so close and so intent on tormenting her that she could feel their out-of-control testosterone and smell their cheap cologne and after shave. It was mixed in with their sweat. And she realised as she listened closely, that she could hear their ragged breathing more distinctly than before. She was trying to maintain her composure while walking at a normal speed when she felt one of the boys get close enough to brush against her.

'That's it!' She said out loud. Celine stopped cold. She heard the boys laugh a little and she turned to face them.

The street where they stood wasn't very busy, but there were tourists and locals alike walking up and down the shoreline, people eating at the food stalls twenty feet behind them and plenty of cars on the road. In that moment, as Celine looked each one of the boys in the face (they had gathered around her in a semi-circle the second she stopped walking and turned to face them), nothing else seemed to matter to her but her own safety. Some of the boys had tiny amounts of facial hair, while others were sporting excessive amounts of teenage acne. One boy was wearing sunglasses even though it was night-time, but he must have thought they went well with his long, spiked hair. Even though it was dark, the streetlights shone brightly enough that Celine could see the thin sheen of sweat that glistened on each of their upper lips and was about to step closer to whom she presumed to be the leader of pack when over the silence of their confrontation, Celine heard the sound of cheap plastic flip flops hitting the pavement in rapid succession, headed in her direction. All Celine could focus on were the five tormentors in front of her. It took every ounce of self-control (and then some), that she had in her body not to teach them a lesson in manners they would not soon forget.

Celine couldn't take her eyes off the pack of young men; they had developed a more aggressive stance toward her in response to her defiance and were closing in around her, but the sound of the shoes on the pavement would not stop. And suddenly, Celine heard a woman shouting angrily at the top of her lungs in the local language. That's when Celine looked up momentarily from the crowd that had gathered around her and saw the woman from juice stand running as fast as she could toward her with something long and shiny in her hand.

The rat-faced kid on the outer part of the circle was the first to turn toward the noise and taking a cue from the look on his face in response to the commotion, the other boys turned also. The chubby kid on the opposite corner had tried to slink away as soon as he noticed who was making all the noise but before he even had a chance, the woman from the juice stand stopped running and was standing directly in front of the group. The woman was waving whatever instrument she had in her hand at each of the boys and intermittently pointing at Celine, then pointing at the sky. The more she spoke the less aggressive each boy became and the lower their shoulders seemed to slump. Without stopping to take a breath, the woman carried on in the same fashion for another ten seconds before each of the five boys in the group had his head bowed low, his hands in his pockets and shame all over his face. The juice lady made one final statement before whipping whatever she was holding across her hand with a loud slap. Each boy jumped in his shoes then slowly slinked away with his tail between his legs back in the direction he had come.

People that had stopped to stare as the drama unfolded carried slowly on their way after realising the show was over when the boys walked away. Celine stood face-to-face with the woman and smiled before she rushed over to her and gave her a giant bear hug. The woman patted Celine's back and said something sweet in her ear before releasing Celine and sending her on her way. As she turned to the direction of her hotel, Celine felt, perhaps for the very first time, that she was a part of something greater than herself. Celine walked the last of her journey to her hotel with a smile on her face, excited for a new day.

Dear Mom,

The rain that was pouring down when I arrived was not an ominous sign after all. The locals have proven to be friendly and helpful, and I had a wonderful sleep when I got here and then an even better massage. On a less-than-friendly note, there are these groups of young men, some of them boys really, that seem to latch onto my scent (the scent of a foreign woman), then follow me around this place like groups of hungry wolves chasing down an injured lamb. They shout, 'hello' and 'missy, missy', then say something in their own language and laugh hysterically amongst themselves. I wonder how they'd feel if I actually turned around and drop-kicked one of them, they probably wouldn't find it very funny. Oh my gosh, I can just hear you now, "Oh, Celine, don't go getting into any trouble!". Sorry to make light of such a serious situation. I can't imagine what you've been through at home by yourself. I wonder what the neighbors think… just kidding! I'm sorry, Mom. But it's been so long since I've felt like I could actually relax and have a real smile on my face.

Have I even smiled since waking up in those woods? Yes, every time I made one of those bastards pay for what he did to me.

I love you, CB

Chapter Eighteen

As it turned out, the lazy island-hopping life suited Celine immeasurably. She loved waking up, having no crippling nightmares that she could remember and loved eating her breakfast at the outdoor patio that doubled as a dining area. Celine, true to herself, believed she had discovered a little slice of heaven on earth when she returned to the jetty and saw a poster that advertised the local wildlife on the island she had just been on previously. Celine bought a waterproof disposable camera and more stale bread for the day's trip.

The moment Celine saw the area where the Monitor Lizards converged and scavenged for food, Celine felt as though she had stepped back in time by about a billion years. The animals looked so majestic and powerful with their perfect scales and forked tongues, their tails were so active and mesmerizing that an hour had gone by before Celine had realised that she had not moved from her spot. But she couldn't stop watching from behind the fence; the longer she stood the more lizards came down from the mountain and wandered in her direction in search of food scraps and hand-outs. The sign posted said not to feed the animals, but Celine noticed a local man holding chunks of barbequed chicken near the area in order to entice the creatures down from their hiding spots. Celine was in heaven. She remembered vividly, a video she had watched with her father shortly after entering high school. It showed South America's black and red aquatic iguanas sunning themselves on the rocky coast-line of the Galapagos Islands, and when she saw them in person a few years later, she was absolutely beside herself. As she stood watching another famous lizard, she felt grateful for the once-in-a-lifetime opportunity that had repeated itself. She wiped a tear from her eye and said a silent prayer of gratitude to her father for showing her so much about life before his death.

Celine returned to her hotel room that day feeling empty and alive all at the same time. She was sick of the feeling that she let creep in; the one where she felt as though she had done so many things wrong and disappointed so many people. And she felt hardened by the thought that what she had done as a result, or retribution, for what someone had done to her, what she had read on the internet one day while looking up revenge behaviour. 'What was it those PhD's had said? That someone who had taken drastic actions after being ignored by police was possibly suffering from, what did they call it? Oh, yes, yes, 'Severe Rape Trauma Syndrome'. Yes, that was it,' Celine thought to herself as she walked around her hotel room, stripping off her sand-covered clothes and turning on the shower. 'How would they know what it's like?' She thought as she stepped under the warm stream of water and began rinsing the sand and salt-water off her body and out of her long hair. 'How exactly would they know what it's like to have some piece of shit guy shove his dick inside you without your consent? And *syndrome*?' She thought angrily, 'How about the feeling of powerlessness that comes after being raped repeatedly, by more than one man? Is that highlighted as part of the *syndrome*? How about never wanting to leave your home again because of the never-ending fear of another unprovoked attack? How about the endless questioning and self-doubt? And when you work so hard to be somebody for so long and all of that is taken away in the blink of an eye because you cannot imagine being worthy of anything else ever again? Is that part of the *syndrome*?'

"Or is it only 'Acts of Revenge'? Because I am more than a woman with 'Pronounced Rape Trauma Syndrome'!" Celine said loudly as the water splashed against the shower walls, and the echoes screamed in her ears. "I am a woman with an anger that is slowly consuming my soul. I am a woman who is standing in a shower on the other side of the world while the rest of my life goes on without me somewhere else far away. A place I used to call home. And I am a woman who just can't seem to take it anymore!" Celine said loudly to no one in particular as she quickly turned off the water and stood naked and dripping in the shower. She stood stock-still for a few moments until a cool blast from the air conditioning hit her wet skin and dripping wet hair and covered her body in gooseflesh. The feeling sent her out of the shower stall in search of a towel. As she dried off in front of the mirror, Celine realised that she could no longer feel satisfied swimming and relaxing on the beach all day. She was restless and bored, and she knew she had to do something. Being frustrated by being so far away from home to begin with, Celine decided that she would visit a travel agent before dinner and book a flight to her next destination.

Celine got dressed in a light cotton dress and sandals, locked her room, then waited for a few seconds at the elevators for the light to blink at her floor. When she got to the lobby, she went to the front desk to retrieve her money from her safe and inquire about booking a domestic flight to a new location. She had her flight booked and paid for within 30 minutes and left the hotel with a feeling of satisfaction that she hoped would last a little while before the loneliness and despair that so often haunted her nights and now visited her days, had a chance to set in.

Celine took the same route she had taken the night previous; she crossed the street at the hotel, walked down the main road, passed the food stalls then the market, only to cross again at a different set of lights at the main intersection and follow the thundering beats to the outdoor bars and restaurants. She found the familiar chicken sign and noticed the name above the door for the first time, "Havana Nights," and walked up the wooden steps to the patio. The waiter, Micah, from the previous night recognised her immediately and ran over to her with a big, warm smile on his face and his arms wide open in greeting. He was genuinely pleased to see Celine and ushered her over to the same table as the previous night. Celine could not help but to smile and feel a warm sense of comfort and belonging so far away from home. The waiter had no idea the positive effect he had on Celine's psyche those few days; it was as if just being near him for as long as it took to order her food, eat and pay could shine a ray of hope through her entire being.

Dear Mom,

The truth is that I feel safe here. It's not only that I'm not constantly looking over my shoulder, praying there isn't police to arrest me and take me back in handcuffs. The men seem different here somehow. Smaller. Less powerful. Not like those evil men I left behind.

There's a man at the restaurant where I've eaten a few times, but although I'm embarrassed to admit it to him, I don't keep going back for the chicken, even though it is delicious. I go back to see him. And no, don't get any ideas, mom. He wears more make-up and spends more time on his hair than I do but, he is just so nice! He is the nicest and gentlest man I have ever met in my life. He's kind to me in a way that I haven't experienced in such a long time. I nearly forgot that men like that existed. There's no threat to me, he's just too kind. He just seems so free, so comfortable walking around the restaurant, talking to customers and singing along with the music. Being himself. It just seems like a dream to me, just being yourself....

I can't believe I am writing this to you from the other side of the planet.

I love you. CB

Celine was sad at the idea of leaving her new friend, Micah, but she knew that she had to move on. She told him when she sat down at the table that she wouldn't be coming back because the flight to her next destination was booked for the very next day. He opened up to her on that last night. Celine heard the sorrow in his voice as he spoke of having to leave his family and friends behind in search of higher wages and a chance at a better life. And she felt the optimism pour out of every fibre of his being when he told her how fortunate he was to be strong and healthy enough to try and achieve his dreams. He didn't know it, but that kind waiter in that tiny chicken restaurant gave Celine a glimmer of hope and a beautiful new perspective about her situation and her life. In those ninety minutes, between refilling her drink and chatting with other dinner guests, he helped Celine to understand that the journey of life doesn't always happen as planned, but if a person has things to be grateful for, then life is definitely worth living, no matter how hard it gets. And coming from a thirty-five-year-old transvestite with a penchant for body shimmer and Latin dance music, those words really hit home as Celine continued to struggle to accept who she had become.

Celine slowly walked back in the direction of her hotel. She thought constantly of her mother and her best friend, Tunisha. She wanted so desperately to tell them what she had seen and what she was going through, and how desperately homesick she was for the life she had left behind.

To my mother,

I wish I could talk to you so badly right now. I'm so happy on one side, the people here have been so nice to me since I've been here. I even went snorkeling today and when I was feeding little pieces of stale bread to these tropical fish, one of them actually bit me! The little stinker! He must have mistaken my leg for a piece of bread. Ha ha! I guess I should work on my tan. Just kidding, I picked up some sunscreen at a shop along the way.

Anyway, I wanted you to know that I'm thinking of you ever step on the way on my new journey. I'm leaving this place tomorrow for what I feel will be my final destination while I'm over here. I wish so desperately that I could tell you where I'm going and where I've been, but it's too risky. It's weird for me to be alone here, so cut off from the rest of the world that I once knew. I think I can give you a hint that only you and daddy would only ever know. This place where I'm going is somewhere that I have dreamed of going to ever since I read of this beautiful animal's plight when I would stay holed up in my bedroom for hours, reading National Geographic magazines.

I love you, CB

p.s. I sat across from a mother and daughter on a boat to the islands today. They looked so much alike sitting there. They were so carefree with their sunglasses and bikinis on. They were so much alike in their mannerisms and their smiles, and it made me so sad to think of you all by yourself. I was so jealous for a moment there as I watched them interact, I was wondering to myself if I did the right thing, or if I hurt you too much because of what I've done.

I wish for so many things right now. I wish I could see you. I left so quickly. Did I even say 'good -bye'? I wish I knew when I could see you again. I wish I knew if the police know anything, and if they do, when things would die down enough for me to come home? I wish I could just relax and enjoy myself, not take for granted that I have a mother who would do anything for me, no matter what.

But most of all, I wish there was a way for me to let you know that I'm doing okay, that I'm safe and happy. Above all, I wish you knew how much I miss you and not a moment goes by that I don't think of you and wish we were together.

I love you, CB

Chapter Nineteen

Celine's flight was less than half-full, and the tiny aircraft still felt cramped. It was sitting on the tarmac and passengers boarded from the stairs outside. She chose a window seat and quickly threw her hair up in pony-tail then used the inflight magazine as a makeshift fan. Sitting in her window seat, Celine was intent on viewing the destruction of the jungle first-hand; she had read many an article describing the devastation that deforestation had made in the lives of the jungle's animal inhabitants. Deforestation was the sole reason why the place Celine was going to even existed. And she was determined to volunteer her skills in the plight of one of the greatest and (she believed), cutest, primates on earth. As the engines rumbled to life and the flight attendants scurried around checking seat tables and seat belts, Celine felt a cool blast of air as the air conditioning turned on overhead and she breathed a sigh of relief.

Celine had not quite processed what had happened to her the night before last. She knew she would be eternally grateful to that brave, kind woman who stepped in and set the matter straight in the nick of time. Celine was deeply certain she would not be sitting comfortably in her seat, on the next leg of her journey if she would have done to those miscreants what her instincts had told her to do in the heat of the moment. In fact, she was sure that she would be sitting in a tiny jail cell somewhere, rotting her life away, wondering further if she would ever see her mother again, and her heart broke at the thought. Celine closed her eyes for a moment and said a silent prayer for the courageous woman who may have possibly saved her life, or at the very least kept her free to do what was on the next part of her journey.

As the plane taxied the runway, Celine looked out the window and thought of her life back home. She wondered how her dear, sweet mother was doing and how she must be feeling, knowing her only daughter is somewhere alone in the world, and may never return to their home as a free woman ever again. Celine wondered if her mother had hope that they would one day see each other again. Although it was difficult to maintain, Celine was hopeful, even certain that they would be together again to do silly mother-daughter things. Anything. And she wouldn't allow herself to think anything to the contrary, it was too painful for her to even contemplate for a moment. 'Besides', Celine thought, as she allowed herself to smile, she felt she was doing the 'right thing', the whole time, so she couldn't believe she would be punished so severely for fulfilling what she thought was slowly becoming her destiny.

As the plane took off, Celine looked out her window to the area speeding by below. She was looking forward to her next destination, she felt that the broken part of her soul was crying out for her to help better the lives of her one true love, animals. Celine nodded off briefly during the two-hour flight but was awoken by a flight attendant just in time to look out a window during the planes decent. Celine moved in her seat toward the window and her jaw dropped open. The sight of the clear cutting she was witnessing was just as bad as it had been described in the literature and research she had read. Perfect square areas of lush, green jungle were cleared away and made room for row after row ubiquitous palm oil trees. Celine could imagine how much of the natural beauty and wonder and life in those jungles had been destroyed in order to make room for something as frivolous as palm oil. She was immediately sickened by the thought that something that she had bought or eaten probably contained the widely popular ingredient. And that was part of the reason for her journey to this faraway land. Celine wanted to see if there was a chance that she could make up for what she had contributed to and maybe give back in some small way. Celine felt any fight for the abused and abandoned was a struggle worth fighting for. She continued to watch, flabbergasted, at the destruction of the jungle below her. It was painful for her to believe that she had contributed to the destruction in any way, even if it was something as simple as buying the wrong kind of margarine or body lotion, or even the chocolate she would gobble down during a late-night TV binge.

When the plane finally landed, Celine needed a moment to wipe the tears from her eyes. As a profound sadness washed over her, Celine slowly got up and gathered her few things then exited the plane. The airport was tiny, probably one of the smallest she had ever been in. The arrival gates were outside of the airport and the entire structure was at street level. Celine waited patiently for her bag, then walked out into the glorious sunshine to find herself a taxi. It was easy; there were about half a dozen lined up at the curb waiting for the tourists to exit the airport. When the next driver in line saw her approach, he quickly flicked his cigarette to the curb and hurried to start the engine. With her bag stowed in the trunk and the driver armed with her destination, Celine sat in the back seat of the taxi and relaxed in the cool, air-conditioned car. She looked around, taking in as much of her new location as she could, as the driver pulled away from the busy sidewalk, and took the road that was needed to get Celine to her new location. Immediately Celine noticed the difference in the places she had chosen to see. The first had paved roads, was much larger, and had more buildings and stores, even a massive, air-conditioned shopping mall. The further the taxi drove, the more apparent it became that the second destination was indeed the poorer of the two. They weren't yet five minutes away from the airport when the paved road with its clean sidewalks and tall buildings were replaced with cracking, damaged roads along dusty lots and ramshackle huts that Celine assumed, constituted as neighbourhoods. There were broken-down food stalls set up on the side of the road where local people were served food at ancient picnic tables, and scrawny dogs and half-naked children wandered around in the dirt beside rickety-looking chicken coops, held together by coat hangers and electrical tape.

The further the taxi drove into the small unknown place, the less vehicle traffic Celine noticed. Cars and taxis were replaced by scooters, but still held the same number of passengers and cargo as a full-sized automobile. Celine could not believe her eyes as she passed a tiny scooter that carried not only what she assumed were 'mom and dad' as the passengers, but also three school-age children and a young baby, along with boxes of food stuff and a tiny white television. When she turned her head back to face on-coming traffic, the driver made eye-contact with her in the mirror; he smiled slightly, shrugged his shoulders as if to say, 'this is how things are done around here, so people make the best of it'. Celine smiled back and continued to be moved by what she saw out the window. The taxi slowed as it got close to a roundabout and Celine saw massive tour buses driving in the same direction as her. They looked to be full of 'Western' visitors with their English signs, and other buses with signs in Chinese Script. Celine was glad that she had a few nights booked at a resort near the jungle where she would hopefully find her way. She was scared about how much she wanted to do and what she had planned. But it was a good feeling though, she told herself.

Weeks before Celine left home, she began to admit to that she may have to go into hiding for the rest of her life because of what she had done. The more she thought about it, the more she realised that just moving to a different town may not be the answer. Her stomach dropped when it finally hit her that she may have to flee the country in order to maintain her freedom. Celine knew that she wanted to help those who were injured or abandoned, and she knew she would fit into that type of environment. It was in her nature and it was the way she was raised. She still wanted to use her skills that she had trained for to give back to others, and that helped narrow her search for the next destination in her life.

After twenty minutes on the main roads, Celine's taxi slowed to a stop and carefully turned down a narrow two-lane dirt road that gave the immediate impression that a jungle lay in wait at the end of it. Celine sat straight up in her seat and struggled to maintain her composure as the end of her journey drew nearer. The trees that dotted the landscape were thicker than any she had seen so far in her life and packs of scrawny-looking dogs ran along the side of the road in search of food. The potholes in the road seemed to be getting bigger by the second and when Celine turned around to look, she noticed a massive dust cloud in the taxis wake.

Finally, after driving for more than twenty minutes, the driver pointed out a sign on the side of the road to Celine that advertised the place where she would be staying. The pictures used as the advertisement on the internet showed a lush jungle resort, but when the taxi pulled up to the front doors, Celine knew immediately that she would be grateful to at least have clean bedding in her room. The driver was quick to alight and half-smirked as he reached into the trunk for her bag, then shrugged as he handed it to her, as if to say, 'it is what it is', then smiled graciously when Celine included a healthy tip in her fee for the ride. He thanked her profusely and wished her luck before he got into his car and drove away. Celine stood completely still for a moment; she noticed instantly as she stood outside of the taxi how different the air around her felt, and she was overcome with excitement to begin exploring her new surroundings. With a spring in her step, Celine walked up the four stone steps and reached for the heavy wooden door that led to the reception area and check-in desk.

The first thing Celine noticed when she walked into the tiny space was the overwhelming smell of mold. It was as if every surface, hidden or otherwise, was infected by the humidity that had been plaguing her straight hair since the moment she stepped off the plane. The entire room felt heavy with dampness; there were heavy carpets on the floor and dark wooden furniture set up against the walls, all over the darkened space. It took Celine a moment to figure out the 'jungle' motif, but once she did, she saw how everything fit together. It was as if she were standing in the main room of a giant tree house. She walked toward the check-in counter and before she was greeted by one of the women in uniform, Celine saw a sign posted on the front desk. It asked guests, quite politely, to inform staff of any 'hairy' or 'leggy' intruders that may be found in their rooms, because it was a preferred practice that staff safely remove all uninvited guests as opposed to them be killed or any paying guest being uncomfortable. Celine thought it a fair and decent request, then crossed her fingers behind her back and secretly hoped she would have no such intruders in her room.

When the women at the counter finally noticed Celine standing there, they smiled warmly and greeted her by name. Celine looked shocked and the women, noticing her panic, quickly explained that the resort was quite small and only catered to a select number of guests at any one time, so Celine being alone, with only one room booked, it was quite simple for the women to deduce who was standing before them. All the excitement of her journey quickly faded as Celine fought to regain her composure; she smiled broadly and said a friendly 'hello'.

"I'd like to know the rate for thirty days total. Cash." Celine said boldly as soon as she opened her mouth. She hadn't thought about it up until that moment, but Celine knew she needed a place to stay and the instant kinship she felt toward those women somehow told her that she was in exactly the right place.

The women smiled back and without skipping a beat, told Celine a total, took her cash and presented her with a key for the room that she would be staying in. The women also handed her a brochure, and quickly explained where and when Celine could get her meals, and the location of the pool, if she fancied a swim. And of course, they told her exactly how she could find what she was looking for; the breath-taking jungle sanctuary that she had travelled half-way around the world to see. The women told Celine that if she hurried, and was so inclined, she would have enough time to get to her room, drop off her things, and get over to the sanctuary for the last feeding of the day. Celine paid, grabbed the proffered key, thanked the women, and hurried out the door to find her room. She was told she would be staying in the second bungalow on the right-hand side of the property. Celine walked quickly and found her room on the first try. Maybe as a precaution, or perhaps a new-found paranoia, Celine knocked on her door before opening it, giving any unwelcome company a chance to scatter before she walked in.

When she opened the door, Celine was completely taken aback by the strong odor of mould. The entire room felt damp and sticky; even as Celine stood in the doorway, she could feel beads of sweat dripping down her back, her long hair plastered to her neck. She stepped inside her room, took a brief glance around as she placed her bag near the bed then turned the light on in the tiny bathroom. That's when she saw it, the uninvited guest. It was the most unusual insect Celine had ever seen with her own eyes. It looked like a miniature black dinosaur, and although she'd never seen one like it to make a comparison, Celine was pretty sure that the end with the sharp looking pincers was the tail. She kept her eye on it as she used the facilities, then promised her little friend that she would be back with reinforcements before the day was over. The insect did little to acknowledge her, but instead maintained its position with its small-but-deadly pincers opening and closing, as if under siege. The 'guest' stayed its position until the light in the bathroom was switched off and could no longer be seen.

Celine grabbed her hat and key, some money, and left her room in a hurry. She followed the inn-keeper's directions and quickly found herself on a newly paved road that led to an Orangutan Rehabilitation Centre that she had seen on a nature show back home while she was away at school. She slowed to a stop under the large entrance sign and wiped a tear from her eye as she took in the stunning photos of the animals she was there to see. Celine felt incredibly grateful at that moment as she regained some of her lost confidence; her feeling as she stood at the edge of the jungle that took her years to get to, was that she was exactly where she was meant to be. Remembering quickly that due to the late afternoon arrival of her flight, Celine only had one chance to view the animals, she looked down at her watch then broke into a light jog and made her way into the area.

Chapter Twenty

The first thing Celine noticed was how well-kept the grounds were. There were manicured lawns, beautiful shrubbery and bright bunches of exotic-looking flowers growing everywhere. There was a large parking lot that as she walked by, Celine counted six foreign tour buses and a few local cars. She saw what she concluded to be administration offices and after 2 minutes, Celine found herself in line with a handful of other eager tourists to buy a ticket and get acquainted with the place.

There were pictures and signs in all directions; Celine could hardly contain her excitement. After visiting the ticket counter, she was told she would have to rent a locker if she had anything on her person that was on the posted list of forbidden items. Celine wasn't carrying a bag, so she didn't have any food or toiletries, and hadn't even thought of using bug-spray and she definitely didn't have any flammable items in her pockets. Security was tight and to be taken very seriously; guests who had any number of items such as purses, or any kind of handbag were not allowed to bring them inside. A visitor could find a row of lockers on the porch outside of the small museum and for a small fee, they could rent the locker for the duration of their stay. The rules, it seemed to Celine were mostly common sense and related to the safety of the jungle's inhabitants. There was no food or drink allowed inside and no smoking whatsoever on the premises. Guests were not allowed to carry cell phones inside the area, and people were warned, from more than one sign, not to speak too loudly after they entered the jungle. Celine could not wait to get to the enclosure.

Celine quickly finished reading the list of rules and regulations, ignored the gift-shop, and looked at her watch before stepping past a few indecisive tourists, on her way to see one of the most amazing creatures in the world, in its natural habitat. From the ten minutes it took for her to walk from her resort, then through the massive parking lot, right passed the ticket counter and gift shop, only to step out on the other side into what could only be described as a lush, tropical jungle. There was a sturdy, impeccably clean, winding wooden walkway that looked like it was suspended amongst the tall trees, vibrant plants and outer-worldly vegetation. Celine stopped at one particular spot during her walk, just to take in the sight and the smell of her surroundings. Every inch of her body was covered with a layer of sweat and the sounds of the cicadas rumbled through the jungle with a deafening timbre. The trees were green in places; either from moss, or old age, or both. Other insects flew around the trees in sheer delight and when Celine looked over the railing, she could not see the ground below; the bushes were too dense for her to make out how high in the trees she really was. And in that moment, Celine forgot to think about herself as Celine Bower, 'Warrior on the Run', hiding from the law in a foreign country, hoping to evade capture and prosecution. Instead, she was Celine Bower, 'Explorer', like she was as a little girl going on exciting adventures with her dad, learning all that the world had to teach her because she was going to rescue helpless animals one day and give them a better life.

Celine looked at her watch and decided to pick up her pace if she was going to get to where she wanted to go in enough time. She didn't know how far into the jungle she would have to walk in order to find the feeding platforms, but her instinct told her that they would be as far away from the human population as possible.

And she was right. Celine walked another ten minutes under the jungle canopy before she saw some signs indicating that she was on the correct path. When at last she found what she was looking for: at the end of the walkway, visitors are blocked from moving on one direction and instead are guided through a maze-like path and forced in another. After one more turn, Celine found what she had travelled thousands of miles to see; an open-air viewing station carefully constructed right in the middle of the jungle. She saw a surprising number of like-minded tourists sitting quietly on thick wooden benches that looked more like really wide stairs, and Celine noticed that some other people were standing casually on a separate platform that was higher than the stairs. She couldn't resist. Celine walked quickly over to the far platform and sat on one of the built-in benches. She smiled at the other tourists that were milling about then focused her attention on the platforms she had come to see. The feeding platforms were built high in the trees and were situated about fifty feet away from where she sat. She strained her eyes as she looked around and noticed thick, long ropes suspended from the highest trees, coming in from different directions, but tied to the same spot. In the middle of the cleared area, directly in front of the viewing platform sat a massive tree, and all the ropes were tied to it. She moved to get a better position, wishing she had brought some binoculars, when she noticed a local man in a uniform, climb a hidden stairwell to the top of the platform. Celine could hear the other tourists begin to whisper excitedly as they patiently waited for the animals to make their way to the feeding area. The group of spectators were barely making a sound in anticipation of what most of them had travelled great distances to see, Celine included. And almost every single visitor sitting at the sanctuary seemed to heed the warning posted all over the visitor platform: that there must be silence at all times so as not to frighten or intimidate the guests of honor.

Celine stood again, she couldn't help herself, as the sound of excited whispering came from some people sitting on the stairs on the other side of the platform. She looked to them, then back to the platform and without seeing anything, she looked back to the ropes. Still not seeing anything, Celine looked to the tourists again and followed their eyes in the direction they were taking photos, then caught a glimpse of the funniest band of rag-tag monkeys she had ever seen. Celine didn't realise she had been holding her breath until a huge smile spread across her lips and she exhaled. Celine watched as a dozen or so, they were too quick to count, monkeys came from out of nowhere, running, swinging from trees and screeching all the way, even passing closely to some bemused, and gawking tourists, all the way to the feeding platform where the man in green dumped a heavy sack of food, descended the stairs and was gone. Visitors were up on their feet, laughing and pointing, while others were snapping photos and filming furiously, the zany show the monkeys put on. One could tell that the monkeys enjoyed their time as much as the tourists did. They had an internal clock that told them when the buffet would open and they knew from past experience, the way one raised in a jungle could, that the tourists loved to watch them do their thing.

The monkeys were cute and lively, bounding around from the trees to the platforms to the ropes and back again. Not one single person dared get too close to the wild monkeys; out of respect for the animals and also out of respect for the warden that had appeared out of nowhere and was instructing guests on how to behave. The woman was walking through the crowds, reminding each guest that they were to keep quiet, and most importantly, to give the animals a wide berth for everyone's safety. Celine could tell from where she stood that everyone seemed to be listening. Just then, another gang of wild and hungry monkeys came running down the platform out of nowhere heading for the food. They made their way through the crowd, all headed in the same direction, to the feeding platform. She looked up and noticed the leaves shake and branches bend as furry grey bullets scrambled by in the direction of the piles of fresh fruit that lay undisturbed fifty feet away from where she stood. They were running and jumping at each other, grabbing at the fruit piles then swinging away to eat their catch away from the group. They would throw the peels off the platform and make a mad dash to the food pile again, rolling and tumbling the whole time. The monkeys put on a show that had people in the crowd in stitches at their ridiculous antics.

Celine watched then gasped when out of the corner of her eye, she spotted something that kicked off a storm of butterflies in her stomach. Some of the other tourists must have noticed too because all at once a hush fell over the chattering crowd. Up in the distance, about seventy feet away, one of the ropes began to show some movement. It began to sway to-and-fro, as if something was pulling really hard on it. The other monkeys on the platform seemed to notice it too, about forty-five seconds after the visitors. At first, the monkeys were eating the fresh fruit with a certain nonchalance, enjoying their time while pigging out on a smorgasbord of easy-access food. The younger monkeys were especially lively, rolling around, chasing each other with reckless abandon while the adults ate sliced fruit then tossed the peels aside, all the while, entertaining the human observers. But when the rope slowly shook high in the distance, all the monkeys stopped to pay attention. They knew what was coming.

Celine stepped closer to the wooden rails, stretched her neck and strained her eyes; she was dying to see an orang-utan in its natural habitat, and when a thick hairy orange arm slid out from the canopy of trees, in the direction of the nearest tree mounted platform, it was love at first sight. Celine's grin spread from ear to ear, and she didn't realise (until she was scolded by the game warden), that she had stepped on the fence. She was dangerously close to falling head over arse to the ground below from leaning too far over the rail in hopes of getting a better glimpse. She quietly stepped down, then smiled through her apology. It took her a moment to realise that the voice that corrected her not only did not belong to a local but had a Scottish accent. For some reason, Celine was even more embarrassed by her actions then she was before she noticed who scolded her. Celine had to speak to someone about volunteering there. She not only had to make her inquiries as casual as possible, but she had to make her case, which, other than her real degrees (that she had carefully stashed in her luggage), was not the least bit truthful. Celine had not yet grown accustom to lying to every person that she met. She pushed the thought to the back of her mind; she was so close to getting what she came for. A chance to work with those magnificent animals.

The light cheering and tangible excitement of the crowd brought Celine back into the present moment. It was just in time to see a mother orang-utan and her young baby make their way thought the trees, down to the feeding platform. Celine couldn't help herself, she oohed and aahed along with the rest of the crowd. It was such a spectacular sight to behold. The mother was slow and purposeful in her movements, and her baby was so adorable in the way it clung to her mother's fur and buried her head as if frightened by the sound of the noise of the crowd and the squeals from the other monkeys on the platform. More orangutans appeared out of nowhere and hastily made their way down to the feeding platform. Celine was pleasantly surprised to see such a variety of animals in one place: as she looked around at all the other tourists, she wondered what reason had brought them to such a remote destination. She could hear all sorts of different languages and accents, people of all different ethnicities, all equipped with photography and video equipment, and she was completely amazed to see the name of her hometown emblazoned on t-shirt that stretched tightly across the beer belly of a large foreign man. They made eye contact, Celine smiled and turned away quickly; she wasn't comfortable with the idea of anything from her hometown being anywhere near her. She stood and waited, casually listening for the man, or anyone in his group to speak. When someone finally did, in obvious German, Celine allowed herself a deep breath.

Suddenly, Celine felt extremely vulnerable amongst all the faces she didn't recognise. She felt stupid for putting herself in jeopardy. While everyone else around her were looking at and photographing the wildlife, Celine quietly walked away. She walked the lonesome path, back through the jungle to the gift shop, out to the parking lot and down the dirt road to her hotel. She walked, looking down at her feet, as tears fell from her eyes and rolled down her cheeks. When she got to her door, she put the key in the lock and turned the handle. She flicked on the air-conditioning, pulled back the covers on her bed, and without even taking off her shoes, fell face first onto her bed.

Celine woke with a start hours later as massive bolts of lightning lit up the night sky. She dragged herself out of bed and found her watch in her bag. The hands said nine o'clock. Celine hurried to the small book near the phone that provided information about the on-site facilities. She scanned the list quickly and learned that she had approximately twenty-six minutes to get to the restaurant and order some food. She went to the bathroom and quickly splashed water on her face, towelled off, grabbed her room key and purse and was out the door. The second Celine stepped out into the open hallway, she stopped and suddenly remembered that she was the closest to a jungle that she had ever been in her whole life and wished desperately that she had brought a flashlight. Celine had stepped out into a pitch-black night, except for the tiny lanterns placed strategically along the wooded walkway, there was not a light to be seen. Celine decided her hunger could wait. She turned slowly back to her room and unlocked the door. As she stepped inside, she promised herself she would not cry; she would not feel sorry for herself, because no matter what she did, what choices she made, that she still carried the haunting scars of a rape victim.

Celine walked into her room, stripped down naked in front of her bed, then stepped into the tiny bathroom and took a shower. When she finished, she dried off, wrapped her hair in a towel, threw on some clothes, and was asleep on her bed before her hair had a chance to dry.

Chapter Twenty-One

The bright sun streaming through the open curtains on her windows and the loud calls from the exotic birds in the trees outside her window woke Celine out of a deep sleep in the early hours of the morning. She rubbed her eyes as she shook off the drowsiness and smiled as she stretched across her bed, thankful for another day of freedom and life. She rose quickly and walked across the room to the window. Looking out, she noticed a sign that she had missed the day before, the directions to the pool. Celine freshened up then found her bathing suit in the bottom of her luggage and put it on. She quietly opened her door, stepped out then closed it behind her. The heat and humidity were unrelenting, even at such an early hour. Celine crept quietly down the hallway till she found the pool entrance. She took a quick dip in the tiniest pool she had ever been in, returned to her room to shower and change for breakfast. When she was ready, Celine shut the door behind her and went in search of food.

Taking into consideration that she hadn't eaten anything in over twenty-four hours, Celine quickly scanned the breakfast menu as soon as she sat down at the table. She ordered a bowl of fresh fruit, eggs, bacon, toast, fried potatoes, juice and coffee and a water, then smiled sheepishly when the waitress asked if anyone would be joining her for the meal. The dining area that was located down a long wooden planked walkway at the opposite side of the resort was deceptively large, with about two dozen four-seater tables scattered haphazardly about. Celine looked at the clock above the bar, it was just 8 o'clock and by the looks of things, the breakfast crowd had not yet filled in all the tables. Celine knew just from the taxi ride over to the resort that options for places to eat for someone without a car were few and far between. The closest thing she saw to a restaurant on her way over were roadside shacks with plastic tables and chairs along the sides of dusty parking lots which also appeared to be frequented by packs of hungry- looking wild dogs. So, with the resort's restaurant being the *only* place she knew of to eat, Celine crossed her fingers under the table and hoped for the best. The waitress returned within moments and dropped off the drinks with a smile. After a few more minutes of waiting quietly, different plates of food began showing up at the table and before Celine knew it, much of the space in front of her had been taken up by her order. All at once, Celine became aware of how gluttonous she must have looked to the wait staff and the other diners, but she smiled as she thanked the waitress then dug in. It wasn't long before she made a noticeable dent in the plates of food, and she was confident she could finish everything in front of her. The waitress returned to her table with a somewhat bemused look on her face and refilled Celine's coffee. Five minutes later, she was back at the table to clear the empty dishes and leave Celine her bill. After fishing some money out of her pocket, and leaving enough for a tip, Celine was about to leave the restaurant when she heard a commotion near the entrance of the restaurant.

A group of young teenage girls had just walked in the restaurant and were looking for a place to sit. The waitress hurried over with menus and led the girls to a table only a few feet from where Celine sat digesting a huge breakfast. Celine must have been blatantly staring because one of the young girls made eye contact with her then smiled shyly before looking away. Celine smiled back then turned to her table and took one last swig of coffee. She sat motionless, preoccupied with the next step of her life. Celine had been moving so fast and to such a far distance that as she sat at her table, feeling full for the first time in days, the world laid out at her feet, she fought hard to silence the voice in her head. The one that said, 'you were raped, Celine. As you sit across from these young girls, in this exotic outdoor dining area, trying to blend in, do you think that they have never been raped? That they feel clean, and that they believe they are immune to the horror you have already faced? Do you think they can tell by looking at you, that you have been raped? Do you believe that you have fought all of your battles, Celine Bower? Do you dare to hope and maybe believe that you will ever be the same? That your world looks better now? Can you ever really outrun what you've done? What you've become? Or hide from your past forever? How far do you think you can run?' The girls sat chatting happily at their table, not noticing Celine or the grimace she had on her face; the girls were eating and drinking and enjoying their time in such a beautiful place.

Celine took one final sip of her coffee and got up from the table. She left the same way she had come in: across the long dining room, past the bar, down the stairs to the walkway. The sun had climbed higher in the sky, almost blinding Celine with the light when she stepped out from under the canopy. Celine walked quickly through the lush resort, back to her room. She was covered in a light sweat by the time she got to her door. As she let herself in her room she contemplated sitting on her bed and thinking about her next move, but she already knew what she wanted, and what she had to do. She also knew if she stopped, she might never get up again. Celine freshened up in the bathroom and took one last look in the mirror before she packed up her things and walked out the door. 'Because', she thought as she closed the door behind her, 'the time for contemplation is over.' She was on the move toward the next phase of her life; the one she hadn't planned for, but knew she had to do. The part she was afraid to look forward to because of what she was leaving behind. She must have had an ominous look on her face as she walked because an older couple that had smiled at her in greeting the day before simply stepped out of her way as she walked past. As soon as she realized it must have been her outward demeanour that they were reacting to, Celine slowed her pace and forced herself to change her mindset; to one that focused on the beauty in her surroundings and highlighted the many blessings she still had to be thankful for.

'How many people do you know that would love to be doing what you're doing in the beautiful place? This is a once-in-a-lifetime opportunity for you, Celine.' She thought to herself as she walked the dusty road in the direction of the rehabilitation centre. 'And what if you *never* got a chance to do this again in your life? What would you be if you didn't enjoy the moment while you are here? Enjoying it for what it is?' She thought as she slowed to a snail's pace.

"My father taught me better than this," She said sadly as she stopped on the side of the road and looked into the tiny stream that ran along the side of her resort; she hadn't noticed it the previous day and found herself drawn to the trickling sound of running water.

'Take a moment to think', he would say, she thought. 'Just a moment to gather your thoughts before moving forward.' And that's what she did. Anyone that would have passed her that day as she stood looking down at the shallow, muddy creek would have seen an attractive blonde woman, standing still, staring at some slow-moving water, maybe guessing she was interested in the local wild-life and watching its behaviour. What they would not have seen was a woman that travelled thousands of miles to escape a past that seemed to creep up on her at every turn. They wouldn't have seen the loneliness that threatened to extinguish the fire that burned so bright deep inside her soul. They wouldn't have seen the thoughts that she contemplated; the thoughts that scared her when she was alone at night before sleep had come. And they would never have seen how much she wished she could have been anywhere else at that moment in time. Because at that moment, on the verge of starting a new chapter in her life, she thought back to what her not-so-distant past had taught her; to fear things she had no control over.

'But you do have control over this, Celine.' A stern voice called out in the silence of the day. She didn't realize she had been talking so loudly to herself until some birds in the bushes beside her shrieked loudly, then took flight at the sound of the disturbance. She quickly put her hand up to her mouth and giggled. She looked around quickly, then shaking her head decided there was no better time than the present to put one foot in front of the other and get started on this new chapter in her life.

Chapter Twenty-Two

When Celine arrived at the Centre, she walked to one of the smaller buildings on the left side of the group that served as the home for the tiny museum they offered. Guests were welcome to look around unsupervised because there were no animals inside. There were several other tourists milling about while some were watching a short video on the history of the land and its peoples, the Rehabilitation Centre and the plight of its inhabitants. Celine finished her short tour then crossed back over to the entrance of the Centre. She paid her fee then followed the signs to the feeding platform. Instead of walking around the different areas, Celine was looking for one vantage point in particular. She was looking for the warden she saw the day before, and judging by the voice and the accent, Celine surmised that woman to not only be someone to speak to, but a foreigner like herself, only Celine guessed the woman to be from Scotland, or somewhere in the United Kingdom.

Celine sat and watched as the woman, in her khaki uniform, purposefully walked from one group of tourists to the next, answering questions in a hushed voice for some and silencing some with a sterner version of the same hushed voice for others. Celine held her breath as the women walked by her and silently prayed that she wouldn't remember scolding Celine the previous day for standing on the ledge. It didn't matter anyway; the longer Celine watched the women the more respect she had for her. Her fear was replaced with respect and Celine found she was encouraged by a woman standing so boldly in the middle of the jungle, commanding silence and respect from people she had never laid eyes on before that moment she told them to 'read the sign' with a terse, accented voice. Celine guessed the woman to be about fifty to fifty-five years old, possibly a former banker, or business executive; the way she carried herself screamed that she had done her previous work in some pretty important places, perhaps with some kind of important job. The woman had short blonde hair and a slender figure under her khaki vest. She was wearing a different colored shirt than she had on the previous day and her work boots looked comfortably suitable for this particular terrain. She also looked hot; her hair, similar to Celine's in texture seemed to be fighting a losing battle with frizz due to the heavy humidity. Celine looked to the trees near the feeding platform but kept the woman in her sights. She needed to meet the woman, but she didn't know how to introduce herself. She knew from her experience the day before that this woman took her job very seriously, and if Celine was hoping to earn any points in her good book, then she thought she had best wait till the animals were long gone. It happened quickly, the way Celine and Penny clicked. Celine was a paying visitor at the Orangutan Sanctuary, and Penny was the 'warden' dressed in green, that made sure all the rules for visitors were enforced and followed. Penny was 'no-nonsense', and Celine felt herself intimidated by a woman for the first time in a long time, not since she met some of her professors at school. Their first encounter, Celine on the platform leaning precariously close to the edge which included a thirty to forty-foot drop to the jungle floor below, and Penny, nearly reprimanding Celine for being so careless. But Penny understood deeply why someone might be so enchanted by the big creatures that their common sense might fly out the window. Celine stepped back, smiled shyly, and apologised, then learned who it was that she was going to speak. As it turned out,

Celine's hunch was correct, and she found the right person to lead her to her goal. Celine liked Penny from the start, even if she had been scolded by her. She liked her terse interactions, how she got right to the point of the matter on any situation as if every second of the day was important and counted for something. Celine thought as she watched Penny interact with tourists of all kinds that it was exactly Penny's 'drill sergeant' attitude that was needed in a place like the jungle.

Penny, without ever knowing it, was the best thing that could have ever happened to Celine. She accepted Celine immediately, and judging by her forthright manner, she wasn't into mistrusting her judgement or playing the fool. The two women seemed to have an unspoken understanding of each other, due to their situations. Penny was, effectively, leaving behind a life that she created for herself, then ultimately decided that she could no longer live anymore, and Celine was running from a life that she didn't know how to live. Both women were smart, fiercely independent, and neither were strangers to the harsh realities of a life of unhappiness. They both set out for their current destination with the burning desire to change something about themselves, that something they could not, or in Penny's case, would not, accept.

Celine felt guilty inside. She struggled with her guilt every time she faced Penny, knowing she was willfully hiding something about herself, and every time she caught a glimpse of her reflection in some shiny, mirrored surface. When she was alone, looking in the mirror, that was a different story. Celine knew who she was on the outside: Celine Bower, twenty-six, veterinarian, the only child of Simon and Molly Bower. She had her mother's eyes and her father's nose. But the other part of her, the one she struggled to acknowledge and accept, was trying at every given moment to be known. This other side of her, this person she had become frightened her and made her question every move. A walk down the dirt road became a myriad of feelings as she tried desperately to relax and admire her surroundings and ignore the urge to stand taller and allow herself to become more powerful.

Celine spent a lot of time alone in Borneo, walking aimlessly, then with a purpose, and sometimes she would stop while walking and just listen as the wind whispered to the trees. The hot sun was so close at the equator that she felt the heat radiate deep within her soul.

Chapter Twenty-Three

They moved quickly into each other's lives, Celine and Penny. With Penny showing Celine, quote, 'a lesson in jungle life', with not only the decent food establishments that were located in the area, only known to locals, but also, 'the dark side', of jungle life. She shouldn't have been surprised, Celine, but it wasn't what she expected to find along her path.

It was the abundance of discreetly placed whore-houses in the little town closest to the jungle's edge that surprised Celine the most. It was her naïve way of thinking, that everyone else who flew all that way, would be interested in seeing anything *but* the jungle. She felt like a stupid, little city-girl when she went for a walk with Penny in the area that was the hub of all the action when the sun went down. Celine discovered after walking around the streets at night with Penny that the sex-trade industry there was alive, and it was *thriving*. Eating its way through people's lives. It rifled through Celine, the contempt, and she tried not to scream and stomp her feet like a child right there beside a tacky souvenir stand, looking around and feeling her head may explode at any moment. As they walked and talked, Celine, who was also actively trying to avoid stepping in any cracks or come in contact with the cockroaches that littered the alleys and corners around garbage bins, saw women everywhere sitting out front of small two or three story buildings, wearing daisy-duke shorts with tiny baby tees, or lace lingerie with high-heeled shoes. Celine didn't notice at first but learned along the way that those women were in fact seated at a strategically placed bar table. Sometimes they would be smoking a cigarette or having a drink while laughing and chatting to the other girls hanging around, the ones wearing the same type of outfit. But the drink was just a decoy, a 'ruse' as Penny called it when they walked by. (There were two reasons the woman sat with a fake drink in front of them-- the first being, if the women were too drunk off cheap alcohol they could not perform properly and the second reason was that most women working in the sex-trade industry could not even afford alcohol, no matter what they were paid by the customer.) All this information was provided very discreetly by Penny, who would speak quietly out of the corner of her mouth as they were navigating the city streets with Celine trying to absorb everything on her path.

The women in the little dresses and high heels were advertising themselves as the wares that the hidden place inside had on offer. They smiled and were friendly, and if you were a man by yourself or in a group with other men, they would get off their chairs and approach you, smiling seductively and asking your name. When the man would stop for a chat the women would try their hardest to get him to go inside. The poor women, doing a bidding and not benefitting in a way that could be considered 'human'.

Penny did not mince words and there was nothing soft or cuddly the way she described how life there truly was to Celine. She did not sugar coat anything and there was almost a 'madness' that would appear in Penny's eyes as they talked about their surroundings. It was as if Penny enjoyed telling Celine just how bad things really were. It was like she was trying to beat the naivete out of Celine and enjoyed herself while doing it. The satisfaction was written all over Penny's face as she watched Celine's heart shatter telling her everything she had seen while living as a white woman in a foreign land.

The stories of the local peoples were glum, and Penny learned most of them while taking up with locals after she landed, hell bent on her own mission to save the world. She told Celine over chicken curry and warm beers one evening that 'there are a few simple reasons as to why those women ended up there. The number one being that their families probably just sold them as young girls into slave labour'. And to Celine, an educated woman from the West, she did notice, and felt deeply, that some people there probably had a very difficult time being able to afford something to eat; she had seen the beggars on the streets, dressed in rags, their feet bare with blackened soles. Celine did not question how a person was to pay for birth control or health care. And with a hardened heart, Celine began to empathize with the parents she learned that had to sell the children they could not afford, or the child they sold to get an even larger sum of money for being that one virginal, pretty girl that they knew would be a prize before she even hit puberty. And the other reason why so many of these women, Celine learned, ended up in the sex trade was because they were the girls whose circumstances, whether of victimization or abuse, were so bad where they came from that they left anyway. But without any support or resources, they ended up having to prostitute themselves to survive. There were girls who tried to help their families get a better life that they quit school early and went to the closest 'city' in search of work as a waitress or cleaner, only to be over-looked or rejected due to lack of experience. They were left with no money, no hope, and no plan 'B'. And they became so destitute that they were forced to sell what they had, their bodies, to survive. Crushingly enough, Celine learned in those few initial outings with Penny that those women and young girls were at the very bottom of a very unholy food chain. They were worth less than dirt.

The sex-trade industry offered them a chance to sell themselves for their next meal and the foreign guys that went there knew that.

The older men that Celine would see walking casually with their arms around some fifteen-year-old girl's waist. Those women didn't want to be there, Celine learned; they were being paid by the hour to smile and stroll, and be groped.

"Those dirty *pigs*", Penny said venomously in Celine's direction. "come here on vacation just to seek out these young girls, these *prostitutes* because they know or have heard how hungry and poor they are. Those *pigs* know that they can get whatever they want because *everybody* has a price, and in this place, it is dirt cheap." Penny said with deep contempt. She took a swig of her drink then carried on while Celine sat in a motionless lump.

"Celine, the men are completely uncivilized. They do sick, disgusting things with teenage girls that they would never be able to get away with back in their home countries. In fact, I am quite certain they do things here that would land them in prison back home… if they were ever discovered and prosecuted. But… they come here knowing and believing this philosophy: spending a little more on a vacation to get somewhere as poor as this is worth it because the people here are so *desperate* for money. They've heard that the women and young girls here will perform any raunchy sex acts, or do the things they've seen on porn, but know they could never damn well get away with their girlfriends or wives back home."

As Celine sat and listened, a little voice in her head reminded her of her past and the one reason why she dropped everything, gave up everything she had ever known, to be there.

"These men that are so *sick* of their demanding Western bitches *who don't know their place* in society, or if you were to ask, there would be at least one acrimonious divorce that would uncover the true misogynist within these men and send them hunting for a cheap sexual playground. Disgusting. And you know what? These women, they get beaten constantly. They get kept in line with fists and cigarette butts and beatings. Do you want to know the most dangerous profession in the world, Celine? Hmm, you probably think it's something like a firefighter or police officer. Well, you would be wrong. The most dangerous job in the world is prostitution. Sad state of affairs these days, Celine, and you better get used to it because *there's* not a damn thing you can do about it." Penny said, then put her hand up to her throat and coughed a little, rubbing her neck and feeling as though she had swallowed a bitter pill.

"You know women who've been hurt?" Celine asked quietly, feeling so completely naïve and out of her element, yet knowing the answer and absorbing every single word that came out of Penny's mouth.

"Everybody does," Penny said quickly, forcefully. It was as if talking to Celine was like talking to a small child. Celine's ignorance toward the situation could not have been more pronounced. "Everyone here does. No matter how humiliated you think you've ever been in your rich, white life, there is no worse treatment of women than there is here. And in other countries as poor as this one. It's disgusting, but nobody listens to the likes of me. No one listens to any of us *because we're women.*"

"What happens to these guys that come here? Do the police ever get involved?" Celine asked quietly, feeling as small as a grain of sand.

"Everyone turns a blind eye because *everyone* is on the take. Some of these women would starve to death, or their babies would die if they didn't make money in the tourism sex- trade. And that's why women *always* get the shitty end of the stick. People... well, women, are a part of an industry here. They are a commodity offered up like cattle. They get in this position because they need to get paid so they can eat. They turn to prostitution where they are degraded and humiliated and treated like absolute shit. It is slavery for the 21st century. There is no other way to put it." Penny said then looked down at her hands. They were shaking, and Celine thought she could only imagine how high the poor women's blood pressure was at that point in the conversation.

"The problem is Celine… that we continue to look at prostitution as a 'women's problem'. We treat prostitution as if the women themselves are somehow to blame. As if those women were given other choices for their lives, but they said, 'nah, I'd rather be raped repeatedly by some old, fat, white piece of shit with a lot of money and severely deranged perversions.' Pardon my language, Celine, but I can't help it." Penny said as her hands continued to shake as she spoke. Celine could see the sweat dripping down the sides of Penny's face as she reached for her glass of beer on the table. Penny spit on the dirty floor with contempt. Never before had Celine seen a woman that was so clearly well-educated, and with what seemed to be an ingrained sense of propriety and decorum, turn so easily mannish and improper at the blink of an eye.

"These assholes," Penny continued, as Celine stared wide-eyed, "are flushed with cash and bereft of morals. That's what I always say. These pigs know that these women are viewed as expendable; they were sold into slavery by their own families, for Christ's sweet sake, and the men that come here to take advantage of them *know* this juicy little tidbit. And they *know* they will never get caught. How's that for sick? Eh, Celine? They are disgusting and they should all be shot… strung up by their balls, then shot. But not before they confess *everything* to their wives, girlfriends and families back home. Wouldn't that be a sight? Then we shoot them." She said as she downed the last of her beer and slammed the empty glass on the table.

"I know you came here thinking you were going to save the world, Celine. But there are more problems here than you and I could ever dream of. It's not like this where we came from; with our free public schools and our access to clean drinking water.

Never mind our police services, subsidized healthcare and all the other things you and I and the rest of the Western world take for granted every day. The poverty here is mind-blowing and that is why it is so easy for them to sell their children to the highest bidder, and to destroy this beautiful, awe-inspiring, life-giving environment. You and I have no idea what it is like to have maybe only that one chance to make money and buy the things that in our culture back home we take for granted. Can you imagine never being able to afford a television, or never having access to a toilet or clean drinking water in your home? We are knee-deep in shit, and fighting a losing battle here, Celine." Penny said then threw up her hands. She looked across the table at Celine, who sat quietly with tears rimming her eyes. Celine knew deep down in her heart, that Penny only spoke the truth. Before Celine could say a word, Penny broke the silence.

"When you are so poor that you cannot afford to eat yourself, never mind feed your children, why would you care anything for an animal? None of us foreigners will ever understand what it is like. And I see you over there, probably thinking that you're not rich... well, you had enough money to fly here, didn't you? And you have stayed in a hotel, haven't you? And you do not look hungry, Celine. Please understand that I am not some horrible person that's trying to hurt you...I just want you to understand...you just have to understand what we are up against here. The poorest of the poor who have every right to want to make a better life for themselves."

"And to be honest," Penny continued as if she had just found her second wind. "I don't know who has it worse: the women or the animals. One has its habitat completely destroyed and the other has its soul annihilated. Life is cheap when you have to fight so hard to survive. What chance do they have anyway?"

"But there are people like you... people who try to make a difference. That's something, isn't it?" Celine said, heartbroken, her voice cracking as she dabbed her eyes with a napkin.

"Yes, I suppose it is. But things around here happen so fast. Huge parts of the jungle get torn down and destroyed and we don't have much time to get in there and save any of these precious animals. Can you imagine? They are some of the most beautiful and serene creatures on earth, surrounded by some of the most beautiful landscapes and it's all being destroyed. The problem is, people don't realise how much their choices, even from so far away, can affect something as precious as *this* eco-system. Who knows, maybe they don't even care. Maybe they just don't want to *see* what is really happening. It's devastation at its worst and we will never be able to get it back. We will never be able to 'fix it', to recreate it again. Once these places are gone, they are gone forever. But our modern world is too fast-paced, too materialistic for these circumstances to even be a blip on someone's radar. How can you worry about a primate in some remote jungle when you are so concerned about making that 'new car payment', or acquiring that 'latest device'?" Penny said, stopping to take a breath and use her bent fingers to emphasize her point. "It's all fast food and fast money, and even faster lives. No one slows down long enough to notice other people's suffering! They don't even stop to watch the news because all anyone thinks anymore is, 'oh great, there's another war someplace far away, or over there… and because they aren't directly affected, they don't stop to notice anything. It makes me insane! That's why I left and that is why it is so easy for me to stay away from a place that was everything I had ever known. The place where it was so easy for me to be successful and gather great wealth. But I couldn't take it anymore. I couldn't take the commercials, telling me to buy everything and more than I could possibly need in this lifetime. I was so God damned sick of competing with everyone over everything I ever had. From my house to my children's school, to my marriage and divorce, and *finally*, to the clothes on my back. I couldn't take it anymore, that race to be the best; to *have it all.* I was done. And I'm glad I did it, glad I left it all behind." Penny said, smiling triumphantly.

"And you know what? Now I do make a difference, and that my dear, is better than anything else I could have made in the life that I had." She smiled, refilled her glass, leaned back in her chair and stared at Celine.

"Why did you come here, Celine? You are an attractive and obviously educated young woman. Pardon me for saying so, but I can tell by your eyes that you have seen things. What would a pretty girl like you, who has the potential to earn a small fortune doing what you are trained for, in a place much cleaner and safer than this be doing here? Why would you leave that affluence behind at such a young age to end up in a place like this?" Penny asked as she looked Celine in the eyes and took a swig of her beer. There was a long stare followed by an even longer awkward silence as Celine looked to the floor.

"Oh gosh, it's not because you thought you could save the world too, is it? Because that would be funny, especially considering how long you may or may not last in a place like this. Take my advice: once you start to really get to know a place like this, it drains you. But then, you become addicted to the rush and you can't stop coming back for more. I wish I would have had the balls to do something like this at your age. Woo hoo! Screw the husband and 'happy mommy' bullshit! If I would have known how much my happiness was going to be sacrificed, I *never* would have said yes when the bastard proposed to me so long ago. I would have told him where to shove that marquis-cut and run like hell in the other direction." She said as she let out a hardy belly laugh, then drank her beer.

"Oh, don't look so shocked, Celine. At some point, *all women know* what's expected of them in a marriage, whether they like it or not. I'm retired, I raised my kids, got a promotion, got a divorce, then jumped on a plane and now I answer to no one. I earned it, Celine, and I fucking love it. And oh… pardon my language!" Penny said then unleashed a laugh that sounded years in the making.

Dear Mom,

I just wanted you to know that I'm sorry for the way things turned out. I'm so sorry if what I did caused you anymore sorrow, because I know deep down, even though you try to hide it, I caused you pain. The problem is, I couldn't help myself. I know I keep going back to that, I know I know I keep saying the same thing. Sorry about that.

I want you to know that I'm safe. I'm happy and I think I'm in a place where no one will ever find me, if they even dared to look. I'm so sorry that I can't be with you right now and I hope you know how much I wish we could be doing all of this traveling and sight-seeing together. Sometimes I can still hear Daddy's voice. He's telling me that I'm not alone and that it's okay and to move on from what I left behind. He says, 'it's okay'. He says, 'I'm okay'. Please take care and don't worry about me.

I love you. CB

Chapter Twenty-Four

Young Woman with Her Whole Life Ahead of Her Found Murdered near A Local Park Police Aren't Willing to Admit There Might be a Serial Killer on the Loose

Lance Williamson

Molly James, 21, had her whole life ahead of her. She was a part-time student at the local university studying for a degree in Education and she worked part-time at a clothing store in the mall. Molly James lived at home where she helped her mother tend to their garden and saved her money for a car. Molly's dream of being a kindergarten teacher was cut short on the night of April 11th, after she left her job to catch a bus at the mall and was never seen or heard from again.

That is, until her lifeless body was discovered in a park not too far from where Molly James went to school. Her family has been left devastated by her death and her class-mates are reeling, wondering what type of person is out there and feels the need to kill innocent women. Police are scrambling for answers but coming up empty-handed, especially considering Molly James is not the first young woman at her school to be murdered and found days later. There was another girl, with a physical description almost

> perfectly matching Molly's found less than a month to the day that Molly went missing.
>
> Police do not want to say it, but this reporter and others like him in the community cannot ignore the facts any longer. We want to know if it is true: if there is a serial killer on the loose in our city, and if so, what are the police, our local law enforcement going to do about it?
>
> Please do not make us wait any longer for the answers, he may just strike again.
>
> If anyone has any information regarding Molly James' last known whereabouts, they are asked to contact Detective Cardosi at the local police station, or the Crime Tips Hotline at: 1 888 444 4444.

Lance Williamson did a final check for spelling and grammar errors before he saved the article then mailed a copy of it to his boss at the newspaper. He was sure he had crossed the line this time, that the local police were not going to be impressed that he had called them out once again for not providing enough answers for the citizens in his town, but Lance thought the people had a right to know. He even called the police station, hoping to speak with someone about his theories, but was told he'd have to wait for a call back that never happened. He was being ignored and he knew it. But Lance couldn't help himself when he had a hunch and he didn't care what it cost him; his job, sleepless nights, even friends, when Lance got a whiff of something newsworthy, he could not let it go.

After hearing about the latest young woman to be found dead, Lance googled her photo, and it was just as he suspected; the women that were murdered only weeks apart and looked almost identical. They could have been sisters as far as Lance was concerned. Both were young, and blonde, and both were strikingly beautiful, and Lance knew from past experience, that there was no such thing as coincidences. He knew someone was hunting these women down and he wanted the police to do something about it.

As Lance switched off his computer he looked over at the table by his window and smiled. Lance trusted his intuition because it always seemed to pay off for him and he was expecting something great for his next pay off. You see, Lance thought there was something to be said for Celine Bower's story, especially once he put all the pieces of the puzzle together. He knew deep down, because his first dream was to be a comic book artist, that Celine's story wasn't exactly his to tell; that would be stealing. But Lance also knew that inspiration could come from anywhere, and Celine's story was too incredible and too important not to tell. So, it was Lance, for the last twelve months, that had been 'telling' Celine's story in a comic book that he had yet to name. He knew Celine's name, or anything that sounded like it, wouldn't be feasible, and he definitely did not want to betray her identity to anyone. Lance felt such a strong kinship toward Celine, almost as if she and her actions weren't real but instead, a figment of someone's imagination that he was in awe of her, even though they had never met. In fact, it took a lot of effort on Lance's part to discover her true identity to begin with. Lots of illegal snooping that Lance wasn't particularly proud of, so he vowed to himself that he would never ever, under any circumstances, reveal Celine's true identity to anyone. That was why Lance was still without a name for the star of his very own comic book series. And it pained him deeply. He needed a name to put to a face that became so familiar to him that he could almost count on seeing her in his dreams at night. So close he felt to her that he drove by her last known address a few times because maybe there was a chance that they could actually meet in real life. But no such luck, Lance had only seen what he presumed to be her mother and he was very aware of how sketchy it might be if he was viewed as a stalker. Plus, not only was Lance in awe of Celine, he was afraid of her as well. He knew what she was capable of having covered her stories personally. Lance felt that he knew her, and after adding his own powers to her creation, Lance became down-right frightened of her sometimes.

So, after he finished his work for the paper, Lance would sit his desk and draw the life and times of a women who was powerful in a way the world had never seen before. He described how she used that power to take back the night for everyone. And by the looks of things, the stories that he created were almost finished and Lance was beyond excited to begin his pursuit of the perfect literary agent to represent his work. He was a pragmatic man, but sometimes he would catch himself dreaming about the exact moment the movie based on his books would appear in theaters around the globe, and he couldn't wait.

Chapter Twenty-Five

"They found another one." Lee James said solemnly as he placed a folder on his desk. He pulled out his chair then sat down beside his partner, Rick, at the station. There were televised reports of a missing local girl on every news station and everyone in law-enforcement was praying that she would show up at home, unharmed. Lee James opened the folder and turned to his partner. Rick picked up the morning paper that had been sitting, folded in half on his desk. He turned it around and showed Lee James the cover. Lee James cringed.

"Molly James, 21 years, worked at a clothing store (The GAP), in the mall situated between her home and school. Molly James, or, M.J., as she was known to her family and friends texted her mother that someone had called in sick while she was at work and she (Molly) had volunteered to cover the shift to get some extra hours at the store (she was saving up to buy a car), and she wouldn't be home till the last bus from the mall had dropped her off a few blocks from her home.

Lee James kept reading; her parents said she had done the route a thousand times since she got the job three years earlier and never had any trouble. Molly was a part-time student and she worked full-time to pay for school, she lived at home with her parents in order to save money to buy a car. Her parents said she never made it home that night and she never contacted them again. Her last message from her cellphone to her mother was at 9:45 p.m. and the mall closed at ten. Molly James did her closing procedures, counting cash and sweeping the store, etcetera, then said good-bye to her coworkers and was reported to have clocked out at approximately 10:36 p.m. The bus picks up passengers at the south-side of the mall at 11:05p.m., and it is the last pick-up of the day.

Lee James let out a heavy sigh as he continued reading, "Molly never made it onto the bus. No one saw her after she exited the mall, cameras show her leaving out the doors, but they do not capture her any time after that. It is almost as if she disappeared into thin air. Molly's body was found two days later in a ravine located a few blocks away from the university; Molly's school. Cause of death was strangulation. There was no foreign DNA found on the body." Lee James said then let out a low breath.

Rick sat thinking for a moment after Lee James finished speaking. "What else do we know about her? Boyfriend at the time? Anyone stalking her?" He said thoughtfully, shaking his head, his heart heavy with sorrow he refused to reveal. The whole town was frightened of waking up and reading about another discovery, and the police were under an immense amount of pressure to find someone, anyone, that could point them in the direction of their killer.

"Molly's mother said that she had always been active socially, it was part of the reason that she lessened her course-load down to part-time status. She didn't want to lower her grade point average; she was interested in attending grad school, but she just couldn't bring herself to give up her social life. Her mother said that Molly was one of very few people from her graduating class (high school) that went on to post-secondary education, and that Molly still spent a lot of time with her old friends. They went to local parties and bars, especially in the school district, and a group of them went camping every summer. But there was no boyfriend, the mother said she was always with a big group of girls. Her mother said she had always been popular. She had a lot of friends that were interviewed, one said Molly was, I quote, "fun and social" but "far from stupid". The friend described Molly, or MJ, as she called her, as being almost weary of new people. That same friend had a hunch that Molly had been, quote, "roughed up" by "some guy", she used to date, but that Molly wouldn't admit to anything."

"That "some guy" turned out to be an assistant manager at the record store in the same mall where Molly worked her full-time job. He claims nothing serious happened between the two of them; said Molly was 'too young and inexperienced' for his liking, so he stopped talking to her when she would come by during her break in the mall. And his alibi checked out anyway… turns out Mr. Experience is a struggling rock star, in a band and there were about a hundred or so witnesses that can place him on his custom drum set until two in the morning doing a show the night Molly went missing. His girlfriend, a self-described 'groupie', says she went home with him at 4 a.m., after they stopped for some food at a diner near their apartment. We showed his picture around and they remember him distinctly, turns out he 'stinks' after a show."

"So… what have we got?" Rick said as he rolled eyes. He looked back with exasperation clear in his voice then rubbed his eyes.

"Absolutely nothing. No one saw her again after she left the mall. Phone records indicate there were no outgoing texts or calls after ten o'clock that night. The last message being to her mother." Lee James said sadly, looking through the paperwork for anything they may have missed.

"But how can she just disappear? Then end up dead? Who took her? And why? What about personal belongings? What was found with the body? Anything?" Rick said, desperately.

"Oddly enough, her mother said everything her daughter had when she left for work that day was found with the body…

her keys, wallet, cell phone, it was all there, even her lunch bag. And crime scene photos show she wasn't 'placed' where she was found. She was dumped and in a hurry. Whoever did it was in a rush to get away from her and it seems as if the killer did not know the victim." Lee James said, as he held down his breakfast. It was threatening to come out of him with the force of a missile. He stopped moving and held his breath.

"She was random? You think she didn't know her killer?" Rick said, making mental notes, hoping for something to stick. It was truly depressing; the walls of the station house seemed to be coated in a matte grey, perfectly matching their moods inside.

"It is believed so, but the whole thing is inconclusive. We couldn't get much from toxicology based on decomposition and her parents had her cremated right away. We didn't know who or what we were looking for before we released the body." Lee James said, then took another deep breath. No one wanted to see these young girls come to any harm, but when it did start happening, it was almost impossible not to feel an intense physical reaction.

"What are you saying, partner?" Rick said rather aggressively, a pain in his temple gathering momentum.

"I'm saying… I think we've got a serial killer on our hands. And the young women in this town need to be warned before the situation gets any worse." Lee James said, furrowing his brows at the thought. Knowing and hating that he was probably right.

"But we don't want to start a panic… we also may not have enough information to warn women with." Lee James continued as he rubbed his brow with his hand.

"We know he likes blondes. Not one of these women drive their own car, or any car, on a regular basis. So… he offers them a ride. They were all students, one high school, two university…" Rick said, opening the file, seeing a picture of a lifeless victim, then closing it with a snap.

"What else? What else do they have in common? We need to liken them to each other. I'm worried about starting a panic, saying something too prematurely." Lee James said, panic evident in his voice. Knowing deep down that they weren't going to win this race, feeling there were too many strikes against them already.

"Look at it this way, you and I both know that there are no such things as coincidences. All of these victims were blonde or had long hair, they were attractive, and they were all young. They all used public transportation, and all were described by their friends and families as being social. And they were all taken then dumped within a ten-mile radius that includes three different towns that all border on each other. It's probably safe for us to figure that he's a local and that he has a preferred hunting ground, and this is it. None of the women's families reported any of them being stalked or harassed, or anything of that nature to anyone. And there were no formal complaints ever made. And there's no one on our radar, it's as if he appeared out of nowhere. These were all good girls who were in the worst possible place at the worst possible time and to me it seems that it is only a matter of time before he strikes again." Rick said, looking around the room. Anywhere but at the files on his desk and the look on his partner's face. He sat, silently contemplating that he wished he had already seen all there was to be seen. Hating that it wasn't true, not anymore.

"One last thing: they must all have quite willingly gotten into his car. There was never any sign of a struggle and no evidence at any last known scene, and with these girls, everyone in their lives notices almost immediately that they've gone missing and then they are reported to their local police. Whoever it is must have something about him that makes these women forget all they know just to get into the car with him." Lee James said after a second of thought.

"Maybe that's it..." Lee James said thoughtfully. "Maybe it's not so much the guy, but the car that he drives. Listen, if someone were to pull up at a random bus stop in a beaten old van with darkened windows, even men would be cautious…because everyone's seen a movie like that… so there's no way a woman would get into that vehicle. But maybe this guy drives something really nice, something expensive or exotic. I'm not saying these women are superficial and that's what got them into trouble, but I remember taking the city bus after I graduated from high school; my old man said he wasn't gonna drive me anywhere anymore. Well, let me tell you, I dreamed of owning a car every single time I stood at a bus stop and waited for the bus to pick me up. In a university town, the buses are almost always full because no one can really afford a car, and parking, and gas and tuition. So almost everybody takes the bus or walks… unless your parents are rich and buy you a car. But even those situations are far and few between. It's not like this is L.A. or somewhere like that. Kids around here come from middle-class families and I can't remember the last time I saw a Lamborghini cruising around town. This guy, whoever he is, has got to drive a really nice set of wheels; something that doesn't draw too much attention, but something that would surely get him some kind of undeserved credit or trust from unsuspecting women. But we don't know make or model, or color. Only that there is a chance that the vehicle is more expensive than your average compact car. Sounds a bit ridiculous to issue a warning based on a car we really know nothing about. I guess it's just a hunch." Lee James said thoughtfully.

"It's a great hunch, it makes perfect sense, and without any evidence or eye-witnesses, hunches are all we have to go on. Let's put it to bed for now, see what we can come up with when we have a rested set of eyes tomorrow." Rick said in exasperation, placing his hand on the file in front of him.

Lee James went home after work to toss and turn in bed the whole night; he couldn't stop with how helpless he felt with the case. He was scared that a serial killer was on the loose and about to ravage his beloved town even more. His fear stemmed from the lack of evidence and the innocence of the victims. He could not get the crime scene photos out of his head. Lee James knew he needed a plan and right before the sun came creeping up over the horizon, he thought he'd found one.

Chapter Twenty-Six

Celine Bower had been planning the attack for weeks. She dreamt of scenarios obsessively and she was finding it more and more difficult by the day to contain her emotions. Every single time she went to the local restaurant off the roadway for Indian food, Celine would see at least three or four of the 'working girls' that were local enough to frequent the place, eating there. And she would be sick. Celine caught herself more than once, staring hard at the poor girls and wondering if there was any way, aside from building a shelter for women and protecting them, that she could possibly help them. And the longer she went without helping those women, the more consumed she became with the thought of doing something, anything, to help their plight.

Every time she saw a foreign man in her daily life, regardless of her circumstances (but she knew who they were, the losers, trying to look tan and relaxed for their vacations, but reeking of false arrogance and bravado. Not realising or caring very little about how destructive their behaviour as a foreign male infiltrating a third world country for cheap sex really was), Celine would stare so angrily that she was sure the men could feel her rage boring a hole into their flesh. All the while they sat in their plastic chairs at any number of the popular, tourist-filled restaurants on the water-front, groping teenage girls that they paid for their company. The men would sit and gorge on their food, feeling like kings because they could afford so much more in such a poor place. Each girl, done up to the nines, with their tiny jean shorts or mini-skirts that were short enough to expose buttocks, along with their breasts in lacy push up bras that had them shoved up to her chin. And their hair was always beautiful, as if the man or his money could somehow demand the length, texture and style of her hair (and from what Celine had heard in her time there, she wouldn't have put it past any man who frequented the area, or the 'working girls').

Sometimes Celine would try to get the girls attention and get them to make eye contact with her, but they were usually too shy or ashamed to look back at her, and instead avoided her glances. Celine could not count how many times she had stopped herself from walking up to some puffy, over-stuffed foreign man sitting at one of the tables with a local girl less than half his age and slapping the satisfied look right off his face, her rage was so powerful. Celine thought of other things she wanted to do to the men but didn't think any of them would be appropriate in public. Celine knew she could never expose her true identity to anyone; she knew she had to stay safe because she felt deep down that there was another way and she just had to find it.

Chapter Twenty-Seven

Fear drove him to it, drove him to risk his professionalism and his integrity. Fear also forced him to search deep into the pit of his soul. Lee James woke early, showered then called Rick at his desk and told him that he would be late. Lee James drove to Molly Bower's townhouse. As luck would have it, his instinct proved correct, she was a 'morning person'. He pulled into her driveway just as she was stepping out of her car.

Celine's mother froze when she heard a strange automobile pull into her driveway. Her only daughter had skipped town and her nerves completely on edge. Any little sound could make her jump, she felt so lost without her Celine. Molly immediately stopped was she was doing to get a good look at the car in her driveway. Lee James switched his car off and opened his door, smiling at Celine's mom. It took Molly a second to recognise his face as he said a kind 'good morning' while he stepped from behind his door then walked up the driveway. Molly let out deep breath then smiled back at Lee James. She collected herself for a moment then resumed loading her arms with grocery bags.

"Let me help you with that." Lee James said quickly as he walked up to the driver side car door that was open. He looked down and noticed that Celine's mother must have been shopping at one of the city's superstores as there were quite a few large, bulky items on the floor of the car along with a few smaller reusable shopping bags. It was as if she did her shopping for the year in one trip.

"Well, um… thank you, Detective. It looks like you got here right on time and who am I to refuse help?" Molly said as she stepped back and gave Lee James space to reach into the car.

"You're welcome, Mrs. Bower. I was just in the neighborhood, so I thought I'd stop by, see how things are going." Lee James said with a handsome smile as he easily lifted a few of the larger items off the floor of the car and followed Molly Bower to the front door of her townhouse. He was careful to take a quick peek into the tiny garage window as he walked by. He smiled when his suspicions were confirmed; tucked under a grey tarp in the center of the garage was Celine's little car.

"Oh, things are pretty great around here." Molly said with a forced smile as she walked past the front of her car to the front steps. She stopped in front of the door and turned to Lee James as she put the key in the lock and pushed the door open. She stepped through the threshold then stepped out of the way to give space for Lee James to follow her.

"You can just put those down there." She said and pointed to an empty space just inside the doorway. Lee James obliged and turned to unload more things from her car.

"You don't have to do this, Detective. I did get them into the car by myself at the store, you know?" She said briskly as she walked back past him and back out to her car.

"It's no problem at all, I'm happy to help. Plus, a lot of these things are heavy, and you probably had a cart at the store. I know my wife will leave heavy things in the back seat of the car until I can get them out for her." He said with a laugh as he bent down to reach for more items. "It drives me nuts sometimes when I go to put something back there and it's full of a jumbo laundry detergent or a box of kitty litter. But what can I do?" He said with a smile. Molly smiled back at him, disarmed by his candor and charm, almost forgetting how they met in the first place. But she could not let her guard down she thought as she took off her shoes. No, she had seen the movies, the TV shows; she knew it couldn't possibly be all fun and smiles.

"Well, thank you very much". Molly said as she regained all of her composure. "But I've been lifting my own groceries since Celine's father passed. I've gotten so used to doing it that I don't even think about it anymore. I'm still grateful for the help, though." Molly said and smiled as she watched Lee James pass her with the really heavy jumbo-sized items she had bought at the store. 'He probably saved me five trips', she thought to herself as she giggled. Molly didn't know why the detective was there, but she had to admit that that having an extra pair of strong arms could really help sometimes.

"Everybody can use a little help sometimes." Lee James said to Molly as he waited for her to get the last of the grocery bags out of the car and shut the door. In that moment Molly was calm, grateful, the detective seemed genuinely happy to help her.

"Isn't that the truth?" Molly said as she walked behind him. When they got inside the foyer, Molly motioned for the detective to place the items in the same spot on the floor and smiled as she thanked him again. He looked around briefly and smiled back at her, shrugging his shoulders a 'no problem'.

"Thank you so much for bringing in my groceries. If you have couple minutes, I can make us a pot of coffee. There are some muffins around here…somewhere", she said as she pointed to some of the bags on the floor.". Molly spotted the container then quickly bent down and reached into a bag. As she stood back up, she became surprised at herself, and her attitude toward the detective. An actual real, live human being in her house. She was almost pulled to the floor with grief as the loneliness she had been feeling snuck up on her. Molly smiled again and turned away from the detective.

"If it's no trouble, a muffin and coffee sound perfect." Lee James said with a smile, relaxing his shoulders and secretly patting himself on the back. He had done it no matter the cost, he was in.

"It's no trouble..." Molly said as she walked in her house.

"And please, call me Lee James. Sometimes I'm just a regular guy that helps women with heavy groceries." He said with a wink and they both laughed. Watching Celine's mother in the small foyer, Lee James wondered how difficult it must have been for her to live through everything she had gone through in the last few years. There was the sudden and tragic death of her husband and then the attack on her daughter. Lee James felt secretly humbled to be in her presence, he felt guilty too.

Molly walked into the kitchen and Lee James followed suit, first removing his loafers and putting them aside, then grabbing a bag of what looked like perishables and following Molly through the pretty little townhouse, and into the kitchen. Molly just finished washing her hands and was putting grocery items in the rightful spots but stopped what she was doing to get the bags from Lee James. He walked back into the foyer and grabbed more items.

When he returned to the kitchen, Lee James noticed Molly had emptied a few of the bags and he could see that she had started a pot of coffee as promised. She turned and smiled at Lee James when she saw what he was carrying and motioned for him to bring the bags over toward her. Lee James complied then went back to the entrance foyer to retrieve the very last of the shopping items. When he returned to the kitchen, he noticed that Celine's mother was nowhere to be found. He placed the items on the counter gently and held his breath as he strained to hear a sound in their house. She was downstairs somewhere and as Lee James stepped further into the kitchen, he noticed a light on and the basement door open. Lee James immediately began a search for anything that might lead him to Celine's whereabouts. Quickly and quietly, with the deft precision of a jewel thief, the detective opened drawers and cupboards, looking for anything. He stopped cold and held his breath when he heard Molly shifting her belongings downstairs. Ever so gently, he turned his head, and craning his neck as far as it would go while he stayed on his feet, he called out in the direction of the basement stairwell.

"Is everything okay?" Lee James said pleasantly as he leaned over and stretched his arms, then began leafing through a stack of papers that were in a neat pile on the small kitchen table.

"I'm okay down here. Just one more minute and the coffee will be done." Molly shouted in response from the bottom of the stairs.

"Can I help you with anything while you're down there?" Lee James asked nicely as he turned, took out the pen from shirt pocket and used it to sift through Molly's handbag that happened to be lying open on the counter near the phone.

"I'm fine, thanks. I'll be up in one minute, Lee James." Molly said cheerfully from the bottom of the stairwell.

Lee James shrugged then turned toward the refrigerator and that's when he saw it. Only half of it was peeking out from behind a take–out menu and a recipe card. Lee James moved quietly and stood in front of the fridge. He held his breath and listened carefully. Molly was not on the stairs yet. The detective didn't make a sound as he carefully lifted the post card off the side of fridge and turned it over. The date-stamp said it had been mailed two weeks earlier and it was written in pretty cursive. A simple message from daughter to mother letting one know that the other was okay. She signed it, 'CB'.

The detective smiled as he struck gold, but the feeling didn't last because all of a sudden he heard a noise. Then he jumped just as the coffee pot started to hiss and steam beside him. Lee James quickly put the card on the counter, then pulled out his cell phone and took a photograph of the post card. The front and the back.

Quickly and very quietly, he returned it to the exact same spot as he had found it. He was casually putting his phone back into his pocket as Molly appeared at the top of the basement stairs. She smiled at him when she saw him then turned to switch off the light and closed the door behind her.

"Oh good, the coffee is ready." Molly said as she crossed the room and reached for the cupboard doors above the coffee maker. She pulled out two mugs then turned to Lee James who was still standing in the middle of the room and said, "talk about perfect timing.".

Chapter Twenty-Eight

Dear Celine,

I don't know how to start. I'm really sorry to be bothering you. I know that we met under the worst possible circumstances because I will never forget the bruises on your face or the fear in your voice. I've spoken to your mother a few times in the recent past; she is probably one of the strongest women I have ever met, but you already know that because you are so much like her. Sorry, I'm rambling, I've never done something like this before and I truly hope that you will forgive me one day. The reason why I've seen your mother is because I had some things to tell you and I didn't know how to find you, other than at your mother's home. I hope that she will forgive me one day too. I wasn't completely honest with her and that's something I'm not proud of.

I need a shot at redemption, Celine. You can call me anything you want, after you hear me out.

Here it goes: When I told Rick that I found some new information regarding your case, we started to look into the names that were given to us by this witness I found. The truth is that we found some striking similarities to each of their fates (we also secretly did a DNA analysis, just to be one hundred percent positive), at the hands of a woman that has yet to be identified. And the thing is, what we discovered only confirmed what Rick and I thought we already knew. That it was you, Celine, who castrated those men. And the reason why you did it is because we let you down. It left you feeling like you had to take the law into your own hands. And just to confirm, Rick and I have NEVER TOLD ANYONE what we discovered. We swear on our lives that we will keep your identity a secret.

This might sound strange coming from anyone else but, Rick and I believe, that you have some kind of special gift and you probably don't even realise how important you are to our town. That is why I'm writing to you today, Celine. I, we, all of us, need your help. We need your special kind of gift.

I have found you because I am a desperate man. You deserve your freedom, but I believe, and Rick does too, that you are our only hope.

Here goes: there is a man that is hunting and killing young women in our town. He finds them, strangles them, and dumps their bodies where people can find them. He has left no trace and not ONE SINGLE PERSEON has ever seen him alive. He's like a ghost, a phantom. People are terrified to leave their homes. Young women are being murdered and families are being destroyed. We need your help to catch him.

Before he kills again.

You can say 'no'. You can tell me to blow it out my piehole, if you want to, and I swear that I will never say anything about you to anyone. Ever. You can see that I have included the newspaper clippings and some copies of the crime scene photos. Maybe it will help you decide.

I would normally never ask you, a private citizen, to do something like this. To risk your life to help us, but women are dying, and I can't do anything to stop it. I need your help. Please.

My number is at the bottom. Call me collect.

Time is of the essence, Celine.

Sincerely,
Lee James Morrison

Chapter Twenty-Nine

Celine's hands shook from the moment she picked up the envelope that sat so innocuously on the front desk of her resort. It was her name in handwriting that she had never seen before. She smiled as the receptionist handed her the envelope. Celine felt like her knees were going to give out and the room was getting smaller around her as she thanked the receptionist, then walked quickly to her room with the enveloped tucked under her arm. It was thick with paper and Celine couldn't begin to understand why anyone would send her anything, when only her mother and Tunisha had any inkling about where she was hiding out. No one around her had discovered who she really was either.

The contents of the envelope made her sick and she needed to stop reading more than once because the crime scene photos were so sterile, so shocking, that she was worried she would vomit all over them. Celine could not believe that Lee James had found her. She couldn't help but wonder what had given her away, and then she realised as she stood there above her tiny air-conditioner trying to cool herself in the vents, that as much as her mother had helped her escape, Molly Bower was no sophisticated criminal mastermind. All it would take was one visit by Lee James, or his partner for a coffee, and Molly would invite them in, probably offer them brownies. 'She must be so Goddamn lonely', Celine thought with a tear in her eye.

"My poor mother," Celine said quietly as she sat down on the edge of her bed and allowed herself a moment to think about the most important woman in her life. "I wonder if she would have chosen any different if she'd had a crystal ball right before she had me or married my father. Would she still have wanted a child if she knew it was going to be me? Would she have raised me any differently? Or moved us somewhere else, just to avoid the tragedy that seemed to be lurking around every corner. Would she still have had me if she would have known what type of person I would have become? Was she still proud to call me her daughter?" Celine said quietly then wiped away a tear that had rolled down her cheek. "Maybe she is proud of me… I know she didn't turn me in to the police, and I wouldn't have gotten away, or even survived any of what had happened to me, if it weren't for her."

Celine paced inside the tiny room and considered her options. She could stay right where she was and be satisfied. She knew she was making a difference; Penny had told her as much. But when Celine looked at the envelope, and recalled the pictures and articles inside, she couldn't get the face of Molly James out of her head. 'Those poor girls, and their poor families,' Celine thought sadly as she struggled with her decision. 'Lee James knew exactly what he was doing when he placed "Molly's" information at the bottom of the pile. He knew that I wouldn't wish what happened to those girls on anyone, but especially my own mother. It wasn't fair, he connected me to them without my permission, using my mother as a lure to get me back into town. What an asshole. You can blow it out your piehole alright, dickhead.' Celine thought bitterly, accepting deep down that she had already made her decision to leave. To go home and help the police, the people that let her down so badly in the not-so-recent past. The people she on occasion, during a moment of weakness, still sometimes blamed for the way things turned out for her. To risk losing everything all over again. But could she really be able to say 'goodbye' to a place that had given her the freedom and anonymity that she had fallen in love with?

Chapter Thirty

Celine packed her belongings quietly and swiftly. She wrote a heartfelt note to Penny, briefly explaining her sudden departure, begging her for forgiveness and swearing to keep in touch. Then she placed everything aside and picked up the other bag she had packed.

Celine walked through the sticky heat to the main road and hailed a taxi. She asked the driver to take her into town. When they arrived, Celine asked the driver to pull over, paid him then stepped out of the car and onto the curb. She walked to the closest hotel and made her way to the entrance where she fell in behind some other tourists, following them into the front lobby. She broke away from the crowd at the elevators and went in search of the women's restroom. She pushed open the doors and once inside, she locked herself in a stall, then opened the plastic bag she had been carrying. Inside the bag were all the items she had arranged in a neat pile and she hurriedly pulled them out of the bag and placed them on the toilet seat. When Celine left her room an hour earlier in an old t-shirt and cotton shorts, she was also wearing a bandeau bikini top with the matching bottoms underneath. She took off the shorts and t-shirt and threw them on the floor, then she picked up the old, khaki board shorts from the new pile and put them on. (She came into the possession of the shorts while walking from the rehabilitation centre back to her room late one afternoon. They were exactly what she wanted. Celine had stopped and looked around quickly before she snuck into the tiny yard where they were hanging stiffly on a clothes-line full of freshly laundered clothes. She looked around again as she pulled them off, quickly rolled them up, then tucked them under her arm as she made her way through the tall grass and back to the road. Celine wasn't proud of the fact that she stole someone else's clothes; she had also shoved a few dollars of the local money in a random pocket of another pair of shorts that were still hanging. Celine smiled as she carried on down the road, the shorts were perfect for her plan.)

Celine picked up the tensor bandage that was also sitting in the pile and began wrapping it around her breasts. (She learned the trick to flattening her chest from a transgendered girl she was friends with while in high school. The girl had the most perfect breasts but would tell Celine how much she wanted to be rid of them because they just didn't suit her.) After successfully minimizing her breasts and fastening the bandage with the clips provided, Celine bent down and picked up the over-sized t-shirt she had gotten from a different hotel giftshop near the marina. It had a picture of a bikini-clad woman lying stretched out on the beach at sunset on it and Celine knew it would look perfect. Lastly, she stepped out of her old thong sandals and slipped on the thick, clunky pair of flip-flops she bought at a roadside stand a few days previous; the day she decided she was going to do something about the atrocities she was privy to since arriving in the small country. Celine gathered all of her belongings, rolled them into a ball, then stepped out of the stall and stuffed everything deep into the bottom of the trash bin. She looked at herself in the mirror, then remembered the last item in the bag. She went back into the stall and found a baseball cap in the plastic bag, then put it on. She went back out to the mirror to inspect her handiwork. Celine adjusted the cap on her head, making sure to tuck her long hair under the cap then pulling a few strands out around her face. When she was satisfied that she no longer looked at all like Celine Bower, the woman because she had even remembered to take the nail polish off her toes and chewed her fingernails down to unsightly pink nubs. Celine was ready, she walked out of the bathroom using the walk she had been practicing for months. Celine had a few laughs at herself looking in the mirror as she practised learning how to walk and hold herself as if she had a penis instead of a vagina. She constantly had to remind herself to avoid things like swinging her hips.

Celine knew immediately that her hard work and determination to look like a man had paid off. As soon as she left the hotel and arrived at the main thoroughfare, she was instantly accosted by some of the women working the strip. Celine had to stop herself from smiling and talking as she carried on her way. Celine was surprised at how differently the world responded to her when she looked like a guy. People, mostly women and old couples moved out of *her* way on the sidewalks and lots of women smiled at her. She felt oddly free and unencumbered with her new identity as she walked the few final steps toward the place she had been eyeing for months.

Chapter Thirty-One

The entrance was hidden behind heavy black curtains that were on the left side of a popular bar, but Celine knew exactly where the door was because she had seen some male tourists stumble out of there then high five each other one evening when she happened to be walking by. She followed them discreetly, listening in disgust, all the way back to their hotel. They spoke in disbelief at how cheap, 'young hot pussy' was in the country, how the best thing they ever did was, 'go to a place where the people were hungry' and 'for a few extra dollars, the local girls would do anal'. They laughed when one of the group's members had thought to mention how their wives and girlfriends at home would, 'never swallow' for any money or gifts they could give them, whereas 'the whores here would do *anything* to buy their next meal'.

While walking behind the group of men, listening to them wax poetic on the virtues of cheap sex, Celine used all of her inner strength to avoid causing a scene by bashing in their skulls with the nearest blunt object. At the time her only concern was rotting her life away in some awful foreign prison and the fear that she might never see her mother again that kept her powers in check. A little voice in her head told her ever-so-quietly that the time for vengeance would come and she should not even dream of doing something before then. Patience, and her will to continue down the right path kept her from beating anyone senseless in the last few months.

The time was upon her. Ten steps from the doorway, Celine slipped into a garbage-filled, rat-infested alley to steal her nerves and double-check that she had everything that she would need. Tucked inside the big baggy pockets of her stolen shorts was a big wad of the local currency, a capped syringe, and nothing else. Celine knew intuitively that she could get away unscathed doing what she was about to do. She couldn't explain it, even to herself, how she 'knew' any of it after she got struck by lightning. She just knew.

Celine took a deep breath, adjusted her hat then walked back out onto the street. Two young women in tight black dresses who were stationed at the door, spotted Celine immediately and smiled as they said 'hello'. The women could tell that the man in front of them was nervous, so the more aggressive of the two (the seasoned veteran who had seen this type of shyness before with many 'first-timers'), walked up to Celine and grabbed her gently by the elbow. Celine's mouth twitched to make the tiniest smile, and she nodded her head when the woman asked if she was there, 'to see one of the beautiful ladies'. The woman said something in the local language and suddenly the black curtains were drawn open and Celine was shifted toward the entrance where another local woman smiled and asked Celine for money. Celine reached into her pocket for the wad of cash, then unfolded a couple of bills to hand to the lady, who grabbed them quickly and shoved them down the front of her shirt. She shouted something that Celine couldn't understand then waited until another woman quickly appeared on the little stairwell and reached for Celine's hand, gently leading her up the stairs.

Celine, holding her breath, could not believe how easy it was for her to get in and get a quick look at her new surroundings. The stairs were short and there were a lot of them. They made a faint creaking sound with every step the women took. Celine could hear the low hum of what must have be multiple air conditioners throughout the place. She could smell cheap perfume in the humid air and could hear the faint sound of music coming from the large speakers in the bar next door. Celine was expecting the entire place to be dark and dirty, considering what went on behind the walls, but found it surprisingly clean and bright when they reached the top of the stairwell.

It was a long white hallway with floors covered in a cheap carpet running the length of it to the window at the other end. There were about a dozen or so, white doors, with equal numbers on both sides running the length of it. Celine immediately thought it to be a converted hotel or boarding house. All of the doors were painted white and all of the doors were closed. Celine could see that there were white hand towels on some of the doorknobs, and as the woman led her down the hallway, Celine could hear lusty noises coming from behind the doors; some laughing, some moaning and other more unpleasant sounds. Celine kept her ears open as her eyes darted around the small space. With the woman still ahead of her, leading the way for her, they got to the middle of the hallway when the woman stopped. She pointed to the doorknobs that had no towels and told Celine to 'pick whichever she wanted and go in.' Celine pointed quickly to one of the closest doors and the woman nodded her head in acknowledgement, smiled, turned on a dime then walked past Celine to the stairwell and down the stairs. Celine held her breath as she watched the woman go.

Chapter Thirty-Two

The doorknob was cold to the touch as Celine grasped it and turned the knob. The door opened silently, and Celine walked through the doorway into the room.

Celine stepped into the room and quietly closed the door behind her. She wasn't satisfied until she heard the 'click', then she stepped away from the door. The inside looked like a cheap hotel room. There was a double bed as the focal point in the middle of the room. It was made up in a cheap satin bedding and covered with a few cheap-looking pillows. Beside the bed was a small table with towels on it. On the other side of the bed was a doorway that led to the bathroom and a small cheap dresser beside that door. Standing beside the bed was a girl of about thirteen or fourteen years old. She had long shiny black hair and she was wearing cheap and tacky lingerie, the same style as the bedding; it was almost as if they intentionally had her attire to purposely match the room and give off an overtly-sexual theme. The girl forced a smile to her lips and turned to face Celine who had just snuck into a whorehouse dressed as a man. The young girl grabbed a towel from the pile behind her on the table and walked toward the door. Celine stepped toward her and the girl recoiled in fear.

"It's okay, I'm not going to hurt you. And I don't want to have sex." Celine said quietly as she stepped closer to the girl. The girl stopped what she was doing and looked quizzically at Celine.

Celine stepped further toward the young girl as she took off her hat and shook out her long blonde hair. The girl stopped briefly and Celine grabbed the towel from her hands.

"I'm here to help you, but you need to be quiet. What's your name?" Celine said quietly as she smiled at the frightened girl.

"Susannah." The girl said so quietly that it sounded more like a squeak than a voice.

"How old are you, Susannah?" Celine said and smiled, hoping the girl would try to trust her.

"Thirteen." Susannah said quietly and looked down to the floor.

"It's okay," Celine said gently. "I'm not here to hurt you, but you have to get out of here. How long have you been here?"

"I've lived here for one year." Susannah said quietly as she looked up at Celine with hope in her eyes. The room was hot and sticky, but the girl had gooseflesh on her arms and shoulders. Celine could see beads of sweat that had gathered at the girl's hairline. Celine could smell the cheap perfume the girl must have been wearing and she almost vomited.

"Oh my gosh. What happened to you?" Celine asked quickly, saddened by what she was hearing.

"My parents sold me to a woman in our village… then they brought me here. They told my family I was going to work in a big house to cook and clean for a rich family, but they brought me here." Susannah said as tears welled up in her eyes. "They took me in a car then they drove for a really long time. They brought me here and I can't get out." Susannah pointed to the window behind the bed and Celine noticed the bars for the first time. The bars were painted white and hidden strategically behind the cheap curtains. Celine never would have noticed them if the girl hadn't pointed them out.

"You must be so scared." Celine said as she looked around the room and took in the shabby surroundings. Her mind began to wonder at the thought of being trapped in a room as a sex slave at the age of twelve. She couldn't imagine her life if she had never had the opportunity to go to school and meet friends her own age. To live with the freedom in knowing she could choose her own path. How devastating it must have been for the girl, knowing that her family had no idea what really happened to her, and probably not even being able to help her if they did.

"I want to go home." Susannah cried to Celine. "They make me do bad things here. They hurt me." Tears fell from Susannah's eyes as she looked at the floor. Celine put her hand out and Susannah took it and held her tightly. Celine shushed her quietly.

Celine had heard enough. She quickly began to undress. She slipped the t-shirt over her head then pulled down and stepped out of the shorts, then untied the tensor bandage. The girl was staring in wild-eyed wonder when the sound of loud voices coming from outside the door startled them. Celine snapped into action, knowing they didn't have a moment to lose. She gathered up her belongings on the floor, grabbed something from the pocket of the shorts, then shoved them into the girl's arms and pushed her toward the bathroom door. The girl turned quickly and scurried to the door and opened it.

Celine could hear the creaking of the stairs getting louder, so she put her finger to her lips and silenced the girl as she stood in the tiny room. The young girl had fear in her eyes as she looked into Celine's face, but she was as quiet as a mouse, somehow knowing it was okay to trust Celine.

"Hide in there and don't make a sound. Don't come out no matter what you hear. Wait for me to come and get you. Okay?" Celine said quickly and the girl smiled before Celine silently closed the door.

The creaking on the stairs stopped and Celine could hear heavy footsteps in the hallway. She looked quickly in the mirror, fixing her hair and straightening her bikini. She went quickly to the bedside table and tucked the syringe under the pile of towels. Celine propped herself up on the bed, crossing her legs at the ankles just in time to hear the door click open.

In walked one of the biggest men Celine had ever seen, explaining the creaking on the stairs. He was in his late fifties, had fair hair that was balding, and at five feet, eight inches tall, probably tipped the scales at around three hundred pounds. He was Caucasian and was wearing a crisp white golf shirt and dark green khaki shorts. The man shut the door behind him then used the same hand to wipe a thick layer of sweat off his enormous brow. His eyebrows raised in a look of surprise, and he smiled showing all of his coffee-stained teeth. He looked Celine's body up and down as if he was getting ready to place an order at a deli, then he spoke in a slow, southern drawl.

"Well, you're not a teenager, are you?" He said as he stepped even further into the room and looked around at the size of the bed.

Celine smiled slightly as she cocked her head to one side and mouthed the word 'no'.

"Well, usually I come here to get some of the younger stuff, but you'll do just fine. But if I find out you're too big for my liking, you'll just have to suck on me for an hour, then smile real pretty when I blow my load all over your face. Sound good, honey?" He said slowly and smiled as he made his way into the room.

Celine smiled and nodded. Then he moved closer toward the bed. Celine smiled more broadly and patted a place close to her on the bed.

"Just you wait a minute there, honey, I've got to take my shoes off before we get started. Sometimes I like to get my toes sucked while I'm here. You know, sucked and fucked, right, honey?" He said with a laugh.

Celine could only nod her head and smile as he sat heavily on the bed, (the whole thing groaned and shifted to one side under his weight), and he attempted to undo his shoes and take off his socks. He stopped what he was doing to ogle Celine's body then he looked around the room. His eyes flickered at the bathroom door for only a moment then he watched as Celine reached over for a towel then got off the bed and sauntered toward the door. In the meantime, the man felt comfortable enough to start taking off his clothes. When he finished, he threw them in a pile on the floor then pulled the comforter down the bed and slowly lowered himself onto the sheets.

Celine watched from where she was standing then opened the door a crack, slipped her hand out and placed the towel on the doorknob. When she closed the door behind her, she turned to him and smiled.

"Get over here and let me get a good look at you." He said as he ogled Celine's body, licking his lips and smiling.

Celine smiled seductively, then sauntered over to the bed and stopped at the end. He raised his finger, beckoning her to come closer and she did as she was told, swinging and swaying her hips with every step she took.

"Vat vould you like me to do first?" Celine said in a pathetic attempt at a Russian accent that she had spent many a night practicing in front of a mirror and hoped it would work. As she got closer to him, Celine could smell his sweat mixed in with cigar and aftershave.

"I want to you to get my dick hard with your tongue before I stick it in your fine ass." He said, pronouncing each word slowly then licked his lips and relaxed further on the pillows.

"Okay…" Celine said, her eyes twinkling.

"And you better do a good job because I paid for double length of service with you, honey. I'm treating myself to extra 'whore-time' with you and I think it's your lucky day." He said, bearing his ugly teeth, the sweat dripping down the sides of his face.

"Oh, how much?" Celine said and batted her eyelashes at him.

"It's gonna be the best twenty dollars I have ever spent, honey. You know, as a Family Court Judge, I see druggie whores like you all the time. Not as hot as you are, or as clean-looking, but I see you in my court room…using your benefits to feed your addictions and fucking any man that will give you the time of day and help you find your next fucking hit. So, don't go feeling sorry for yourself when you realise that your time and body aren't worth more than I will pay for my next meal. So get your skinny ass over here and suck my dick." He said, as the color rose up in his cheeks. "You know, the sad thing is, that I have to come all the way over to this third world shithole to have my dick sucked by young whores when I see them all the time in my court room and can't do anything about it because it would really upset the wife. Too bad. Now, get over here."

"Okay," Celine said and smiled as she got close enough to the side table to reach and grasp the syringe. She jumped on the bed and straddled the judge around the waist with her legs. He began rubbing his hands all over her body then started moaning as Celine began kissing his neck. She was giggling and making loud sucking noises as she brought the syringe up to his neck and plunged it into his flesh. He coughed and choked and raised his hand to his neck while trying to buck Celine off his naked body. He was grunting and spitting while trying to understand what was happening to him.

"What did you do to me?" He demanded and tried to grab her as she jumped off his writhing body.

"I did you a favor." Celine said in her normal voice.

"What?" He thundered at her as it became clear she wasn't who he thought she was.

"I'm a judge, goddammit! What did you do to me, you whore? I'm a judge, for Christs sake!" He stammered as he tried to raise his massive bulk off the bed.

"Well, then I am your worst nightmare… bitch." Celine said as she stepped further away from his flailing arms and body.

"What? Who are you? You're no Russian. Argh, what did you do to me? I feel like I'm having a heart attack." He said as his eyes began to bug in his head and his breathing became more labored. He stared wild-eyed at Celine looking for an answer while she stood there casually, waiting as the drugs worked their way through his system.

"I can assure you that you are not having a heart attack." Celine said calmly as she smiled at him. For a moment, just as her words sank in, he looked relieved and smiled back. "But you are, in fact, dying."

"What?" He said angrily and began to struggle once again to lift his body off the bed.

"But, if you think about it, I'm actually helping you… Judge." Celine said and smiled at the look of fear and confusion that spread across his face.

"What are you talking about?" He said angrily. He was winded and had stopped writhing about on the bed.

"Well, I'm putting you out of your misery. It must be awful to walk around, to simply exist with so much hatred inside yourself." Celine explained calmly as she looked at her nails and picked off a stray piece of skin, then looked back at the judge that lay before her dying.

"You bitch!" He tried to shout loudly but came out as a lonely little whisper. "I'm dying."

"Well, isn't that just your luck, *honey*? You go on vacation in a third world country to have paid sex with underage girls, although as a judge, you know damn well how illegal and immoral that is, and you end up choosing the room with the one woman here that can do something to stop you and your sick, disgusting ways. And other guys like you. Isn't just your shitty luck that you go out to get your fat, bald ass 'fucked and sucked' as you so eloquently put it, and now you are going to die? Like, what are the chances, right, Judge?" Celine said as she watched the light fade from his eyes. She knew he had only moments left on earth and she wasn't quite finished. She leaned over his body and whispered in his ear.

"Just think about this, Judge… what on earth will your wife and kids think when this is where they are going to have to pick up your body?" She said as she heard the Judge's final breath escape his body.

Chapter Thirty-Two

John Scott used to be an attractive man. He was never a good person but, with his chiseled jaw, broad, muscular shoulders and thick hair, his appearance made it obvious as to why some women would be attracted to him. Initially, of course, because once he began speaking and the real 'John' came out; the misogynistic, ignorant bully of a man turned off more women than could be imagined. Not all of them of course; some women felt they could 'change him', others believed he was a good person 'deep down', and that maybe they could 'give him a chance', but for all the women that he pushed around and all the prostitutes that he beat up, there was the one woman that decided that John Scott had done enough damage to innocent women that he came in contact with, and had hurt enough of them too. And because this woman in particular suffered terribly at the hands of John Scott, perhaps more than any other woman he had ever encountered, she felt it her civic duty to ensure that a monster like him was never going to be able to hurt a woman ever again. See, what John Scott didn't realise (or perhaps he just didn't care about), when he and his friends made plans to drug, kidnap, and rape Celine Bower, was that maybe, just maybe, karma, or something like it, was going to catch up with them. That one day their luck would run out. The group of men didn't believe in anything supernatural, or maybe they had just gotten away with being sacks of shit for so long, that they became arrogant, and believed themselves invincible. So, when John Scott woke the morning after his night with a stunning brunette named, 'Scarlett', that he met and got drunk with at a bar, even he knew deep down that his life had been changed forever. And when he absolutely refused to take part in any police investigation, he once again considered that his own actions had sealed his shitty fate.

John Scott never gave up his attraction to women after his testicles were forcibly removed, but he found life in the fast lane too difficult to enjoy the way he used to. Although he tried, and tried, he just couldn't get over the fact that he had an ugly scar proclaiming that he raped women on his back, and he couldn't get over the fact that it was true, that someone had made him accountable. John Scott looked at it in the mirror after every shower for weeks on end until he eventually stopped looking and refused to be near any reflective surface without his clothes on or his back turned. Then there was the fact that he no longer had his testicles to speak of. The doctors at the hospital tried their best to counsel John about the physical effects that a castration would have on his body. Never being the scholarly type, or the type to give a damn about what anyone said, John let the information they were trying to share with him go in one ear and right out the other. He didn't bother to go to any recommended therapy sessions and he never filled a single prescription the hospital had given him before he was discharged. All in all, John Scott was probably the lousiest patient the hospital had ever seen, but their hands were tied the minute he signed his discharge papers and walked out the double doors.

The problem for John was denial. He was so deep in denial that he refused to see that anything about his appearance had changed due to the lack of testosterone that would normally be running through his body. He was still the same ugly, mean, bigot of a man inside, but he wasn't as scary as he had been before, nor as physically threatening. You see, where John was once solidly built and muscular, his body had changed and he was, for lack of a better word, flabby. Where there was once an abundance of defined muscle, there was now a sort of pudgy, soft flesh where the muscle had once been. And through his denial he managed to completely ignore the fact that he himself had developed a lovely set of man-boobs, and they continued to get bigger regardless of how he tried in earnest to deny their existence. The last symptom that John Scott ignored on a regular basis was something that scared him initially but since he had 'calmed down' and became less aggressive, it was easier for him to deal with. The terrible hot flashes and night sweats that woke him up almost every night since the hormone testosterone, had been removed from his body. And it was all due to the fact that he had been castrated by Celine Bower, a woman he had once drugged and gang-raped with his friends. If one were a betting person, one might surmise that many of John's previous victims would have loved to have seen him in the state he was in just a few months after he left the hospital. Maybe some of them would have even loved to meet up with him. Holding a baseball bat. In a dark alley. Just to inflict some more revenge. Maybe for people like John Scott, it was just better to let karma catch up with them, instead of getting blood on your shoes.

John hadn't had sex since sometime before the night he woke up with his body mutilated, bound with ropes and a shock collar in an abandoned shack on the outskirts of his town. He hadn't even really thought about it either, considering any female that he was going to have sex with was going to have to see him somewhat naked, a thought that scared him. His arrogance having faded away months ago. John Scott didn't really feel like having sex, at least not the way he had had before. A thought that frightened the once chauvinistic John; he couldn't have a woman see his scar, or the empty space between his legs where his testicles once hung so freely. He felt it made him look freakish. Sometimes he felt like a dog that thought it was going out for a joy ride but was really being dropped off at the veterinarian's clinic to have his once manly testicles removed, and with no say about it (because he had no say about it, something else he also tried to deny). John's self-esteem had plummeted so drastically since he came to the realisation that a woman had gotten the better of him, that he decided that he would never be able to face any woman if he had had sex with her ever again. It was strange for John, because before his unexpected surgery, he was the guy that would just shamelessly sleep his way through the female population of any place he was in, but his new identity left him feeling more like the person that never got laid. Ever.

With only his internal dialogue to guide him, John resorted to one of his old standbys to try get his needs fulfilled and feel somewhat normal. Instead of driving around to do it though, because he was worried about being seen, John used the internet and found himself a website that offered patrons interested in having 'the company of a beautiful woman'. You just choose your date online from a series of photos and she would show up at your door at anytime. All anonymous, guaranteed. John had figured it out. He looked through a series of photos and found a picture of a hot blonde that he thought would be able to entice him enough to 'get it up'. At 6:45 p.m., she showed up at his door.

Chapter Thirty-Three

John's escort knocked at his door and he opened it wide to let her in. The woman walked by him and stopped. She announced that she liked to be called 'Charity' and her payment was to be given up front. John stopped in his tracks as he took look at her; she did not look anything like her on-line profile picture, and he was just about to say as much when she spoke.

"I know what you're thinking." She said in a husky voice. "That I don't look like I did in that photo. Well, let me tell you somethin, honey, with the way I do things, it don't matter what I look like cuz you're gonna be cross-eyed anyways from so much pleasure." Charity said as she stepped further into John's tiny apartment and ran her finger down his chest to the button on his jeans, all with a ravishing look in her eyes. She was short, fat, and dumpy. His brows furrowed when a faint smell of her breath finally hit his nostrils.

Startled and perhaps a bit unprepared, John stepped back and thought for a moment. A sly smile appeared in the corner of his mouth as he came to a distinct realisation that he was, without a doubt in his mind, a million times better looking than the woman that stood before him. There was no way she was going to affect his confidence in any way, shape, or form. 'Tonight', he thought, 'might just be the sex I need to get this mojo back up and running'.

"Alright," he said, stepping way back to give Charity more room, "Let's see what you can do." He said finally with false bravado, a tentative smile on his face.

Charity took a look around John's tiny apartment then asked him to take her to the bedroom. As he got closer to her John, could have sworn he smelled more than her breath, which he thought was very foul, and turned him off a little bit, but he reminded himself that he needed to start somewhere if he was ever going to have sex with women again. John led her to his bedroom and stepped inside. The room was dark and small and smelled of man-sweat and cheap cologne, as if the person living was trying to hide the odor behind the fragrance, but it just made the whole room smell rancid and stuffy. It was no matter to Charity; she had been in and seen much worse. She just smiled and once inside the room, kicked off her shoes and plopped herself down on the bed.

John looked frightened and Charity smiled harder; she just assumed that he was a 'newbie', a first-timer. Being a seasoned veteran, she just figured she could accommodate the situation accordingly. Charity patted the bed beside her, and John moved closer to her in the room. Then he stopped suddenly and began fanning the air in front of his face, in less than a second he was covered in sweat and Charity, still sitting on the bed, looked completely alarmed.

"Hey man, are you okay?" She said cautiously, looking up at John with a funny look on her face. She looked ready to catch him if he were to fall over, or at least ready to jump out of the way before he landed on her.

"Yeah, I'm fine. Just got really hot all of a sudden." John said breathlessly, desperately looking around his room for something that might help circulate the air.

"Well, you don't look so good… you sure you're okay?" Charity said to John as she watched him look around frantically with a panicked look on his face. Charity had heard many a stories about customers dropping dead on the women that went to service them, and she was scared shitless of something like that happening to her.

Charity did not want to have to explain to anyone why a man she had never met collapsed and died in front of her. She continued to look at John with a strange look on her face.

"Yes, I said I'm fine and I am, dammit!" John said loudly as he tried to wipe away the sweat beads were developing on his forehead and upper lip. Charity could see a sheen begin to cover his whole body. She began to panic herself. She motioned to get off the bed, as if to help him but his demeanor scared her into submission. Charity had also experienced a few nasty beatings at the hands of Johns and did not want to explain a shiner away to anyone, let alone her pimp that was waiting outside in a car parked down the road.

"Okay, I'm just checking. Sheesh. You're not my only customer for the night, if you know what I'm saying. It's not real lady-like if I show up somewheres else and I have the flu that I caught from you." Charity said sternly, looking John up and down.

"I don't have the fucking flu! Why don't you just shut up, you fat pig!" John said from his position at the dresser; he was burning up and knew his only relief was to take off his clothes, right down to his underwear. So, John did just that.

Charity watched as her customer quickly tried to remove each article of clothing on his body. He ripped off his jeans and flung them to the other side of the room then tore off his t-shirt and chucked it over her head onto the bed.

"Hey!" She shouted as she ducked out of the way. John was just about to lean in and raise his arm to her when he noticed her looking at something in the mirror that hung on his wall across from his bed. As he turned to look, he noticed the look on her face turn from surprise and fear, to one of complete and utter amazement.

Charity grabbed her shoes, got up off John's bed and crossed his bedroom in three quick strides. He watched her walk out then followed her in his saggy, grey underwear. She was in the kitchen, leaning on a chair, quietly putting on her shoes. She stood as she finished while John walked in the room.

"Just where the hell do you think you're going?" John said with a growl as he stepped closer to the hooker that he had ordered to his apartment an hour earlier.

"I'm outta here." Charity said as she stepped toward his apartment door. John reached for her and she turned away from his grasp and grabbed something in her bag. When Charity turned to face him, she was holding a canister of pepper spray and had it pointed directly at his face. "Don't you even think about touching me, freak. I'll fuckin blast you." Charity said and John stopped in his tracks.

"I know exactly who you are," Charity said with a mean snarl across her lips. "You're that piece of shit that some woman hated enough to chop your balls off. You fuckin raped that woman and now you can't get it up because…because she cut your nuts off." Charity said as the heat began to rise in her chest. She was ready, willing and able to hurt John, she wouldn't think twice about it.

"You shut up." John said as he once again stepped toward Charity. He stopped in his tracks as she raised the pepper spray and pointed it directly between his eyes.

"You just stay where you are, freak. I'm getting outta here." She said with a smile as she took a better look around his apartment. Even with her education, or lack thereof, Charity had seen enough in her young life to know that a person that lived in the conditions in John's apartment: floors covered in filth, take-out containers littering the kitchen counters and the stench of loneliness and despair that coated every surface, was suffering from some type of mental illness or depression. And it didn't bother her one bit. John stood in his underwear and Charity laughed loudly in his face as she turned and opened his door. He could have sworn he heard the words, 'pathetic loser', from her mouth before the door slammed shut in his face. He was left all alone in his small, dirty, and unwelcoming apartment. As he stood sweating, panting and choking for air, he listened to her heavy footsteps going down the hallway outside his door, the loud echoing sound triggering a memory from a year before where John was also shaking and grasping for breath.

The first thing the police constable saw when he walked cautiously up to the shack was a small, dirty, broken window. And as he got closer to the building where he had been sent to by dispatch in response to a call about a disturbance, the police constable observed what appeared to be a man sitting in the middle of the room, unconsciously hanging his head on his chest. The man looked to have some ropes or collars of some sort fastened around his neck, suspended from either side of the thin wooden walls. And he appeared to be naked from the waist up. The constable stepped on some twigs while he was walking, and the birds screeched in the trees high above. The man looked unconscious but jerked suddenly when he heard the constable's footsteps approaching. He turned his head in the direction of the crunching gravel and howled like a wounded animal.

"Help me! Argggghhh! Somebody help me!" the naked man cried from inside the shack.

The constable walked a little faster toward the frightened voice coming from inside. He quietly stepped onto the tiny porch and nervously peered through the dirty glass to indeed see a man that looked in distress.

At his discovery, Police Constable Cloward quietly stepped back off the porch onto the gravel to put some space between him and the small building. He walked to his patrol car, reached in for his radio and called for dispatch to request backup to the address. He also asked to have an ambulance waiting down the road just in case one was needed. He hadn't been on the force long enough to see all there was to be seen in his hometown, but he would always listen when the other cops told stories of the characters they encountered on a daily basis. The young constable had no idea what had happened in the shack with all the crazy sex games people were into nowadays, but he thought that just maybe the guy's sex partner had just gone out for breakfast that morning and had forgotten to untie him.

The constable stood safely behind the door of his patrol car as he listened to the man who was still wailing from inside.

"This is the police. Sir, are you okay?" he asked loudly over the sound of the man inside the shack.

"Help me. Get me out of here." A weak voice came from inside the small space. Police Constable Cloward stared hard at the exterior of the cabin.

"Sir, are you alone in there?" Cloward asked slowly, trying to maintain calm over the situation.

"I don't know. I think so. I can't see," the man said stupidly. He sounded as though he had more than his fair share of alcohol the night before. 'Maybe that's how they do it', Cloward thought to himself. 'Get really plastered then play a few games of slap and tickle.' But Cloward wasn't there to judge, he had a job to do and that was his first priority.

"Sir, are you blind?" Cloward said in a clear voice from where he stood.

"No, I'm not blind! I can't open my eyes. They're…stuck, or something," the man replied angrily to the police officer. Cloward was taken aback by the ferocity of the response but maintained his focus and composure.

"Okay, sir, calm down. Have you tried to open them?" he asked, thinking the guy needed to stop being so angry at the only person there to help him.

"Of course I have tried to open them. I can't. I can't see anything. Help me, you asshole! Get me outta here!" the man yelled at the officer in a fit of rage. Birds in the trees near the shack took flight out of fear at the disturbance. The strange man sounded desperate to get out of the place and regain his sight.

"Sir, I'm here to help you, but you've got to calm down. I can't do anything more until help arrives."

"God! Can you just come in and help me? I don't even know where I am. What is this place? It smells funny in here," the man said, and Cloward could hear the confusion under the aggressive tone.

"You don't know where you are? Sir, you're on Old Garner Road, about two miles down from Holly Lane."

"Old Garner Road? Holly Lane? What the hell? How did I get here?" the mysterious man's voice rose higher sounding more confused with every question he asked the officer. "Can you please come in here and help me?" he whined in a pained voice.

"Sir, I have to wait until backup arrives. They won't be long now. Can you tell me your name?" Cloward asked calmly, trying to soothe the man and not overreact himself. The officer was growing more concerned for the man's welfare and the fact that he didn't know what to expect behind the closed door. He was a consummate professional with controlled responses and training for every situation he should find himself in, but he was uncomfortably aware of his inexperience as he waited for his backup to arrive.

"My name is John Scott and I'm in pain, you son of a bitch. Can't you just help me outta here?" John said angrily. He didn't care who was speaking to, he wanted to get out of the shack more than anything he had ever wanted in his whole life. He was not only cold, naked and unable to see, but he felt like he was experiencing the worst hangover known to man.

"Okay, *John*. It won't be long now. I'm just following procedure. Are you sure there's no one in there with you?" the officer said patiently as he turned and nervously looked up the road.

"Don't you think *I would know* if someone else was in here with me? I'm alone. All. Alone. So, get in here now and get me the heck out of here," he said sarcastically, and Cloward could hear the scraping of his seat on the wooden floor as John began to lose patience with the officer.

Cloward stood behind the door of his patrol car, watched the road for his backup and wiped sweat from his brow. The morning had started off cool, but the thermometer was steadily rising, the heavy humidity made the officer particularly hot in his uniform. He could hear John mumbling to himself inside the shack and sometimes howling in pain. Cloward tried to ignore the sounds as he waited patiently for his backup.

The next two uniformed officers to the scene found the shack on the first try and pulled their car in formation in the lot beside Officer Cloward's. They approached him quickly to get information from their colleague.

"There's a guy inside. His says his name is John. White, male, appears to be in his late twenties to early thirties. From my initial inspection, he appears to be tied up by his neck on either side of the walls by rope or something to that effect. He is completely naked. He says he's in pain and has been screaming intermittently since I arrived. I've maintained a visual with the shack and have spoken with him somewhat. I have not yet entered the premises. He seems to think he is alone in there. He says he cannot see at the moment but has assured me that he is not blind. He says his eyes are 'stuck', and he can't seem to open them. I have an ambulance on standby. How should we proceed?"

"We should speak to him some more and see if he can tell us anything further. Then we go in." The other officer who arrived at the scene had more experience than Cloward did at the time and saw more too; he had transferred to the police department from a bigger city east of Norfolk Falls that had a much higher crime rate and was notoriously rough around the edges.

"John, can you hear me? This is the Norfolk Falls Regional Police. I'm Officer Cardosi. We would like to help you, but we need you to answer some questions first. Sir, are you alone in there?" he asked in his deep, calm voice as he stood a few feet away from the entrance of the shack.

"Yes! I'm alone in here. Like I told the other guy, I can't see but I know there is no one in here with me. Can you just get me outta here?" the voice said from inside the shack. John sounded as though he was going to cry. He was traumatized and sobering up and was more uncomfortable than he could put into words. He just wanted out and was frustrated by the officer's need to follow protocol. John had never followed protocol in his whole life and at his weakest moment on earth, he was forced to comply with every single thing the officers said.

"Okay, sir. Just calm down. We're going to come in and get you out. Just stay where you are," Cardosi said to John. Cloward just shrugged his shoulders as he stood there and listened as John told his colleague what he had told him and in the same tone of voice.

"I can't move, or I wouldn't be sitting here waiting for you assholes to get me out. Just hurry up! Arrrghhhhhh," John growled then shouted in pain as he tried to free his body from the ties that bound him.

Cloward and the other officers made eye contact with each other, then mentally prepared themselves for what decided they were going to do. They walked slowly up to the small porch and looked through the dingy window to the tiny interior of the cabin. There did not appear to be anyone else inside, so they gathered toward the door. They announced to John that they were coming inside, and they heard a loud sigh of relief. Cloward grasped the doorknob with a sweaty hand. He took one small step forward with his shoulder on the cracked wooden door and gently pushed it open. The door creaked loudly as it gave way to his body weight and he slowly stepped one foot over the threshold. The officer pushed it further and suddenly a click followed by a whooshing sound came from directly above. Cloward barely had time to focus his eyes toward the sound when he saw an old silver bucket tip forward and dump its contents directly on the man in the middle of the room, covering his naked body and drenching the surrounding area with a clear liquid.

The instant the liquid touched John's flesh his body shot up right and he shrieked as if he had been dipped in a vat of acid. The sound of his painful screams reverberating off the walls and shocked the police officers into action. John kept screaming, louder and louder, until he unknowingly hit a note in his throat that set off the bark collar that was fastened tightly around his neck. His body threw itself forward again in a fit of shock, and the officers, startled by his sudden and violent reaction to the mysterious liquid, removed themselves quickly from the scene. They turned and ran out to the safety of their patrol cars in the weedy drive and radioed for more backup. They also requested that an ambulance come as quickly as possible.

The officers patiently waited by their patrol cars as John screamed and howled from inside the shack. Two minutes later another police car entered the scene. The two detectives got out of their car and quickly headed toward Cloward, who was the closest to the shack. They spoke in hushed tones as they relayed information and developed a plan of action. The five officers split up and surrounded the shack with their guns drawn. They slowly crept up to the front and back windows and peered inside. John sat on his stool and cried softly; his body, now wet, glistened and his hair was plastered to his forehead. The officers looked inside the shack for any other hidden traps or surprises. They finished their search and once again made for the only door. The ambulance pulled into the gravel driveway just as they walked toward the door of the tiny, old building.

"John, my name is Officer McKlintock. I am here to help you. I understand that you cannot open your eyes and that you are in pain. We are coming in to secure the scene and if we decide it's safe, the EMT's will get you out and take you to the hospital," he said with a strong voice of authority from the edge of the porch.

"Well it's about goddamn time! I am dying in here," John said in near hysterics as he cried real tears for the first time in his adult life.

The three officers walked slowly, cautiously into the shack where John was still wailing in pain, while the other two remained in front eyeing each other nervously and praying for more backup to arrive. Once inside, they looked around the room from the floor to ceiling. Matthew Cloward, the first officer to arrive on the scene slowly walked up to John sitting on the stool and looked at his body. He saw a heavy steel pronged dog collar around John's neck along with a bark collar. He could see that John's eyelids were sealed together. He walked around to the back of John's body and noticed deep, red scratches that upon closer inspection were actual words carved into his flesh. Matthew silently signaled to another officer with his hand to look at the words. They gasped aloud and stepped back in shock as they mouthed the words, 'I RAPE WOMEN', written in perfect script in the man's broad back. The officers looked at each other then stepped quickly away from the area. They no longer considered it a sex game gone terribly wrong. They had just trampled over a crime scene that was now covered with their big, dusty footprints. They quickly signaled to the other officer in the room to go to the door.

"Okay buddy, we're just going to step outside for a minute and speak to the tech guys. We won't be long… and someone will be right in to help you," Matthew Cloward said to John hurriedly as they retreated to the porch, leaving John by himself.

The three officers converged on the porch and silently closed the door of the shack. The other officers who had been outside walked up to them to partake in the conversation and to learn what they had seen. They spoke in low voices and discussed their next move. The crime scene guys were called to the old shack, so they waited for them to arrive, which they did very quickly. The tech guys were briefed by Cloward, they then walked quickly into the shack accompanied by a senior detective and all of their investigative tools. John had been sitting the whole time on the stool in his ropes and collar moaning softly. He was drifting in and out of consciousness and had mucus and other fluids running down his face and onto his chest. The tech crew went to work, photographing the interior of the shack and John's position. They signaled for Officer Cloward to come back into the shack and join them.

"This is a hell of mess you guys made of this place. Does someone want to tell me what happened? And where the hell the vinegar came from?" the detective said sternly to Cloward who was feeling a bit sheepish over the way he handled the situation. It was a big mess, the kind of which none of them had ever seen before.

"Well, Sir, I responded to the call and came out to find a building matching the description from dispatch. I approached the scene, determined that a person was inside and called for backup. I did not enter the premises until they arrived. We determined through our observation that he was the only person inside, so we then entered from the front door. When I pushed the door open, it triggered a pulley system that was rigged to the ceiling. That's when a bucket dumped of what you just identified as vinegar, onto the man and the surrounding area. In the confusion that followed, we retreated back to our patrol cars, called in for more backup then we went back into the shack. I stepped into the liquid to get a closer look at the guy's body, and read the words, 'I RAPE WOMEN', on his back. That's when we knew a crime had been committed, so we called you." Cloward tried to sound as professional as he could because he wanted to cover his tracks. He certainly wasn't expecting to find a guy tied up with ropes in an abandoned shack, in the middle of nowhere, and enter it only to discover it had been booby-trapped by some highly-skilled assailant.

"We've been waiting outside ever since," he said and exhaled a deep breath. He had forgotten to breathe while he was giving his report and didn't notice until his lungs finally screamed out in pain.

"Yeah, well, now our guys are securing the scene both inside and out. But we'll need a full report from you," the detective said over the sound of John's whimpers.

"Detective, you had better come take a look at this," a crime scene technician said from the entrance of the shack. He was standing in the small doorway looking as if he had just seen a ghost.

The detective left Officer Cloward and walked toward the shack. He stepped onto the tiny porch and walked in though the open door. John heard the commotion and stirred in his stool as the two men moved around him.

The detective walked over to the front of John's body and looked down where the technician was pointing. His eyes widened in disbelief as the color drained from his cheeks. He slowly turned to the technician.

"What the hell is that?" he said quietly as he pointed to a small glass jar that was positioned between Johns hands. It was in between his legs and appeared to be glued to John's skin. John's head was slowly lolling back and forth on his shoulders, sometimes resting his chin on his chest. The officers didn't know he was listening so intently.

"I think that those are his testicles," the technician said in a low, frightened whisper.

"What?" The detective said shocked and looked down again.

"I said, I think those are his testicles in that jar," the technician said quickly while his hand unconsciously grazed the front of his pants.

"Holy shit, I think you're right," the detective said as he bent down for an even closer look.

John had been drifting in and out of consciousness but heard the last fragments of the officer's conversation. His body froze at the last words as he digested their meaning. He furiously tried to move his hands to feel in between his legs but he could not. The officers reached down to calm him but could not see a place to put their hands. John stopped moving and spoke in a hollow voice.

"What did you just say about me?" John said in a hoarse whisper to the two men standing above him.

"Well, John, maybe it would be better if you waited until you got to the hospital to hear the full extent of your injuries," the detective said in an unnaturally calm voice, looking from John to the technician that stood beside him. He stepped back quietly and inhaled a deep breath, slowly exhaling like a winded rhino.

"I want you to tell me right now. Tell me what you see," John said suddenly alert.

"John, this is hard for me to say but, it appears that your testicles have been removed from your body. They are in a jar in your hands," the detective said as calmly as could. He was struggling to maintain composure and hold down the vomit that was threatening to spray uncontrollably all over the interior of the room.

"What? You're messing with me. Tell me what you see, man!" John said angrily; birds that had returned moments earlier to the calm of the bushes once again took refuge in the trees high above.

"It's true, John. I'm sorry I have to be the one to say it," the detective said in a soft voice as he looked from the jar to John's glistening body.

"No! This can't be happening to me. Argh!" he screamed loudly as he sat on his stool.

"Calm down, John. Take it easy," the detective said pleadingly, hoping that John wouldn't hurt himself any further.

"Calm down? Are you kidding me? My balls are in a jar, and you're telling me to calm down? Are you crazy? What the hell?" John bellowed as he lost control. He bucked on the stool but his neck was still tied. He was almost hyperventilating as he screamed out and through the confusion and chaos of having just learned that a part of him had been surgically removed, John hit a note in his throat that activated the forgotten collar around his neck. His body sprung forward with the force of lightning and at once his shouts were silenced and replaced with a soft whimper. Tears poured from his eyes and snot ran down his face. He sat heaving and sweating as the two policemen walked to the door of the shack; one to hail the ambulance personnel and the other to walk to the side of the building and vomit his breakfast all over an anthill in the shrubs.

The ambulance personnel worked quickly in the shack to get John loose, then carefully lifted his body on its side onto a stretcher and into the waiting ambulance where a sheet was placed over him. The ambulance turned on the siren and lights and drove quickly out of the gravel drive toward the only hospital in town.

The detective rode in the ambulance with John to the hospital. He looked down at the pathetic shape bundled under the white sheet and mentally prepared himself to ask John questions. Never in all his time on the police force had the detective seen something so cool, so mythical in its proportions. As the ambulance drove down the city streets, he racked his brains for the correct protocol, something he was trained to never forget.

"John, do you have any idea who would do this to you?" the detective questioned finally as he pulled a notebook out of his pocket.

"No," John said, and the detective thought he heard fear in the man's voice.

"Those are some pretty serious injuries you sustained back there in that shack. Why were you out there? What did you do last night? Can you think of any reason why someone would want to do something like that to you?" the detective said finally catching his stride.

"I can't think right now. Just leave me alone, okay?" John said quietly in the direction of the voice. He still couldn't see what had happened to him and his limbs felt the residual pain of being bound in the same position all night.

"I know you must be in some serious pain, John, both physical and psychological. And I know you can't see right now, so I'm going to tell you what is on your back. Maybe it'll help you remember who did this to you or why it happened. You have the words, 'I Rape Women', carved deep into your skin. It's probably why it hurt so much when the vinegar poured on you. That's a pretty harsh statement, John. Can you think of any reason why someone would say that about you? You will probably be scarred for life. Why would someone do something so violent to you?"

"I don't know who'd be crazy enough to do something like that to me. I never hurt a woman in my life. I certainly ain't never raped one," John said defiantly with the last of his adrenaline slowly dwindling.

"What were you doing before you got to the shack last night? I don't think you walked out there all by yourself and I didn't see a car." the detective said with a tiny hint of a smile in the corners of his mouth.

"I don't remember. Look man, just leave me alone, alright? I'm not answering any questions, so just piss off," John said and attempted to turn his body away from the detective but could not move. He was trapped in his own thoughts and scared to death over what he had just experienced. Always the bully and never the victim, John Scott began hyperventilating as fear, real fear, entered his consciousness for the first time in his adult life.

Even after all the scars healed and he returned to his life, John Scott could never get over the powerlessness he felt when he looked at himself in the mirror or remembered the things that had happened to him that night. He could never get over the fact that *she* got him back for the things that he and his friends had done to her. And a few nights after Charity's sudden and somewhat insulting departure, neighbors in John's building called the police to report that they had heard a gunshot coming from John's apartment. When police and paramedics arrived, they discovered John Scott's lifeless body in a pool of blood, and they found what police on the scene described as a suicide note.

In it were the words,

I hate myself. Fuck you, world.

John Scott

Chapter Thirty -Four

Celine stepped out of the airport and squinted her eyes in the bright sunlight. The cops, in particular, Lee James and Rick Hamilton did not know that she was home… yet. She called Lee James shortly after his letter arrived and told him that she would help, that she would get a flight out as soon as it was possible to pack her things and say good-bye. He thanked her profusely and she never contacted him again; she could still feel the resentment boiling her blood if she thought about things for too long. Celine still couldn't believe what they were asking her to do, and risk, in order to help them.

"Celine, I can assure you that there is no active investigation that you are involved in. You have been gone long enough. The case and all the noise died down not long after you left town. There have been a few inquiries and suggestive articles in the local paper. All written by the same guy, every once in a while, but he seems to be a part of your fan club, as opposed to someone that wants to see you punished. He is a local reporter, Lance Williamson, who has been publishing all these theories about you. I actually feel bad that you and your mother have been dragged through the mud so much when the two of you should have peace above all else." Lee James said quietly into the phone.

"What are these theories this guy has?" She responded plainly.

"Well, I think he's really into superheroes, or Gotham City, or something out there like that. It's almost as if he compares you and your story to other famous superheroes." Lee James said in all seriousness. He didn't want to keep her on the phone for too long; he could feel the tension that surrounded her like a thin veil.

"Really?" Celine said, daring to crack a smile, completely oblivious to the effect and influence her actions have had on those around her. Celine spent so much time in the recent past feeling guilty for abandoning her mother and the job she thought she was devoting her life to that she never dreamed that anyone, let alone a random stranger, especially a man, would think anything positive about her. It made her smile, loosened the tension around her just a bit.

"Yeah, he's really latched onto your story. You should check him out sometime, his name is Lance Williamson. He's local and really vocal about you and your story. Listen, Celine, I… we, this whole town, cannot thank you enough for what you are about to do. And for what you have already done. I just wanted you to know that." Lee James said quietly, almost as if he just realised what she had done by coming back there, that she was willing to risk her own life to help the police find the person responsible for murdering the innocent young women in their town.

'Well, I haven't done much of anything yet, so keep your 'thanks' for later. It's really my mother you should be thanking… it's her strength that has always inspired me. She deserves all this gratitude, not me." Celine said.

'Have you spoken to your mother since you've been home?" Lee James asked her quietly, although he had a feeling that he already knew the answer.

"No, she doesn't know I'm here and I'd like to keep it that way for now. I don't want her to worry about me anymore than she already has. I think it would kill her to know what you guys have asked me to do. How I have agreed to help you. I can't put her through anything anymore. She's seen enough." Celine said sadly, feeling lower than dirt at the thought of her mother, sitting at home and feeling secure in the knowledge that Celine was tucked safely away at some sanctuary on the other side of the planet, risking nothing more than humidity-hair and heat stroke, while in reality being a few blocks away from their home after having agreed to fly back and work with the cops to hunt down a serial killer.

"I understand completely." Lee James said, feeling guilty himself. He genuinely liked Celine and her mother and still had a difficult time sleeping at night, knowing how dangerous Celine's mission really was. He knew she was risking her life for them and he didn't know if he would ever be able to face Molly Bower if something terrible, something more terrible than being kidnapped or gang raped, happened to her daughter. He pushed the thought out of his mind and continued with his conversation with Celine.

"When can we meet, Celine? We have some things to discuss and I think it would be better in person so if you have any questions, I can do my best to answer them." Lee James said.

"I will think of a place and get back to you. I am really tired and need to rest." Celine said wearily, running out of steam; not having a moment to process anything that she had done in the last week.

"Sure, I understand. That's a crazy flight. So where are you staying?" Lee James asked her politely.

"Yeah, I don't think so, buddy." Celine said and laughed. "Just make sure you keep your ringer on, and you'll hear from me soon." Celine said then pushed the button to disconnect. She looked at the receiver in her hand. She hadn't expected so much compassion from a cop, especially one that admitted to knowing the crimes she had committed, she thought as she put the phone on the receiver.

'Maybe he isn't so bad,' she thought as she stripped off her clothes and prepared to take a long hot shower. 'Then again, look where you are, Celine. *Look at what you are doing*. You are risking your very life for the people that you thought would help you but instead, it's you… helping them. Do you think they know how difficult your life has been since you woke up on that cold, wet earth that morning in nothing but a jacket? Do you think they have any idea what it's like to leave your home and all that you hold dear to try and forget everything you have ever known because you did something that you felt was right, but it could land you in prison for the rest of your life? Do you think these cops have any idea how *used* you feel right now, Celine? Again. How cheap they made you feel when they had the audacity to contact you in a place where you never wanted to be found? How they manipulated you and your mother into thinking that they actually cared about you? And how stupid you feel right now because you did agree to help them, but you actually have no idea if you will do anyone any good. Do you think they know had sad you are right now, knowing that your poor mother misses you so dearly but because of what you agreed to do, you can't tell her you're home and go see her, hug her and tell her you love her and that you're alright, that you survived? Do you think they get it, Celine? Do you think they care?'

Chapter Thirty-Five

Celine slept that night at her hotel as if she hadn't slept in years. Maybe it was being back in her hometown that gave her a sense of comfort and relaxation, or maybe her body and mind were so exhausted after what she'd seen and done in the last seven days that made her pass out so effectively. Regardless, Celine awoke with a start and had an early breakfast at the in-house restaurant before calling Lee James on his cell phone from her room. They agreed to meet at a coffee shop that morning and when Lee James pulled into a spot and saw Celine standing out front of the building, he was surprised to see how stunningly beautiful she looked. He couldn't remember the last time he saw her in public, but he was sure she didn't look so healthy and relaxed. Her hair was clean and lightly bleached from the sun and her skin had taken on a warm honey glow. Her body was toned and fit and he could have sworn he smelled some kind of tropical oil emanating from her when he got close enough.

"How are you?" Lee James said as he approached her cautiously.

"I'm fine, thank you." Celine said, she was already holding a take-out cup from the store and took a sip after she answered. "I'm sorry I didn't get you anything. I don't know what you like. I'm just dying for a coffee. This jet-lag is killer."

"No problem. I'll just go inside and get something… then maybe we can get out of here? I have somewhere in mind because I think we could use some privacy. Can I get you anything else, a cookie or a muffin?" Lee James said tripping over his words, smiling and thinking he sounded like a fool on a first date with the hot chick from school. He caught himself and changed his demeanor back to one that was a bit more acceptable for a happily married man.

"No thanks, I'm fine." Celine said and smiled. She could tell he was feeling awkward, but she was an icy calm, and felt no responsibility for putting him out of his misery. Celine had a powerful dream during the night while she slept. Her father was there with her, he sat on the side of her hotel bed. He was visiting her, he looked young and healthy, exactly how she remembered him as a child. He told her that he thought she was very brave and strong, and that she must always remember that as his beloved daughter, she was never alone. That he would always be by her side, cheering her on. He said he was so proud of the fact that she was willing to help others in need. He asked her if she could look at the situation with grace and compassion and find it in her heart to forgive those who had wronged her. Her father told her he was afraid that the bitterness in her heart was going to consume her, and that he was scared he wouldn't know how to help her anymore. Celine truly believed that he was really there with her. When she rubbed her eyes and reached out for him in the darkness, she could have sworn that she caught a faint hint of his favorite cologne in the air and she knew deep in her heart that he had visited her. She loved him for it. As she stood there, watching the detective that so desperately needed her help, she thought maybe it would do her good to let go of the bitterness and focus on the things she should be grateful for; her life, the love of her mother and the fact that she had made it this far and was still around to tell the tale.

Lee James returned after a few minutes with his hands full of coffee and a paper bag and walked toward his car.

"I'm assuming you didn't drive here, if your car is still parked at your mother's?" He said and smiled at Celine.

"Well, you would be correct, Detective. I got a ride from the hotel shuttle, so you get to drive me around today." Celine said casually, as if speaking to an annoying ex-boyfriend.

"Hey, no problem, it's the least I can do." Lee James said with a smile then unlocked the car doors. He opened his door and motioned for Celine to get inside.

"Where are we going?" Celine asked as she sat down in the passenger seat.

"There's a few things I have to tell you before any of this gets started. I know a good park bench where we can sit undisturbed and discuss what's going on. But I need you to know, Celine, you can back out at any time. I thought about all of this last night, actually all night, and I realised my mistake in asking you to put your life in danger. I'm really out of line here and you have every right to be pissed off at me and Rick… and you really need to understand that we both know that you don't owe us anything." Lee James said as he turned to Celine. He waited for her response before he started the engine.

"I really appreciate you telling me that… but I know I don't owe you anything." Celine said dryly. "Sometimes, when I was away, I really felt like you *owed me*. I felt like it was you who didn't care enough about me to do anything to catch those guys… and I really hated you for that. But you know what? I have never been one to back down from a challenge and I was raised to help others whenever I can. So, I don't feel like I'm helping *you* necessarily. I feel like I did when I castrated those men… that I don't ever want anyone else to go through what I went through and if I can help some poor girl by saving her life, then I'm going to do it. I owe it to her, whoever she is, to help. Not you, or your partner, Rick. I owe it to the next innocent girl that accepts a ride from a stranger and ends up dead. *I owe it to her*." Celine said calmly, then wiped a tear from her eye.

Lee James smiled briefly and promised himself he would never forget this conversation for as long as he lived. He knew he was a part of something special. And he would honour and be grateful to Celine and her parents both, because without them, he knew, she would not even exist. He started the car and said a silent prayer of gratitude to the universe, before pulling out of the parking lot in the direction of the park bench.

Chapter Thirty-Six

When they got settled on the bench, Lee James turned to Celine with a deadly-serious look on his face.

"Before we get started discussing the matter at hand, I feel I have to tell you something that's really important. I tried to tell your mother when I found out this information, but she wouldn't have it, in fact, she barely let me in the door that time I went to see her. If you do speak to her again while you're here, would you please tell her I didn't mean to scare her by showing up unannounced and I never meant any harm." Lee James said as he looked at Celine and watched for her reaction. He didn't concern himself with specifying which time he meant, and he hoped it would pass by unnoticed.

"Okay," She said and smiled briefly but there was a hint of fear in her voice, as if she knew what was coming, or maybe it was the way Lee James said 'if' she were to ever speak to her mother again that frightened her.

"Celine, we know what happened to you that night. We know what those guys did to you." Lee James said.

"You do? How is that possible?" Celine said in complete shock as she quickly turned to face him, her eyes wide as she searched his face for answers.

"There was another guy there that night. That's what I wanted to tell your mother. That there was someone else there." Lee James said finally. He was bursting at the seams to tell her this vital piece of information, hoping it would mean something to her. Give her some peace.

"There was?" Celine said with sadness in her voice. She leaned back against the bench and closed her eyes. Lee James took a sip of his coffee while he waited to speak.

"Yes, and he finally came forward. I guess the guilt had been eating him alive. He said he couldn't take it anymore." Lee James said slowly as he turned and faced her.

"Why did he wait so long to say anything?" Celine said suddenly opening her eyes, feeling no mercy toward someone whose knowledge could have saved her whole life as she knew it, could have changed the course her destiny had taken.

"He was afraid." Lee James said, remembering the tears in Frankie Angel's eyes as he told his side of the story.

"Afraid of what?" Celine said quickly, turning to Lee James with anger in her eyes, wanting to jump off the bench and take a healthy swing at whoever this person was. "Well, John Scott threatened to kill him if he ever told anyone. John went to his apartment and promised to end his life if he ratted him out to the cops. He was pretty scared and took John's threat seriously. He was new to this town and completely alone. He didn't do much but work and watch sports at the bar before John and his friends invited him out that night." Lee James said calmly, feeling her rage, and hoping to explain as best he could. Sometimes Lee James couldn't even make sense of it all, no matter what people told him. But he would never betray Celine, he couldn't and he didn't know why.

"The night they raped me?" She said quietly.

"Yes," Lee James said, looking down at his shoes.

"Then why come forward at all? I already gave John and his friends what they deserved." Celine said, unable to feel anything but anger. She wanted to be alone with what she had just heard, she wanted to sort her feelings, process her 'what-ifs'.

"He has a younger sister. And he couldn't stop thinking about her, if something like that were to happen to her. Said he didn't know what he would do if it was her in that position instead of you. He said he couldn't live with himself anymore." Lee James said, then realised he was pleading with her to understand. He almost cried, he felt so terrible about the situation he was in.

"Yeah? But he probably wasn't worried about John anymore, was he?"

"Yes, but I think it was more than that, Celine."

"Really? How so?" Celine said, remembering very briefly the visit from her father the night before, but finding in real time that it was very difficult to let the bitterness out of her heart.

"He said he never wanted to be there, Celine. That those guys tricked him, lied to him even, just so he would go and be a part of it. He said that he never would have agreed to any of it, and…"

"And what? You're telling me you actually believe him?" Celine said, not even acknowledging the bitterness that was there. Wanting to leave, to get up and walk away. To never see Lee James' face ever again. But she didn't move.

"Yes, I do… he didn't have to come forward. But he did. He needed to get it off his chest so he could move on with his life." Lee James said.

"Well, I'm so glad he feels better. You make sure you tell him that for me, okay? That I'm just so stinking glad he's all better now." Celine said, sarcastically, still unable to tap into the compassion her father said she had. It was still buried too deep to feel.

"You don't understand… he tried to stop them, Celine. He tried to end it before it began. But he was out-numbered and out-manned. Those guys would have beat the shit right out of him and kept on going…" Lee James said, completely surprised at himself and the stance he had taken in defending Frankie Angel, right down to the bench they were sitting on that Frankie had shown him.

"Like the way they beat the shit out of me?" Celine said almost reading his mind, still shocked at the effort Lee James was putting in to defend this guy that she knew nothing about.

Lee James put his head down at the truth; he knew she was right. And he suddenly realised how pathetic he must have sounded to her. But he respected Frankie Angel and he owed it to him to tell his side of the story.

"They let him leave, and he tried to get them to stop. They were going to beat him up, so he just walked home. He walked eight miles home in the rain. It took him all night to get there, but he couldn't take you with him..."

"He didn't think to call the cops when he got home?"

"He thought about it, and he wanted to call but he was scared. John was..."

"I know exactly how John was..." Celine said bitterly, then spat on the ground beside the bench. She was unable to get the bad taste out of her mouth.

"I know, I know, I know you do. Please believe me, I'm not trying to upset you or justify anything that happened to you. And I'm so sorry about what happened to you. But, he tried, Celine. He got home from work the next day and John was already waiting for him. John said he'd kill him if he said a word to the cops and he was scared of John. He felt guilty ever since."

"Is that how you knew it was me?" Celine said smiling.

"No." Lee James said quietly.

"No?" Celine said, her eyebrow raised.

"Rick figured it out shortly after the attack at the strip club. Put everything together himself. Damn... he is good at his job." Lee James said, the truth dawning on him for the first time at that very moment.

"Then what?"

"Then we tried to contact you but…"

"You mean you didn't tell *anyone* else?" Celine said as she turned to face him. Staring at the detective, forcing him to tell her the truth.

"No, I swear… we didn't. Rick and I wanted to talk to you first. We wanted to see if we could help you, Celine." Lee James said, pleading for her to understand, for her to believe him.

"Help me what? How?" Celine said, incredulously, her eyes filling up with tears, the events of the last year flashing quickly in her mind, threatening to bubble uncontrollably up to the surface of her life. She was about ready to get up and leave. Leave it all behind.

"Well, we didn't really know how we were going to help you. We didn't even know if you would ever trust us enough to use our help, but we wanted you to at least know that we weren't going to tell anyone that we thought it was you. And we certainly weren't going to help anybody find you; that is for damn sure. You probably won't believe it, but most of the people I work with in law enforcement never really tried all that hard to find you anyway. You're like some kind of hero to us, Celine. Some kind of legend. And now we need your help more than anything." Lee James said on the verge of tears, feeling as though he may have just messed up the most important case of his career. He ran his fingers through his hair then took a deep breath through his nose and exhaled loudly.

"Now you need my help again?" She asked.

"Yes, as pathetic as it sounds… we need you, Celine."

"Well then, I think there's something you can do for me… should I decide to help you."

"Anything, truly…you name it." Lee James said and turned to her and smiled.

Chapter Thirty-Seven

Troy Alexander drove around his town with music playing loudly from the car speakers. He was trying to drown out the voice that he kept hearing in his head, but it wasn't working. All he could hear, the only thing that kept playing over in his mind was that he could not stop killing, that he could not stop. Troy had no power over his need to eliminate, or kill his 'mother', over and over again. He would lie awake at night in his big mansion trying to remember a time when he felt like he was really a part of something, a unit, a family. But all his mind kept playing was one of his worst possible memories of childhood. Troy remembered his nanny dressing him in his most expensive clothing, warning him sharply to not soil anything because she wanted him to look his best for his mother. Then she placed five-year-old Troy on a large wingback chair on the landing outside of his mother's bedroom and told him to sit quietly until they called for him. He remembered being excited, thinking that he would not get dirty, that he would sit in that big chair, be a perfect little gentleman, ready for the door to open. Troy Alexander imagined, as he sat there, the door opening and his mother, smiling warmly as she looked down at him and took his hand. Then he, her son, with his clean and pretty clothing, would climb as fast as he could into his mother's loving arms, and snuggle into her warm embrace. He would look into her eyes and feel her love, and she would smile and giggle, then tell him over and over, just how much she loved him. How she loved her son. But it never came. Troy sat on the chair, in that big, lonely hallway, until he eventually dozed off. His nanny had forgotten about him until hours later she finished whatever chores she had been doing and remembered her charge. She ran upstairs, saw that he had not even moved a muscle and shook him awake, disappointed herself that he had not seen his mother because she went through a lot of effort to have him ready for that day. And it broke his nanny's heart into a million pieces when he asked her quite calmly why his mother didn't love him.

Troy never forgot how he felt. Broken, but young enough to keep trying for her attention, to be like one of those other families, the ones he would see when he was at school. He would watch his classmates squeal with delight as they looked for their parent's in the audience of a Christmas concert or play at school. Troy would stand in the back in his costume, his face painted, and look at all of the faces, trying to spot his mother and father, just one time. But *she* never came, it never happened like that. It would always be his father, sometimes accompanied by one of his nannies. After a while his father stopped coming too. Troy would look out into the crowd, just to see his paid caretaker looking at her phone, not looking for him or waving like the other parents. He was embarrassed and ashamed, and by the time he was nine, he gave up. Troy never got over it, but instead of looking for love and companionship, Troy grew up a loner, consumed by hatred. He drove around town, after his dinner was finished, looking for something to fill that never-ending void left by a mother he knew never loved him, her only child.

Troy wasn't stupid, he knew what the papers had said about him. He read the articles that screamed a serial killer was on the loose. Troy knew that the police had no idea it was him committing the murders, strangling those women, his mother's look-a-likes with any chance he got. He also knew that with a car as nice as his, and someone as good-looking as him would never be suspected.

Troy knew that all women cared about was money, so getting another unsuspecting female in the passenger seat of his car would be no trouble at all, because as long as she needed somewhere to be, he would be there to offer her a nice, clean ride, for free. Troy didn't scope out his usual haunts; he knew better than to push his luck, but he couldn't silence the voices in his mind either. When Troy got to the end of his grandfather's street, he put on his indicator and turned left instead of right and drove down the road. The sun had already begun to set, and darkness was beginning to settle over the town. Although Troy had already eaten, he knew of a popular place that served cheap and satisfying pizza to the students around the area and decided to drive there. He pulled into the parking lot of the mini-mall and spotted her. She was exiting the pizza place and walking in the direction of the enclosed bus stop that was on the main road. Troy slowly pulled into a parking spot a few car lengths down from the stop and carefully watched her as the traffic rumbled down the street in front of them. He sat in his car for a few moments then decided that she was the one. There was no one else waiting for the bus, so Troy got out of his car and walked up to the stop in the direction of the girl.

"Excuse me," He said politely as he approached her. She turned to look at him and smiled. "Could you help me? I was supposed to meet my friend here… but it looks like I've missed him. What time does the bus usually get here?" He said with a smile as he looked at the sign with a glance.

"It's actually coming right now." She said as she pointed down the road. Troy watched as she reached into her handbag and pulled out her wallet as the bus came to a stop in front of her. The doors opened and she got on without a look back in Troy's direction. His smile couldn't hide the anger he felt inside, so he turned quickly and walked back to his car and got inside. Troy slammed his hand on the steering wheel, started the engine and drove out of the mini-mall. He turned left, a direction he didn't normally drive and looked on his right for another bus stop. It wasn't long before the winding road became less populated and as he was just about to give up and go home to fight the voices in his head alone when he saw her. Young, blonde, and waiting for the bus in knee-high boots, a skirt, and a cotton bag over her shoulder. He smiled to himself as he drove slowly up to the curb. When he got directly in front of her, he rolled down the passenger window and smiled. She smiled back when she noticed him and walked toward his car.

"Can I help you?" She said with a friendly smile, the light breeze blowing tendrils of long hair around her face.

"Hi, I don't know if you can help me…I'm looking for a friend that said he would meet me at this bus stop, but I don't see him. You didn't happen to notice a sorta dorky-looking guy standing here about ten minutes ago, did you?" Troy said casually, as he looked in his rear-view mirror for traffic.

"No, sorry. I've been waiting out here for about twenty minutes, and I never saw anyone who looks like that here." She said and smiled. Troy smiled back and she moved even closer to his car. She had perfect teeth, bright green eyes and a great figure. She also had glorious long blonde hair. Troy couldn't believe his luck, that he had found 'her' again, that he found a way to silence the voices again.

"Well, it's my lab partner and we're supposed to be going over some work tonight but… I guess I'll have to try to his cell again. Wait, did you just say you've been waiting out here for *twenty minutes*?" Troy said and looked past her to the sign.

"Yeah," She said and laughed. She leaned into Troy's open window and smiled. "But twenty minutes for this bus isn't that bad. I take them all the time. At least it's not raining today." She said as she looked down at her watch. She stood back up and straightened her bag on her shoulder, then once again looked down the road for the city bus.

"Well, I drove all this way looking for my lab partner, but he's nowhere to be found. *I* could give you a ride somewhere. I'm already headed in that direction." Troy said and smiled.

"You wouldn't mind giving me a ride? I was just at my friend's place...we finally finished our project." She said and smiled. She was wearing a jean jacket and tried to tuck her hands in the tiny pockets. The temperature dropped as the sun went down, and Troy could see goose-bumps all over her bare legs.

"I don't mind at all," Troy said quickly, and looked in his mirror for traffic. "Get in." He said and unlocked the doors with the press of a button.

"Thanks," She said as she slipped into the passenger seat. "I don't know how much longer I could have waited out there. My friend said the bus was usually on time, but I don't know." She said and she reached for her seatbelt as Troy pulled away from the curb. "Nice car, by the way. My name's Sloane. What's yours?"

"It's Troy." He said and smiled as he looked in the rear-view mirror.

"Nice to meet you, Troy." She said and smiled as he turned up the dial for the heat.

"I like that name...Sloane." Troy said as he drove along with the flow of traffic, hiding the giddiness he felt deep inside.

"Thanks. It was my mother's pick. My dad was angry, of course. He thought it was a boy's name, so he always called me, 'Sloaney'. And now, it is what it is." She said and turned to look at him. He turned in her direction and smiled. She was perfect, almost a spitting image of the women that came before her, she looked identical to his mother.

"I think it was the right choice...you look like a 'Sloane'." He said and watched as she reached into her pocket and pulled out her cell phone. She looked at the screen and when she felt his eyes on her, she pressed a button, the screen went black and she shoved it back into her pocket with a smile on her face.

"Well, Troy, no one is trying to get a hold of me, so I don't know about you but, I just finished a bunch of really annoying shit, and I could totally go for a drink right now…" The blonde passenger said to Troy with a smile.

"Me too." He said and smiled. "Were you looking to go somewhere, or, my place is just around the corner…we could go there for a drink, if you want?" Troy said calmly, smiling at her.

"That sounds okay…I guess. My place is definitely out because my roommates are home and everyone's hittin the books. So, it wouldn't be any fun." She said with a laugh as she looked out the window and smiled.

"Well, there's no one at my place. I could give you a ride home whenever you want, I'll even pay for a cab…whenever you want to leave." Troy said as he pulled into a lane of traffic and turned at the lights in the direction of his grandfather's mansion. "I'm only about five minutes from here."

"Sounds good to me." Sloane said as she smiled at Troy, then stretched out in her seat. Troy noticed her long legs and smelled the perfume she was wearing. He smiled to himself as he drove the five minutes to the top of his grandfather's street, signaled, and pulled down the road.

"Woah, this is your place?" She said as he pulled into the large driveway and pressed the button on his visor to open the garage door.

"Yeah, it's mine. It's not too bad." He said and laughed as he pulled carefully into the garage.

"Not too bad?" She said and laughed. "Wow, it's a really nice place."

"I inherited it. I'm a student too. My grandfather left it to me." He said dryly.

"Nice grandfather. Does your family live here too?" Sloane said as she watched Troy turn off the engine and open his door. She opened hers and got out.

"No, my parents are dead." Troy said, solemnly as he walked around the front of the car toward the door of the house. He beckoned her with a wave of his hand, and she followed closely behind him.

"I'm really sorry to hear about your parent's. Gosh, that must be terrible." She said as she followed him into the kitchen.

"It's not really as bad as it sounds…I wasn't close to them anyway. Look, I have lots to drink here, what do you want?" Troy said as he walked in the kitchen and opened the fridge door. "I've got some wine coolers, or beer," He said as he held the door and looked through the shelves. "I think there might even be some red wine left over from the other night."

"I'll take a beer." She said and smiled. He turned and looked at her and was again pleased with himself. She was beautiful, a bit taller than his mother had been and her legs had more muscle, but the blonde hair and the bright eyes made her perfect. He smiled a hallow smile as he reached into the fridge, grabber her a beer, twisted off the cap and handed it to her.

"Thanks." She said and took a sip. "What are you gonna have?" She said and smiled as she looked around the large kitchen and surrounding hallways.

"I like whiskey. But it's in the study. I just need a glass with ice, then we can go sit and drink." Troy said as he reached into a cupboard, pulled out a glass then held it under the ice- dispenser. When he was satisfied, he smiled at Sloane and led her down the hallway to his grandfather's study. Troy hadn't been in the study for a few days and when he got into the room, he noticed that the cleaning staff had been there and tidied it. Everything in the room sparkled, from the framed photos on the walls to the items on the big mahogany desk where he kept the decanter of whiskey. He stopped and poured himself a drink then walked into the middle of the room and sat down on the sofa. Sloane followed him but stopped at the wall with the photos and began looking at each one of them. Troy watched her as he sipped his drink.

"These are really nice pictures…it looks like you have a lovely family." Sloane said as she turned to Troy. He wasn't smiling when he looked at her, but staring at her with his cold, empty eyes. "Um, do you have a bathroom I could use? I really need to go." She said finally when he didn't respond.

"It's in the hallway, on the left…" Troy said in a hollow voice as he stared at her. It was as if a masked shadow had taken over his face. Once he stepped into his home, he didn't appear to be anything like the guy that stopped and picked her up.

"Uh, great. Thanks." She said as she looked for somewhere to leave her beer. She could feel his eyes on her, so she kept the bottle in her hand and walked out of the room, into the hallway. She found the door to the bathroom, walked in, and closed it behind her. She turned the lock on the handle and put her bottle on the counter. She quietly put her foot up on the counter and pulled a little white syringe out of her boot and put it in her jacket pocket. She flushed the toilet, washed her hands, then checked her reflection in the mirror. She was still the same Celine, she told herself, she just acted differently because people needed her help, at least that's what she told herself as she took a deep breath, unlocked the bathroom door, and walked down the hallway to the study where she found Troy waiting for her on the sofa.

"Is everything okay?" She said as she walked back into the room, her eyes never once leaving his face.

"It's fine," he said as he looked up at her. "I was just thinking about how much you look like my mother. Her eyes weren't green, they were blue, but you still look so much like my mother."

"Oh, that's nice… was she?"

"She wasn't anything, I never saw her," Troy said as he got up from the sofa and put his glass down on the desk, then turned toward Celine. "I hated my mother."

"That's really sad," Celine said as she looked at Troy and stepped back a foot away from him.

"I really hated my mother." He said as he walked slowly toward her. "Oh, it looks like I forgot my beer in the bathroom…" Celine said quickly as she turned in the direction of the hallway. Troy jumped at her and grabbed a fistful of her hair. Celine stopped moving, reached into her pocket, and pulled out the syringe. Troy caught a glimpse of the shiny metal in her hand and shoved her down away from him.

"What the fuck are you doing?" Troy shrieked in disbelief as he watched her fall to the ground.

Celine fell hard then immediately jumped back up. She had the syringe in her hand and slinked towards Troy, a fierce, determined look on her face.

"You're the guy. The ones the cops have been looking for." Celine said as she crouched and studied him, ready to attack at a moment's notice.

"I said, 'what are you doing', Mother?" Troy screamed as tears rimmed the corners of his eyes. He stopped to look at the photos and Celine stepped forward and took a swipe at his arm. He turned quickly then pushed her away from him. Celine turned back around just as Troy swung his arm in her direction. The glass paperweight that he had picked off the desk weighed over five pounds. Celine didn't have a second to block him. He smashed her face and she fell to the ground. Troy jumped over her and ran out to the hallway. Celine shook off the hit, touched her cheek and saw blood. She pushed herself up off the floor and looked for the syringe. Her eyes watered as blood dripped down her cheek, onto her jacket.

She pulled out her phone and dialled 1. Lee James picked up on the first ring.

"I'm inside! Trace my phone. He's running! He's getting away!" Celine said breathlessly. She could feel the burning sting of where the paperweight had cut her face. She stopped, held her breath and listened to Troy running through the big house.

"No, Celine! Where are you?" Lee James said in a panic.

"Trace my phone. I gotta go!" Celine said and shoved the phone back into her pocket. She stepped into the hallway and listened. Troy was one floor above speaking incoherently, opening, and closing doors. Celine ran to the plush, carpeted stairwell in the main hallway, grabbed the curved wooden banister as she jumped on the stairs, and took them two at a time. When she reached the landing two flights up, she ran down the long, carpeted hallway with the syringe in her hand. She heard a door close and ran toward the sound. She didn't have time to react. Troy was waiting for her. He stepped out of the doorway of the room and swung the heavy wooden oar with all his strength as Celine ran by. Celine went down hard, and the syringe flew out of her hand as she landed on the floor. Troy jumped over her and ran down the hallway to another doorway, down the back stairwell that led into the kitchen.

Repeated buzzing from Celine's phone roused her. She rolled over onto her back and remembered where she was. She flipped onto her stomach and pushed her body up with her arms. Celine ignored her phone as she scanned the large area, desperately looking for the syringe. It had rolled under an ornate chair across the hallway, Celine spotted it, walked over, bent down and picked it up. She Troy heard mumbling and another door open. Celine ran to the stairwell at the end of the hallway. Slowly and cautiously, she crept down the stairs. Her instinct told her that he was the one they had been looking for, that he would kill her, if he got the chance. She got to the bottom stair and looked around the room.

It was the opposite end of the cavernous kitchen. Across the room, she spotted a glass door open a crack, as if someone had just used it. Celine stepped silently through the spotless kitchen and peeked her head out the door.

Night had fallen and Celine didn't get a good look at the house when they pulled in the driveway. She had no idea just how vast the back of the property was. Celine stood on the large stone patio and held her breath, her heart beating a million times a minute. She saw the tops of tall trees and the stars in the sky. As she listened quietly, she thought she could hear Troy's voice in the distance. She looked for a way to get closer to him without being seen. She ducked down then walked quickly across the patio to the stairwell on the other side and opened the gate. It was difficult for her to see as she walked down the steps, but she followed the sound of his voice. Every hair on her neck stood up as a gust of wind blew through the trees. When she got to the bottom Celine stopped. She squinted her eyes as she silently tucked herself behind a large bush. Celine held her breath until she heard the sound of a shallow creek somewhere in the distance, at the bottom of the hill.

Troy was down at the water, she just knew it. Celine carefully gripped the syringe then crept silently through a dirt path in between the trees. She could hear Troy crying as she got closer to the creek. He was talking to his mother, cursing her and begging her to love him. Celine was getting closer to him with each step. Creeping low and silent, treading lightly on the dark ground, Celine saw Troy standing at the water's edge, shouting and crying up at the sky. She crept closer, then stumbled on a tree root. Troy turned, startled by the noise. He stopped shouting and squinted in her direction. Celine froze, but he saw a flash of her blonde hair before she had a chance to duck and hide completely.

"I know you're there, Mother! You can't hide from me!" Troy shouted as he sloshed through the creek bed. He was breathing heavy and wiping his eyes. Celine moved only an inch and held her breath.

"I know you're there, you bitch!" Troy shouted. He was crying and wiping his eyes. His hair was messy, and his pants dragged along in the frigid water. "I know you're there!"

"You hate me, Mother! *You've always hated me*… that's why you're hiding." He said moaning, then slipped. He fell face first into the water. He was sobbing as he tried to get back on his feet. Troy mumbled incoherently, his teeth chattering, not focusing on anything, but reaching into the front pocket of his pants. Celine took it as her chance and emerged from behind the bush, then crept to the water's edge, syringe in hand.

Troy forced himself up then stopped moving. He was silent as he turned to Celine. His eyes glazed over as he looked at her. She stepped closer to him as he stood in the middle of the creek.

"You killed those women." Celine said as she stepped closer to Troy, her boots getting wet as she walked into the cold water that lapped at the edge of the creek.

"Who are you?" Troy said indignantly as he stopped moaning and looked at Celine.

"I'm your worst fucking nightmare, pal." Celine said with a smile as she cocked her head to one side. "You're done. Well, first, you're gonna take a little nap", she said as she held up the syringe in her hand. "And then you're gonna come with me." Celine said as she stepped a little closer to him and raised her arm.

"I'm not going anywhere with you, bitch." Troy said, then charged.

He crashed into Celine with full force; she had crouched, bracing for impact but he still knocked her off her feet. He landed on top of her and raised his arm and punched her in the face. That was enough for Celine. She took the hit then pushed him off with incredible strength as she simultaneously slid from under him. Back up onto her feet, Celine turned as she kicked him in the head. He fell to the side, his head smashing into a large rock and Celine ran toward him and kicked him again, and again. Anger, and the pictures of the girls he had murdered flashed in her mind as she stomped on his head, his face getting slammed against rocks, sloshing in and out of the creek bed. Troy Alexander hadn't been in a single fight in his entire life, he had gotten manicures since his was fifteen years old, and he never had a real job. But when he thought of Celine, with her long blonde hair then felt pain as her boots kept smashing into his face and neck, pushing him into the water, and him struggling to catch his breath as he choked and gasped for air, Troy looked like a street-fighter as he pushed up off the creek bed and lunged at her. They both flew back, and the syringe flew out of Celine's hand. She pushed out from underneath him again then scrambled back up onto her feet. When he stood up and faced her, she landed a perfect right hook, before he could hit her again.

"Stop it, Mother," Troy cried in a whiny high-pitch voice, as he quickly stepped back from Celine and raised his arm up to touch his face. He had tears in his eyes and his hands were shaking as he looked at the blood on his fingers. Troy cried out into the dark night. "Stop it, Mother."

Celine began to approach Troy again, she was cold, bleeding and dripping with water, but she was determined to get him, even as he stepped further away from her on the creek bed.

Troy's shoulders slumped as he looked down to the ground, then he raised his head and turned to Celine with a crooked smile on his face. Celine felt her legs go numb as she watched Troy pull a shiny, snub-nosed revolver out of his pocket. She had almost turned to run when she heard him whisper 'Goodbye, Mother', then watched in horror as he put the gun under his chin.

"I hate you," Were the last words Troy Alexander said before a shot rang out in the night. He blew his brains out and his body fell to the ground with a sickening crash.

Chapter Thirty-Eight

"Celine! Are you okay?" Rick said as he threw his arms around her in the pitch-black night. He quickly wrapped a blanket around her shoulders then, grabbing her by the arm started walking with purpose up the creek bed, toward the houses.

"Oh my gosh…oh my gosh. I couldn't stop him, Rick." Celine cried as she allowed herself to be directed by Rick's strong arms. "I didn't see the gun. I couldn't stop him."

"Its okay, Celine. It's okay." He whispered in her ear and moved her swiftly toward the far side of the property, away from the body. He knew that she was in shock because of what she had just witnessed; he had seen it himself a few times during his years on the force.

"But… I couldn't stop him…" She said as she turned back to look where Troy Alexander lay dead. A cavalry, led by Lee James, was on the way to the creek bed from the other side of the property. Celine tried to stop walking, to get a look, but Rick gently eased her to keep going. He led her up a public walkway on the other side of the mansion and sat her in his waiting police car. Celine stared out the window, her eyes blank, as Rick drove cautiously through the city streets to the hospital. When they arrived, under the cover of night, Dr. Natarajan was paged over the intercom and she met Rick and Celine in a tiny room. Rick said he would wait outside while the doctor stitched up the cut on Celine's face. When the doctor finished, she asked Celine to wait while she got her a prescription for antibiotics, and when Dr. Natarajan returned to the room, Celine was gone. Rick had his back turned and was completely heart-broken to hear from the doctor that Celine was nowhere to be found. He was scared for her and he wanted to thank her personally, but he never got the chance.

Though, they never said Rick was a good detective for nothing.

A newspaper article was published; a wealthy, young student, named Troy Alexander, had taken his life. He was found lying dead in a creek bed with a very rare, very expensive, antique revolver beside his body. Inside the student's mansion was a journal and in the journal were entries, written the day after each school-girls murder. The town decided it could relax once again.

Rick couldn't. He tossed and turned the night he missed Celine at the hospital. And it weighed heavily on Lee James as well. They both asked Celine to risk her life, and they both *knew* they owed her a debt of gratitude that went beyond time and space. And Rick, being the man that he was, had an idea as to where he might find their hero.

Rick drove his own car to the cemetery. He stopped for flowers on the way and bought two bunches. Then he pulled into the spot that he always used when he went to visit his wife's grave and parked his car. He grabbed the flowers and walked the same path that he had taken every weekend for over twenty years. He knelt down at his wife's headstone and placed one bunch of flowers gently on the ground over the inscription. He told his wife he loved her and that he could not wait to see her again. Then he asked for her forgiveness for what he had done to Celine. Rick wiped a tear away from his eye, then got back up and gently kissed the top of the headstone. He whispered 'goodbye', picked up the other flowers and walked slowly in the opposite direction of the cemetery.

"Thought I might find you here." Rick said to Celine as he approached her. She was kneeling on the ground in front of a gravestone marked, 'Simon Bower, Loving Husband and Father'.

"Rick..." She said as she turned to him and smiled. "How did you know?"

"I am detective, Celine. I...I'm sorry to disturb you, but Lee James and I..." Rick said, slowly.

"It's okay. I understand. I just had to go. Sorry about that." She said and whispered to her father's gravestone. She kissed her hand and placed it over his picture, then stood up.

"You don't have anything to apologise for anything, Celine. It's us who..." Rick said, as he choked out the words.

"Its fine, Rick. Really. I was just shaken up, that's all." Celine said and smiled. Rick smiled back then looked down at his hands.

"These are for you...' He said as he held up the bouquet of flowers. "Well, I mean, they're for your father. I was just here visiting my wife and I..."

"Thank you, Rick. They're beautiful. I'll just put them here." Celine said. She wiped a tear from her eye as she bent down and placed the flowers at the base of her father's gravestone.

"Listen, why don't you let an old man take you out for a coffee? What do you say, Celine? These old bones of mine can't take the cold anymore, and I could really use a drink. What do you say?" Rick said and smiled nervously. Then offered her his hand.

"I say, that sounds great." Celine said as she took his hand and stood up. "I know just the place."

"I'll meet you there. Actually, I'm gonna follow behind you, tail you, if you will. I don't want to lose you again." Rick said and laughed. Celine smiled, told him the name of the coffee shop then waited for him to pull behind her rental car before they exited the parking lot.

When they arrived, the place was nearly empty. Rick and Celine both ordered a coffee and a muffin and Rick paid. They chose a booth at the front of the coffee shop and sat down.

"I just really want to take this opportunity to thank you, Celine. You have no idea how much you've helped us." Rick said in earnest. He was almost in tears as he looked at her face and then in her eyes. He felt like he had seen her grow up and he loved her like he thought he would have loved a child of his own.

"You're welcome." Celine said and smiled. She took a sip of her coffee.

"I don't know how we will ever be able to repay you." Rick said quietly.

"You don't have to repay me, Rick. I don't mind helping out, but… I just want you to know something." Celine said, holding back tears.

"What is it?" Rick said, quietly.

"I didn't choose any of this…any of this." Celine said and lowered her head as tears came to her eyes. She sniffed loudly, then looked on the table for a napkin. Rick handed her one and she wiped her eyes.

"I know you didn't. I know this isn't easy for you either. I'm about to retire myself. I can't take it anymore. And my job here is done. That's why I wanted to talk to you. You need to know that you will always, always, have a friend in me. I love you like a daughter, and I feel responsible for what's happened to you. I'm sorry about that mark on your face. It just kills me." Rick said sadly.

"I thought no one would notice…and thank you. What you said… that means a lot to me." Celine said as she wiped a tear from her eye then smiled shyly. She turned her head toward the window to avoid eye contact with Rick then let out a small squeal.

"Oh my gosh!" Celine said and jumped, as the color rose to her cheeks.

"What is it?" Rick said in a panic as he turned from left to right, then patted himself, ensuring his gun was always where he left it holstered.

"Jason." Celine said in a faint whisper.

Rick looked out the window and his grimace turned into a soft smile as he watched a handsome, young man walking on the sidewalk outside of the coffee shop stop in his tracks to look at Celine. The young man waved and smiled and pointed to the door. Celine waved back to him and when she turned to Rick, she was beaming.

"Celine, is that you? I can't believe it's really you. I mean, I went by the clinic looking for you and they said you had taken some time off. I just wondered if I would ever see you again, but here you are. I…" Jason said as he walked toward their table. He got there in five steps and smiled at Rick and Celine. Rick smiled back at him and nodded 'hi' in greeting. Jason nodded back and turned to Celine. She turned and looked up at him with a shy smile on her face.

"*How are you*?" Jason said loudly, then stopped. "I'm so sorry, I didn't mean to interrupt, I…" He said as his cheeks turned a beautiful shade of crimson. "I didn't even…I wasn't thinking…I.'

"It's okay, Jason." Celine said quickly and smiled. She turned her face to get a better look at him and Jason looked closely at the painful, red cut on her cheek.

"Woah, how'd you get that big cut on your cheek?" Jason said and looked closely at her with a pained expression on his face.

"Cat fight." Rick said quickly then smiled at Jason.

"Huh?" Jason said and looked from Rick to Celine.

"Big cat." Rick said and winked at Celine.

"That's right. Big cat." Celine said and winked back, then she turned and smiled at Jason.

"Listen, I really gotta run." Rick said quickly as he began to gather up his coffee and muffin. "There's a lot of paperwork that goes into catching bad guys. You understand, right Celine?" Rick said and smiled. He didn't wait for her response. He just grabbed his coffee, slid out of his seat and turned to Jason. "It was nice to meet you." Then he turned to Celine.

"If you ever need anything…*anything*," He said as he looked at her. "Do not hesitate to call me." Rick said and slipped a card from his pocket onto the table in front of Celine. She thanked him and Rick waved a good-bye as he scrambled to the door. As Jason took off his jacket and began to sit down, Celine turned the card over. Written in Rick's terrible scrawl were the words,

'Don't lose touch'.

Chapter Thirty-Nine

If there was ever a piece of shit that walked this earth, it was Adam Johnson. Not only did he rape a woman along with a few of his friends, but when the time came for said woman to get even for the rape, Adam resorted to defending himself, or his testicles, with a canister of pepper spray that he stole from his girlfriend's gym bag. Not only did he steal the pepper spray from a woman to use on another woman, in order to defend himself, and boy did he defend himself, by leaving a woman writhing around in pain on the ground in a parking lot and then running away, but he also, in the same night, tried, and mostly succeeded, in beating the shit out of his live-in girlfriend, who also happened to be the mother of his child. Now, they say that children don't remember much of their early lives, but no child should be witness to her mother being slapped around by her father, ever. So that was Adam's claim to fame: rape a chick, spray a chick with pepper spray, beat another chick with a child watching, then get arrested for domestic battery and assaulting a police officer. Have one's ass taken to the police station in the back of a patrol car, booked, and sentenced. Sent off to a penitentiary to serve said sentence and pay for the crimes committed.

Adam didn't really like being in prison, not that too awful many people do, but Adam had his world, a world where he never got in trouble for anything, beating women, raping, driving drunk, etc., turned completely upside down when karma came a calling.

And he was scared. It didn't take much of an imagination to think about what other prisoners thought about 'wife-beaters' in the clink but especially rapists. Adam had never been formally charged with rape, a mercy he believed he deserved, so therefore, the only way someone might learn about his crime was if Adam was stupid enough to tell someone himself. Which he wasn't. Adam was a lot of things, but stupid wasn't one of them. So, he accepted his sentence for what it was and he enjoyed the little bit of street cred that he got from assaulting a police officer, and he basically kept his nose clean so that when he became eligible for parole, that he would be outta there as soon as humanly possible. And it worked, he was quite nearly a 'model prisoner' and what no one in the entire establishment knew was that Adam was guilty of a more serious crime that he had been convicted of, not that beating your girlfriend wasn't as serious as a heart attack, but rape was in a different category altogether, another fact that never once slipped Adam's mind. Especially after he witnessed a known rapist take a beating from some other inmates and not return from the infirmary for over a month. He was sufficiently scared. And he was thanking his lucky stars that he would be released without injury to his person, or his ego. He hid his guilt well.

Till one day that karma came a knocking. Adam had been keeping his head down, he made a few friends, and he was counting down the days till his release. Lawyers are expensive, every minute of their time will cost you, so when Adam was summoned by one of the guards, he wondered what on earth his lawyer had to say to him that he didn't already know. He assumed it was a lawyer because visiting hours were finished, and another day had gone by with no one close to him having gone to see him. He recognised the guard, an older man, but still tough and as mean as a snake, that called to him in his cell area. Adam responded with a grunt and the guard called him over. He was being taken to a private room, and that was all the guard knew. Well, Adam's mind began to race, he knew his parent's, as kind and as generous as they were, were not going to take any more money from their retirement savings to help him out of trouble. And he knew his ex-girlfriend wasn't going to do shit for him either, so Adam, on the way to an interrogation room, was extremely nervous about the meeting.

Adams lawyer was a somewhat sleazy-looking guy with bad taste in shoes and a speech impediment, who specialized in getting wife-beaters the shortest sentences possible. Adam's parents, who footed most of the bill were initially skeptical of the man with the ugly blue suede shoes, but when they realised he had gotten their son a reasonable sentence in a prison close to their hometown, they signed over the last of the payment and prayed Adam would survive his time while incarcerated. When Adam's sentence was handed down, his mother cried, of course, and his father told him to keep his nose clean and stay the hell outta trouble. And that's what Adam did, and he had only a short period of time left to serve, not that he was counting, so he wondered what his lawyer had to say to him.

Adam reluctantly followed the big burly guard down the bland grey corridors till they finally reached the hallway that Adam barely recognized. He had only seen his lawyer one other time during the duration of his stay and spent most of his time in the lock up, so when the guard pulled out his keys and opened a door to an interrogation room directly in front of Adam, he just pointed to the opening and Adam went inside. The door slammed loudly behind him and he could have sworn he heard the guard chuckle. Once inside Adam realized he was not there to meet his lawyer (he was nowhere to be found in the tiny room), and that perhaps maybe the guard had gotten his identity wrong because from where Adam stood he only saw one other person in the room; it was a petite blonde woman that was standing at the furthest wall from the door and had her back to him. He thought for a moment that it was his lucky day, because a mix-up that involved an attractive woman was the kind of thing incarcerated men like Adam only dreamed of. That is, until she turned around. It was precisely three seconds till Adam realized who exactly was standing before him, and he did not like what he saw. You see, Adam, one of the four men that raped Celine that night so long ago, was the only one of them that still had his testicles intact. Something of which he took pride in, he being the only one that defended himself, out-smarted her and got away unscathed. He would never admit it to anyone, he was still full of himself, even though his only wardrobe selection was an orange jumpsuit and he never got to pick what he watched on TV, he still had an arrogance about him, it was evident in the way he walked and held himself. But now, as he looked from the fresh cut on her face to her rather tight, muscular frame, to the hatred that burned in her eyes and the smirk that sat on her lips, Adam felt a whole bunch of his self- confidence fade away. Although he tried to hide it, Adams shoulders sunk as beads of sweat began to gather on his top lip. He thought he was hiding his fear, but the stench began to fill the tiny room and couldn't be ignored.

Celine watched his demeanor change as soon as he recognised her. She felt sick looking at him, looking at the last piece of shit whose face still haunted her dreams. Even after all she had just been through, from being gang-raped and left for dead before giving up everything she had ever worked for and running from the law to the other side of the planet, Celine found it difficult to be in such close proximity to Adam *and* maintain control of herself. But she promised Rick that she would only talk to Adam, not disfigure him when she would so easily be caught, and have her identity revealed. Deep down, Celine still blamed Adam and his friends for what she had become. And she seethed, standing there, trying to remember what she was like in life before her encounter with them, before her thoughts of committing revenge on John and Adam and the other two had completely consumed her and helped turn her into the person she had become.

The rank smell of the small room began to bother Celine and as she continued to look in Adam's direction he moved toward the table in the center of the room, pulled out one of the chairs and sat down. His legs began to shake inside his prison uniform, but he absolutely refused to show her any fear. He didn't know she could smell it. Celine walked closer to the table but didn't sit down.

"Do you remember me, Adam?" Celine said with little hint of emotion in her voice, her eyes piercing his.

"No." He said defiantly as he shifted uncomfortably in his chair.

"You sure about that? Why don't you take a good look at my face?" She said as she straightened her chin and looked down her nose at him.

He straightened in his chair and met her gaze and held it. "No, I don't know you."

"You're a liar. You know exactly who I am. I am the woman that you and your friends completely drugged, and gang raped that time. Remember? You threw me out to die like a piece of trash. You don't remember, Adam? Or have you raped so many women in your lifetime that all our faces blend into one?" Celine said staring at him, remaining calm on the outside while a fire burned deep in the pit of her soul.

"I don't know what you're talking about." Adam said, looking at her face but avoiding direct eye contact with her eyes. His gaze stopped momentarily on the scar on her cheek, then his focus slowly drifted to the wall behind her head.

"That's not very convincing. In fact, I know you're lying, you son of a bitch. You know exactly who I am." She said, looking him straight in the eyes and fighting the urge to jump onto the table and smash his face off the wall. She could feel her blood pressure rising and she struggled to breathe deeply.

"Oh yeah?" He said, not looking directly at her and becoming increasingly agitated, evident by the way he shifted in his seat and rolled his head on his shoulders. They were both trying to remain calm at that moment.

"Yes," She said loudly, slapping her hand on the table and watching him jump. "I also know that you almost finished your sentence here, Adam. Pretty good lawyer you got yourself there, specializes in getting wife beaters the minimum sentence under the law. Oh, and we cannot forget the additional charge you got for assaulting a police officer. Hmm, hitting a cop? That's pretty ballsy for a guy that usually beats on women. What happened, Adam? You thought you'd finally pick on someone your own size and he thought otherwise? Shitty, isn't it? Sitting here in that ridiculous orange jump suit while the world goes on outside these walls as if you never even existed. As if everyone forgot about you." Celine said with a disgusted look on her face. She was running out of patience with him, and therefore running out of control.

"How do you know why I'm here?' He said as he sat up in his seat, somehow aware of how increasingly angry she was becoming.

She held up her hand to silence him. "I'm not finished." She said with a smirk in the corner of her mouth, the anger she felt, blazing in her eyes. He said nothing, just sat there, surprised at how quickly her demeanor had changed. The beads of sweat had returned to his lip and he began to twitch his leg under the table.

"You say you don't remember raping me and we both know that's a lie. So let's try this: do you remember a night a few months ago when you went out to a bar looking for your friends, but you couldn't find any, so instead you had a conversation with a group of people from a place called Jacksonville, Florida?" She stopped talking and watched as a flicker of recognition flashed over his eyes.

His hands gripped the table as he attempted to put some distance between them.

"Then," She continued, "You met a cute little librarian named, Lisa, and you took her outside to smoke a joint." She said and smiled as she bobbed her head from side to side in an excellent rendition of the last role she played at the infamous sports bar.

"Guard." He said in a hoarse whisper, his eyes wide, as he attempted to push his chair away from the table and stand up. She leaned over the table, close to him and spoke in a low voice. He stopped moving and watched her mouth.

"Then something happened that I am sure you were dreading because you came prepared that night, Adam. Instead of taking your chances and defending yourself like a real man would AGAINST A WOMAN, you sprayed me in the face with pepper spray because it was your only chance to get away from me still intact." She said as she half-stood, her palms resting on the table, her chair two feet behind her. It clanged loudly in the tiny room. The sound made Adam jump and he suddenly found his voice.

"Guarrrrd." He said loudly, craning his neck toward the door, not daring to take his eyes off her completely.

"I'm not finished with you, Adam…and he won't come until I call. I came here to tell you that I haven't forgotten about you. No, you're not getting off that easy. You might think that because you're in here that you got lucky and you'll remain intact for the rest of your days. But that won't be the case at all. You should enjoy the rest of your time here with your little balls because the day you do get released, I'll be waiting outside those gates for you, Adam. I will finish what I started and there's nothing you can do about it. Because you can't run from me forever."

"Guard! Get me outta here!" Adam screamed as she moved closer to him. She stopped leaning and stood straight up, smoothing her jacket and picking a miniscule piece of lint off her sleeve.

It was that moment the guard chose to return. He peeked through the tiny glass window at Celine and she nodded. Adam and Celine heard the click of the door and then watched as it slowly opened. The guard walked toward Adam and reached under his arm to help him up. He was about to lift him clear out of the seat and guide him toward the door when Celine spoke.

"One more thing I want you to remember while you're finishing your sentence here in this shithole, Adam." Celine said calmly. The guard and Adam stopped.

"What?" He said quickly, attempting to shuffle toward the door but unable to do so due to the strength of the guard.

"Payback's a bitch… and so am I." Celine said and smiled. Just then, the smell of urine filled the tiny room as a darkened stain began at the top of Adam's leg and ran slowly down to his ankles, right into his prison-issued, white cloth sneakers.

It's not the same as being 'out'. Prison. You are your uniform, what you are in for, and how much money goes into your canteen. Granola bars are worth their weight in gold. Pecking order absolutely dictates everything. Make friends, keep your nose clean, and get out in one piece. And never, ever, tell anyone that you are a rapist. Unless you plan to spend all of your time in Solitary Confinement, because that's where the rapists and diddlers go. The prison guard tasked with leaving Adam in that room with Celine had casually let it slip to another guard what he had overheard; that Adam wasn't just a 'wife-beater', he was also a rapist. And there are a few things lower than that, especially in prison. No one really cares who you are when trapped behind cement walls, especially when you are a rapist. It started small, after the rumor got out. There was a little push here and there, sometimes a harder shove when he wasn't looking and before he knew all of Adam's things would be destroyed when he went out to the courtyard for exercise. No one saw a thing, until one day Adam caught a guy red-handed.

Stealing his food and pissing on his bed. There was a struggle, and before the guards could stop it, a fight broke out, that grew into a massive brawl. Adam bled to death in the ambulance on the way to the hospital. He had gotten shanked in a fight that had broken out over who's turn it was to clean the toilets.

Chapter Forty

Molly Bower woke up to the sound of her own voice. She could feel her heart thumping wildly in her chest. When she opened her eyes and looked around her bedroom, she saw her bedsheets twisted in piles around her ankles, her comforter in a pile on the floor.

"Argh," She screamed. Then wiped her eyes. She must have been crying in her sleep again. The last thing she remembered upon waking was calling Celine's name, but never getting a response. Molly Bower shot up quickly and sat with her legs hanging off the side of the bed.

"What am I going to do?" She said aloud then buried her face in her hands and wept. She hadn't heard from Celine in weeks and when the letters stopped coming, her thoughts began to torture her.

The townhouse was in a complete disarray, and Molly's face was gaunt. Her cheekbones becoming more pronounced with each passing day. Her fingernails were bitten down to the quick and her cuticles were bleeding and raw. The unknown was eating her alive; Molly Bower was wasting away.

"These old bones." She said quietly as she pushed herself up off the bed.

"What am I going to do?" Molly Bower said as she took a deep breath and walked over to the tallboy dresser that was against the opposite wall. She picked up a framed photo. It was her, Celine and her late husband gathered around a campfire. Her hand flew up to her mouth as tears sprang from the corners of her eyes.

"She can't be gone…she just can't." Molly said quietly as she traced their faces in the photo behind the glass frame.

"Oh God, what am I going to do?"

Molly Bower showered and got dressed, then she went downstairs and made herself a cup of tea and a slice of toast. She sat at the table and sipped her tea deep in thought, while she pushed the toast around on her plate.

"She can't be gone…" Molly said then got up from her chair, walked to the front entrance, grabbed her coat, car keys and walked out the door.

She pulled into her usual spot at the cemetery, dried her eyes with a tissue, then got out of her car. Molly walked slowly to her husband's gravestone, dragging her feet as she went, feeling the full sorrow of her life. As she got closer, Molly noticed a small bouquet of white flowers at the base of his headstone. She knelt down on her knees and reached for a single flower. As she picked it up to smell it (they looked so perfect), Molly Bower heard leaves rustling a few feet from where she knelt motionless. Molly placed the rose back on the headstone and turned immediately to the sound, when she heard a small voice.

"Mom?" was all she said.

THE END